DARK ROOTS

THE THORNHILL VAMPIRE CHRONICLES
BOOK ONE

LUCIUS VALIANT

THORNHILL PUBLISHING

In memory of Anne Rice, the true Queen of the Vampires

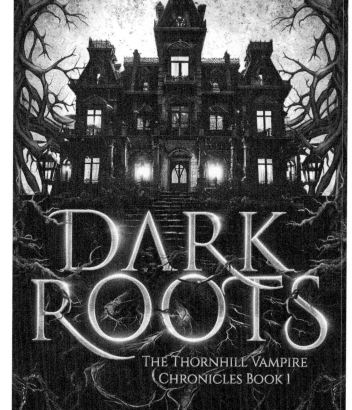

DARK ROOTS

THE THORNHILL VAMPIRE CHRONICLES BOOK 1

LUCIUS VALIANT

CHAPTER

ONE

Traveling up the tree-lined gravel path to the base of operations for the Van Helsing Society always felt like coming home - and considering how much time I'd spent there over my 27 years of life, that made sense.

On this particular August morning I arrived in one of the Society's sleek black Lincolns, my fellow hunters Jed and Carmen riding with me.

Jed's large, powerful frame was folded in behind the wheel, his deep-set eyes gleaming with mirth in the rearview mirror. Carmen was in the seat next to me, her long ebony hair streaming around her face in the draft from the rolled-down window. The night's hunt had ended in triumph and the collective mood in the car was elated.

It was still dark, but with a rift of pale gold daylight bleeding through the horizon as the familiar sight of the three story building came into view. It was an old Scottish country house turned occult fortress, its facade lit up by floodlights. Instead of traditional gargoyles, werewolves, basilisks and other mythical creatures perched on the roof -

each of them a reminder of the supernatural nature of what the Society dealt with.

The building housing the Van Helsing Society was built in the 1500s but had been beautifully restored and modernized since. The Society itself had been established in 1899. Its name was a playful nod to the fictional vampire hunter and scholar Abraham Van Helsing from the then recently published novel, Dracula.

Back in the early days of the Society's existence, you had to be a pureblooded human to be allowed to join. Back then, the merest drop of supernatural beast in your blood was enough to disqualify you. The theory was that if you were more beast than man, your integrity would be automatically compromised.

The rules had been relaxed considerably in recent years. If the Van Helsing Society had to keep excommunicating its best hunters when they got bitten by werewolves or grew scales after handling cursed objects, the turnover would simply be too great.

Excommunicating members used to be less of a problem, because it was easier to recruit. One of the Society's elders, Miranda Minerva, herself a retired hunter, had wryly lamented, "People are less adventurous these days. They'd rather play computer games than put their lives on the line for the greater good."

I was one of the exceptions. You could say I was compelled into this line of work by fate. My family were all killed by vampires, and I was saved by one of the Society's most legendary hunters. I'll get back to that. For now, let's just say that joining the Society had been inevitable, and that chasing supernatural monsters consumed my whole life.

But where was I? Oh, yeah. I counted five figures

standing on the front steps, apparently waiting for us. The hunt we'd just come back from had been a success, but the Society usually didn't do fanfare. So why were they here?

Before Jed had brought the car to a full stop, I'd flung my door open and stepped out onto the crunchy gravel. Behind me, I heard Jed's and Carmen's car doors shut as they also got out.

The Society's chief librarian, Ramsay Fairweather, stepped down and effectively blocked my path, his pale blue eyes flashing with barely concealed glee.

I'd never interacted much with Ramsay, thank heavens, but we seemed to have reached the shared conclusion that we hated each other's guts. The few times we'd been forced to occupy the same space or exchange words we'd been like two bushy-tailed cats circling each other.

Ramsay was tall, willowy and pale-skinned. The short-cropped, moonlight colored hair that crowned his head accentuated his sharp, angular features. He had a way of always looking snooty, as if whatever conversation or action he was engaged in at any given moment was beneath him.

The Fairweathers were one of the old families that had been involved with the Van Helsing Society for generations. In fact, Forthilda Fairweather, Ramsays's great-great-great grandmother, or something like that, was one of the Society's founding members, a fact he never failed to harp on about.

Ramsay seemed to think that his family name granted him the status of royalty. It didn't help that, for about a decade, he could also claim to have been the Society's most promising hunter. That was until his vampiric blood count got too high. I didn't know the details because everyone's files are confidential, but the rumor was that he already had a little vampire in his blood to begin with, and that a hunting accident had caused it to soar past the strict 30% threshold.

So the details were shrouded in mystery, but the outcome was clear. While still a member of the Society, Ramsay was no longer allowed to hunt.

Relegated to the role of librarian, he now sulkily presided over the Society's wealth of occult tomes, scrolls and artifacts. It was a hallowed position, sure, but it wasn't the same as being a hunter. Out in the night, chasing after supernatural beasties was where the adventure was at. Ramsay hated no longer being part of it, and for this one thing I couldn't fault him.

There had been an incident a few months ago at a Society formal dinner where both Ramsay and I had overheard Minerva, usually tight-fisted with praise, describing me as the most promising hunter she'd seen in her time. It's no wonder why Ramsay resented me even more after that - I would too, if the tables were turned.

"Harlan, welcome back, and good morning." Ramsay took another step down and stopped directly in front of me. His aura was so frosty that I half expected the steps to be slippery with ice. He fixed me with an equally frosty glare. Didn't acknowledge my fellow hunters with as much as a nod.

"Is it a good morning, Ramsay? I thought you hated mornings." I gestured to indicate the slight rose tint that had now saturated the horizon. If he had been all vampire, he would have had to start worrying about getting away from the sun. But as it was, only strong and direct sunlight troubled him.

Ramsay's pupils narrowed, as if he was reading my mind. Hell, he probably was.

Out loud he said, "Don't worry about me. I've got time. Besides, I really wanted to deliver the news myself."

"What news?" I gave him a smirk intended to annoy him as I tried to walk around him. "It's getting light, so walk and talk with me. Let's get you inside."

"Not so fast."

As if on cue, four butlers (a somewhat misleading term for the Society's staff of muscle) stepped down on either side of Ramsay to block my path. "You can't go in."

"What do you mean we can't go in?" Jed's voice rose behind me with a note of tired indignation. "We need to get in, give our reports and clean up our weapons."

"Well, *you* can go in, Jed. You and Carmen. It's just Harlan who can't." Ramsay didn't even look at them while saying their names. His attention was still firmly locked on me.

Despite my back being turned, I could sense Jed and Carmen tensing up behind me. I shrugged. I was as clueless as they were.

"Care to tell me why I can't go in?"

Judging by the amused glimmer in his eyes, Ramsay was savouring the moment.

"I'm afraid I've got some bad news for you." Instead of just saying what it was, he paused for dramatic effect. The smug attitude was getting on my nerves. "Well, I've got some bad news, and some even worse news. Which would you like first?"

I looked up at him, tilting my head to one side. "Just spit it out in any order you like."

"I guess I'll just tell you." He sighed and, maddeningly, paused again. He gave a casual shrug and said in a nonchalant tone that conflicted with his words, "I hate to be the bearer of bad news. Miranda Minerva suffered a stroke a few hours ago. It was pure luck that Denise found her in the library before it was too late. She was, of course, immediately rushed off to hospital."

I stood completely still, as if struck by lightning. I could feel Carmen placing a soothing hand on my back, and Jed gave my shoulder a squeeze. They both knew what Miranda Minerva, my direct superior and an important mentor, meant to me. She was a stern and commanding woman who, despite her age, seemed timeless and immortal to me. Despite being in her 70s she didn't seem like someone who could have a stroke.

"What?" The word came out jagged, filled with tension. He had to be joking.

"Is she going to be alright?" It was Carmen's turn to speak up. "She hasn't - has she?"

"Ah, no. No, at least not yet. But her situation is... critical."

I finally managed to snap out of it and demand, "So where is she? Is she here or at the hospital? I've got to go see her right now, before anything else."

"Still at the hospital," Ramsay confirmed, "Where she'll be for quite some time until she's made a full recovery. *If* she makes a full recovery. There are no guarantees. But this isn't all," he added, clasping his hands in front of him, a prim smile spreading from ear to ear. "I did mention that I've got two pieces of news for you, didn't I? I'm suspending your hunting license pending an investigation into your conduct."

I opened my mouth to protest, but he held up his hand, demanding silence as he continued, "Minerva has long been turning a blind eye to your excessive and unnecessary use of violence when dealing with members of the supernatural community, but while I'm in charge, or excuse me, while I'm stepping in to look after everything here while Minerva recovers her strength, I won't be. I, along with a committee consisting of the Society's elders, will be conducting a formal hearing. You'll be able to defend yourself and respond to any of the points of concern that we decide to raise. In the meantime, you're denied access to any of the Society's premises, equipment and resources."

The flow of words was delivered with relish. My guess was he had been rehearsing them in his head for hours, bursting to let them out.

"I'll park all this for now, if you don't mind. I should go see Minerva. I should be there when she wakes up."

"*If* she wakes up," Ramsay corrected me. "As I said, she's in an extremely critical condition. Hovering between life and death. You stomping around in there, stressing her out, is the last thing she needs. So stay away from the hospital."

"You didn't even tell me which hospital she's in!"

"Precisely."

We had reached an impasse. I'd been hell-bent on pushing my way past him and getting into the building to deliver my report and be done with this latest mission. But now, that no longer mattered. My hunger, fatigue and need for a shower also seemed to have evaporated. I needed to know that Minerva was going to live.

Again Ramsay seemed to be reading my mind. He pretended to be buffing his glass-like fingernails on his lapel, but really he was watching me like a hawk.

"I know how attached you are to Minerva," he said, apparently mulling over the possibilities this entailed. "But I'm your elder now, at least for the time being."

"You're kidding me." I was probably not being very respectful, but in the face of the avalanche of bad news that had just hit me, did it really matter? "You can't be my elder when we're practically the same age. You don't have the experience, your misgivings about my conduct have no legs to stand on and besides, Minerva will probably be back in action before we know it."

That last sentence didn't sound as self-assured as I'd hoped. It hung in the air between us like a question mark.

Ramsay took a deep breath, eyes flashing as he regarded me. "Age," he pointed out, "has got nothing to do with it. I've got the experience, the ability, and now the jurisdiction. Besides, I know you haven't forgotten what I am. It follows that I'm not as young as I look. What all of this boils down to, for now, is that you won't be coming in. Not today, Harlan, and not before I explicitly request your presence for your hearing. And after that, who knows?"

I was dying to grab him by his lapels and throw him down the stairs into the gravel, just to wipe that self-satisfied grin off his face.

"You do know, don't you, that any violence I've ever inflicted on members of the supernatural community, as you call them, has been in self defence or to protect human life?"

Ramsay looked unmoved so I added, "I don't use unnecessary violence, I use necessary violence."

Carmen gave my elbow a nudge, as if to suggest that maybe I wasn't helping myself.

Ramsay sighed, "Let's not have this conversation now. Save your breath and your convincing arguments for the hearing."

Suddenly one of the Society's trained ravens swept down from the paling sky and landed on Ramsay's arm. It squawked once, as if in agreement with him, and when it opened its beak I caught a glimpse of the round eye-shaped camera lodged within it. Ramsay plucked the tiny camera from the raven's beak. He lifted a pale eyebrow. "I'll be reviewing this later. If I find anything particularly damning it'll be brought up at the hearing."

The Van Helsing Society had lots of these ravens, specially trained to follow us hunters to make sure everything happened according to the book, which of course, it rarely did. If there's one thing you can count on when dealing with supernatural forces it's that they don't play fair. Because of this, the elders usually allowed for a bit of leeway and flexibility when it came to adhering to the Society's rules as written.

Most of the elders were retired hunters themselves, their personal experience having taught them that we were dealing with vampires, werewolves and such, not lap dogs.

Ramsay understood this, too. His days as a hunter weren't far behind him. But he seemed intent on making life difficult for me, just because he could.

"The camera won't tell you anything I'm not willing to admit," I said, trying to connect with the part of him that was human. "There were a bunch of missing children carried off to a crumbling bell tower by a bloodthirsty vampire. I arrived first, and yes, I rushed in there without waiting for the others. I acted both quickly and violently without asking politely first. It was the children or the vampire. I made a judgement call."

"I disagree." Ramsay's voice was chilly. "You could have waited for backup without risking the children's lives. Isn't it true that this particular rogue vampire had been abducting toddlers from around Edinburgh for *days* without killing any of them yet? There was no urgency."

"Sure, that's true, but when I arrived he was about to sink his fangs into one of them. I had to act. What should I have done instead, sat there and watched him suck this toddler dry? I did the right thing and I'm not sorry."

Carmen and Jed both began raising their voices to back me up, but Ramsay lifted his hand.

"Shh," he shushed them as the raven flew up from his arm and settled in the branches of a nearby oak tree. "Harlan, you don't need to be sorry. You just need to hand me your hunting license and go home."

This was unbelievable, but that seemed to be the theme of this conversation.

"You can't suspend my license," I protested, reflexively reaching into my jacket's inner pocket and closing my fingers around the thin silver plate with the hunter's symbol, two stakes crossed, engraved on it.

"Oh, but I can, and I am. Hand it over. Why not take some time off? Consider it a holiday."

"I know Minerva is going to agree with me, not you." I said. "When she returns, reinstating my license is the first thing she'll do."

"Well, she and I will have to figure that out when she returns. For now, I'm in charge."

Ramsay held his hand out to me, palm up.

Technically, I had no choice, but I still looked around at the others assembled. None of the butlers made any move to defend me. In fact, they were helping Ramsay to block my path with their mere presence. It was clear where their loyalties lay.

Ramsay sighed. "Harlan, I am asking you nicely to hand over your license. Don't make this difficult for yourself, and try not to worry too much about it. You'll get it back again, most likely, though of course I can't make any promises."

"But I've had my license for nearly a decade without

suspensions, and tonight wasn't the first time I've had to make a quick decision and act on my feet."

"Oh, I am aware," Ramsay was getting impatient. "That's a big part of the problem."

His hand was still extended, floating in mid-air between us in silent command. I looked over my shoulder at Jed and Carmen. They were flanking me, both looking as tired and annoyed as I felt.

"We vouch for him," Carmen said, "He did the right thing. He did what any of us would have done."

"Any one of us with enough guts, at least," Jed added.

"Well of course the Three Musketeers are always going to back each other up." There was more than a hint of irony in Ramsay's voice."And I'll make sure your points of view are heard at the hearing. But for now, Harlan, you really have no choice but to surrender your license. Don't make me ask one more time."

With this, the butlers flanking Ramsay seemed to straighten up. One of them actually rolled his neck until it made a wet click. I was usually on friendly terms with the butlers, but apparently that didn't count right now.

My fingers were still coiled around my license in my pocket. Slowly, reluctantly, I drew it out and watched the silver gleam as it caught the floodlights. This little piece of metal was one of my most prized possessions in this world and handing it over to Ramsay was causing me physical pain.

Excruciatingly slowly, I placed it on Ramsay's open palm, and he closed his fingers around it, instantly snatching it away from me.

"Thank you, Harlan. I appreciate that. There's no need to cause a scene."

"If you didn't want a scene, you wouldn't have met me

like this on the front steps with a whole committee," I pointed out. I should have probably stuck with just thinking it, but oh, well.

"I suggest that you go home, get cleaned up, and try your best not to make any more trouble for yourself than the trouble you're already in. And don't try to find out where Minerva is! She can't handle any visitors right now." Ramsay winked at me before finally turning to my two companions. "Carmen, Jed, you two come with me."

The gravel crunched as one of the Society's sleek black cars drove up and parked, with the engine still running, in front of the one Jed had been driving. A butler I didn't recognise was behind the wheel, his eyes covered by dark glasses. The automatic car door opened from within, seemingly on its own accord.

"Bye for now, Harlan," Ramsay said, "I'll see you at your hearing. Until then, I don't want to see you at all. Don't contact me, or anyone else here for that matter. We'll contact you."

Dazed, I stepped back down from the stairs and folded myself into the car. It set in motion immediately.

CHAPTER

TWO

W hat the hell had just happened? I flung myself back against the thickly upholstered car seat with a disgruntled sigh. Of course, my driver offered no answer. The Van Helsing Society's drivers never do. Not asking questions is part of their job description. No matter what they might see or hear, they remain completely stoic and unmoved. Whether that's to preserve their own sanity or part of the training they receive, I couldn't tell you.

"Where are we going, Mr. Thorne?" the driver asked in a smooth, polite tone that went perfectly with his flawlessly pressed uniform. He was young, probably younger than me, but the formal suit he wore combined with his professional manner made him seem somehow older and more distinguished.

"To Romerstadt's place." It was either that, or back home to my own little flat in Edinburgh where my personal demons would be waiting for me.

I should probably get a pet to ward them off. But would I really look after it? With my unpredictable schedule, I didn't even feed myself three meals a day, and I could never predict when I'd be around. No, I probably shouldn't get a pet. A cactus, maybe. And once I'd acclimated to that level of attachment, I could consider scaling up to a pet, and maybe after a decade graduating to a relationship. A stable one this time.

We had already set off in my desired direction; the car was moving so smoothly that only the changing landscape outside indicated that we were moving. Fields upon fields of various crops, here and there clusters of trees, and a couple of lakes, all softly lit by the early morning sun.

How dare Ramsay do this to me? And the butlers, how dare they just go along with it? I understood that Ramsay was covering for Minerva while she was hovering between life and death in the hospital. That part of it I could understand and even halfway accept. But what business did he have suspending my license?

Jealousy had to be the answer. With his own license suspended for good, Ramsay would never be able to add to his achievements as a hunter. Ensuring that my license was suspended, too, was the only way he could stop me from overtaking him by a country mile.

Ramsay's only reasonable hope of one day being let back out of the library was the Society relaxing its rules further. It wasn't an impossibility, but it was highly unlikely.

All Society hunters had our blood tested every three months, and the last time I checked, the cutoff point for being a hunter was 70% human, 30% other. If you exceeded that, you were out of the hunting business forever.

Werewolves were, of course, the exception to the blood percentage rule. The beast in their blood ebbs and wanes with the moon, meaning you can't get a reliable test result.

How the Society handles its lycanthrope members is by banning them from hunting three days on either side of every full moon. That seemed to work. Werewolves weren't the problem. Some of the Society's best hunters have historically always been werewolves.

In general, the blood percentage requirements had always been more lax concerning Society members who weren't hunters. It was only really us hunters that had to be pureblooded humans, or close enough. Different rules applied to the scholars, investigators and exorcists.

The debate often got heated when questions about the ethics of accepting members that were more monster than human were brought up at the monthly Society dinners. The Society was essentially a conservative organization, but there were those who were in favor of a more inclusive approach.

Sure, I could see the usefulness of the Van Helsing Society being more welcoming of non-humans. Why dismiss truces and alliances? But at the same time there had to be a line drawn. The way I saw it, giving any vampire the keys to the Society's front doors or to the vaults filled with secrets and occult objects was bound to backfire.

You could even look at this from the monsters' point of view, I suppose, if you had to. Supernaturals that collaborated with the Van Helsing Society risked being ostracised and attacked by their own kind. Maybe that would be different one day, as a result of the Society's efforts to not merely hunt down and slay the monsters, but to build bridges and form alliances with them. I doubted it, though. My life experience had taught me, time and time again, that the only vampire you can trust is one you've just nailed to the floor with a stake.

My thoughts circled back to the matter at hand. What

about me? No one had ever asked me to hand over my hunting licence before. My entire identity and life revolved around being the Society's rising star hunter. If I was no longer that, what was I? What was I supposed to do with myself?

I'd repeatedly been told by the few people in my life that really mattered to me (almost all of them connected to the Society in one way or another) that I was an obsessive workaholic. They were probably right, but I didn't know how to be any other way. Putting your life in jeopardy on the regular doesn't make much sense if you're not fuelled by an obsessive flame.

It was no mystery how this flame had been ignited. My parents were killed by vampires when I was very young, or at least, too young to remember anything more than shadows, screams and otherworldly laughter.

Eli Romerstadt, the vampire hunter who found me and prevented me from suffering the same fate as my parents, was my only semblance of a parental figure. Eli had raised me, trained me, honed me for what I'd become.

But even he didn't fully understand me. Even he cautioned me to be more careful, kept telling me I'd end up burning out or getting myself killed by going as hard as I was. But I knew I'd burn up if I didn't. This was why I didn't do holidays and always accepted every assignment that came my way. It was why I was so good at this. I wasn't really afraid of dying. I was afraid of standing still.

It was always in the empty, quiet moments that what I considered my personal demons would appear. They were the shreds of memory that I had simultaneously tried to piece together and keep at bay. They were a veil of dread always billowing in the corner of my vision.

"Mr. Thorne, we've arrived."

"What, where?" I jolted upright, my senses jumbled from the abrupt awakening. Apparently, I had dozed off during our journey through the rolling countryside, placing my trust in the stranger behind the wheel. Evidence, I suppose, of the level of faith I had in the Van Helsing Society and its members.

"We've arrived," the young driver repeated, his face an impassive mask as he watched me in the rearview mirror.

I peered out the window, squinting against the sunlight that danced off the white walls of Eli Romerstadt's country house. Nestled within serene Scottish woodland, it exuded tranquillity that I had never been able to find anywhere else.

The only sounds as I emerged from the vehicle were the melodic chirping of birds perched on branches above me. From the outside, the windows of the house looked vacant.

It'd been a little while since I'd been back at Eli's house. Like the Van Helsing Society headquarters, Eli's house was surrounded by trees, but the house itself was smaller and more homely. Or maybe I just thought of it as homely because it was the closest thing to a childhood home I'd known.

The last time I'd seen Eli, we'd kind of ended things on a sour note. My ongoing request and his ongoing refusal to formally adopt me had polluted our connection for years. Still, I couldn't think of a place I would rather go to lick my wounded pride. And I was looking forward to seeing my reluctant father figure.

Eli was always up to something, always riveted by the chase of some creature, object or secret. He was one of the relatively few hunters that worked not only for the Society, but for whichever private clients found their way to him. And after a prolific 50 years as a hunter, it was fair to say he'd amassed quite the magnetic reputation.

In fact, he was one of the few hunters whose reputation was more extensive than mine. In a profession where most don't live to see their fiftieth birthday, a fifty-year career is a complete anomaly.

Eli himself was a living, breathing anomaly and enigma, his lifespan rendered unnaturally long by the supernatural blood in his veins. His werewolf status gave him an edge and advantage over those who had only their human lifespans and bodies to rely on. You can afford to take more risks when you're closer to being immortal than the average person, simple as.

I reached into the backseat and grabbed my bags. The butler must have loaded them in - I'd been too distracted by Ramsay to even notice. The bags almost only contained weapons. Everything else I owned was back in my flat in Edinburg or inside Eli's house, where I still had a room. Apparently, he was happy for me to have a home under his roof that I could return to any time I wanted. I could always rely on him in an emergency, and he'd practically raised me. But signing the formal adoption documents was where he drew the line.

Actually, maybe I was reading too much into the room. The inside of the house was deceptively large. It had six bedrooms, so it was hardly like he was going to miss one. Still, it was uncharacteristically sentimental for him to have left it unchanged after I moved out somewhere around my 18th birthday.

I hadn't called ahead, but Eli's beloved vintage car, a 1930 Packard 740 Roadster, deep bottle green in color, parked in the driveway told me he was home. Strangely, though, there was a second car parked next to it. A cheerful orange VW Beetle that I didn't recognize. Definitely not Eli's.

I turned around to look at the driver and thank him for the ride, but before I'd even opened my mouth, he said, "My pleasure, Mr. Thorne." He then shut the door behind me. The car glided away, its sounds fading behind me as I ascended the front steps.

This time, there was no welcome committee, no humiliating relinquishment of my license. It had been a bad morning, but there was solace in knowing tragedy could only strike once on the same day. Probably.

As my hand reached for the door knocker, shaped like a wolf's head with a magnificent aged green cast, the door swung open from within. Eli loomed in the doorway, larger than life. Despite having grown into adulthood myself, Eli still seemed of mythical proportions to me, both literally and metaphorically.

Going by physical appearances, it was clear that the two of us weren't blood related. My mentor stood at well over six feet, his physique solidly built, his chestnut curls with only a few iron gray strands, brushing against his broad shoulders. No matter the season, he was always deeply tanned, which made his husky blue eyes look all the more vivid and striking. An aura of absolute vitality surrounded him at all times - even when the moon was waning.

I wasn't naturally built like a warrior. Every ounce of lean muscle on my 5'8 frame I had I'd had to work for. I wore my cinnamon coloured hair just long enough to sweep it behind my ears and out of the way of rather elfin features and large amber-colored eyes. Silvery scar tissue criss-crossed my arms, chest and the left side of my neck, left there by the hostile beings I'd hunted and in most cases slain.

All hunters of supernatural fiends end up with their own unique collection of them. On Eli's tanned skin they should have stood out with greater clarity than on mine, but his werewolf blood meant he didn't scar easily.

I expected surprise from Eli when he opened the door and saw me standing there, but none registered in his weathered but still handsome face. "Harlan, there you are," he greeted me, the words hanging in the air.

"Here I am," I responded, lingering on the doorstep, a deliberate pause. I wanted him to bridge the gap, to reach out. And true to my expectations, he did, drawing me into a one-armed hug, enveloping me in his familiar scent of wood smoke and pine needles.

"I can't say I've been expecting you," Eli admitted, breaking the hug. "But someone else has."

I looked up, honestly surprised. I wasn't in the mood for any more surprises. The ones I'd already had today had been more than enough.

"What do you mean?" I asked.

"Some solicitor," Eli said, his tone gruff. "He's in the conservatory right now, waiting to speak with you. He insisted on waiting for you - he seemed to know you were going to show up."

That couldn't be right. I didn't have a solicitor, unless you counted the ones working for the Society. Sensing my surprise, Eli's alert eyes scanned my face with just a hint of concern. "So you haven't invited him here?"

"Of course not. I wouldn't invite anyone to come here, especially not without telling you. You know that."

"You better find out who he is and what he wants, then, don't you?" Eli stepped aside, allowing me to enter the hallway fully. It was as if he had been hesitant to let me in before confirming whether I had compromised his privacy.

Like I said, Eli Romerstadt had a reputation. He had helped countless grateful clients over the years, but he had also angered many non-human entities. If you wanted a long and illustrious career as a hunter, you didn't make a habit of giving out your home address to strangers. You never knew who, or what, might one day show up at your doorstep holding a grudge.

I noticed that Eli was wearing his long, heavy leather coat inside. The solicitor must have arrived while he was somewhere on the grounds. It was either that, or he had thrown it on when he heard the doorbell. Whenever Eli donned his signature coat, I knew he was armed. Concealed within its voluminous folds and pockets were knives, possibly a stake, and undoubtedly a gun, all at the ready.

I followed Eli down the long hallway, past the rustic kitchen, the sitting room, the small library with its soot-blackened fireplace and into the conservatory at the back of the house. There, seated at a small round wicker table on a wicker chair, was a bird-boned older man, in his late 60s or early 70s.

The solicitor wore a dark gray suit, and a pair of small round wire-framed glasses. His hair, also gray, was neatly cut and combed so that it looked like a steely helmet. He appeared slightly uneasy amidst the various carnivorous and poisonous plants that filled the werewolf's conservatory.

I took a step into the room, and immediately, the man stood up. He seemed relieved to see me. Anxiously, nearly toppling his wicker chair in the process, he extended his hand in greeting. I hesitated for a moment, but there was something about his appearance and demeanor that made him seem utterly harmless and inviting. I offered my hand, and we shook.

"Harlan Thorne," he said, his voice filled with a surprised delight as if he were shaking hands with Mick Jagger. "I cannot express how pleased I am to finally meet you."

I must have looked puzzled because he continued, "My name is Jeremy Gently. As I believe your... father told you, I am a solicitor. I work for the Thornhill family and I'm here on their behalf."

"Eli isn't my dad - more like a mentor. But, it's good to meet you, Jeremy Gently. Did you say you're here on behalf of the Thornhill family?" I turned the name over in my mouth. An interesting name, prickly and ornamental.

"Yes, indeed. I work for the Thornhill family - I have for a very long time. My errand here is on behalf of Lyrica Hartenbrook. Well, technically she is a Hartenbrook, but she is the only member of the Thornhill family who remains. She desperately requires your expertise, your unique services. She's prepared, I should add, to reward you generously for your trouble."

"Okay, tell me what she needs my help with?" I pulled out the wicker chair across from Jeremy Gently and took a seat. "I'm listening."

"My employer requires your assistance with," the solicitor lowered his voice, as if wary that dark forces might be listening in on our conversation, "a vampire problem."

CHAPTER

THREE

"And what makes your employer think that I can help with her vampire problem?"

I darted a glance over at Eli, who was still standing in the doorway as if undecided on whether he should join us or busy himself elsewhere.

To be honest, he looked like he could do with some fresh air, or maybe some rest. His skin was much paler than usual, and if I wasn't wrong, sweat was forming on his brow.

Oh, but of course, how could I forget? The full moon was tonight, and he seemed to be already fighting against the tide of his inner beast.

"I understand that my presence here and my errand require a bit more explanation," said solicitor Gently as he sat back down in the wicker chair. His voice was as cultured as you would expect from his appearance. "As it happens, Ms. Hartenbrook is a great admirer of your work. She has been following your career for some time."

My throat felt dry, and my spine tingled. Something about the urgency in Gently's tone made me think that whatever was going on here was crucial, for better or worse.

"I suppose I have a lot to tell you," the solicitor began.

"I suppose you do," I agreed. "I don't exactly advertise what I do or how to find me, so I wonder how she knows. She must be well-connected."

"That she is," Gently conceded. I wanted him to continue, but I didn't push. Instead, I sat back, all my senses alert.

"As you can probably appreciate," he went on, stirring two glittering cubes of sugar into his teacup with a silver spoon. The spoon had a wolf's face engraved on it, a nice little touch, "My employer places great value on privacy and discretion. In other words, I cannot tell you everything that she might choose to disclose when you, hopefully, agree to meet her in person."

I nodded. I understood. The handful of times private clients had sought out my services outside of the Van Helsing Society, they too had come to me discreetly, and in a few cases, almost ashamedly. After all, most people aren't happy to admit that they are dealing with a supernatural problem. And at the other end of the spectrum, of course, are those who convince themselves that they're haunted or cursed when really they are neither.

"There is much information I could give you, but I will try to make myself relatively brief," Gently said, taking a careful sip from the fine china cup.

"Take your time," I said, leaning back in my chair and crossing my ankle over my knee, draping my arms over the back. "I have all day. "Actually," I cast a glance over my shoulder at Eli, "for this, I have all the time in the world."

"The Thornhill family is a very old family," Gently leaned forward confidentially over the table. "Briefly put, they built a fortune on trading sugar and coffee during the 1800s. The family seat, Thornhill Mansion, still sits on top of Highgate Hill in London, overlooking the cemetery. The Mansion is old, was in fact built at the same time as the cemetery, and the grounds that the cemetery occupies used to belong to the Thornhills. I'm saying this to illustrate how deeply embedded the family is in London's history, how influential they were."

I nodded. "Sure. Now, where does the vampire problem come in? And does this have anything to do with the so-called Highgate Vampire?"

The Highgate Vampire was one of the many supernatural case files I'd studied during my time at the Van Helsing Society. It was often used as an example of a minor supernatural disturbance that had spilled out into the public and ballooned to massive proportions. Another similar case was the Enfield Poltergeist, which had also caused a media circus in the 1970s. Of course, the actual entities behind both phenomena had turned out to be negligible supernatural pest problems that had soon been subdued once real hunters and exorcists appeared on the scene. The legends they'd inspired, though, lived on.

"Well," Gently knitted his brow, "The Highgate Vampire is nothing more than an urban legend, at least as far as I know. To tell you the truth, when I was a young man, I was rather fascinated by the supernatural, the occult. But I'm a grandfather now and would rather not dwell on these things. Still, handling this errand for Lyrica Hartenbrook is part of my professional duty, so I suppose I must. This I can tell you with certainty - things began declining for the Thornhills right about the time when the cemetery was built. Of course, all this happened over a hundred years before the Highgate Vampire legend took off in the media.

What I am saying is, the Thornhills have been plagued by darkness long before the Highgate Vampire legend was even a twinkle in the eye of the media machine."

Jeremy Gently heaved a sigh and looked as though he was reaching deep into his memory and dragging out something particularly unpleasant. "Most of the Thornhills died tragically and mysteriously over a brief period. It was speculated that they might have... stirred up something when the cemetery was built."

He paused for a beat and took another sip of his tea, as if to steady himself before venturing into the next sentence. "It seems they angered someone, or perhaps something. I won't theorize on precisely what happened or why. This is for you to hopefully discover if you accept this assignment. All I can say for now is that Thornhills started dying as soon as the cemetery had been built. First, there was the murder of Algernon Thornhill, which was never solved. Not long before his second wedding, his body was found mauled and decapitated on the staircase outside the mansion. It would appear that he had been trying to flee his attacker, an endeavor in which he'd obviously failed. Algernon Thornhill had been the one to take the family business and turn it into a veritable empire. An admirable man, certainly, but not a well-liked figure. Oh, not at all, from what I've heard."

Gently had become quite animated as he spoke and had abandoned his half-empty cup of cream tea.

"Algernon was prone to drinking and had a notorious temper. He was even rumored to have killed Helen, his young first wife and the mother of his first child. My point being that there are any number of people who might have wanted him dead and gone. And his descendants, too, perhaps. As a cutthroat businessman and womanizer, Algernon Thornhill was a thorn in the side of many of his contemporaries in Victorian London. But I'm getting sidetracked. Algernon was murdered in 1860. His killer was never found. Stranger still, within a year of Algernon's death, the rest of his family, well, almost all of them, were also dead. That's what the record shows."

Sensing my eagerness to break into his stream of words, Gently lifted his hand slightly. "I know you are probably getting impatient and want to know how all of this ancient history ties into the present, how any of it is relevant to you and to your own discoveries."

At this, the solicitor reached into a bitter chocolate-colored leather briefcase and produced a thick manila envelope.

"These are photographs, daguerreotypes. Some of them are quite faded, I'm afraid."

I accepted the envelope. Its thick cream paper made it seem antique, but it was new. I cleared some space on the small round table between us and upended the envelope on the glass. I shook it with the gentle respect its contents seemed to command until a small flurry of sepia-toned daguerreotypes poured out onto the table.

I still didn't see how the Thornhill family's history tied into the present, but on the other hand, I knew that vampires and other supernatural problems are less constrained by time and space than problems that are merely human. It was probably all going to start adding up.

I picked up one of the daguerreotypes. They were all faded with age and all different sizes. The one I'd picked up was the largest one, not quite the size of an A4 sheet. It showed a family in Victorian dress standing in a lush garden, a big mansion house in the background to their left. I let my eyes move over the photo as if searching for some clue, which I suppose I was.

I'd never seen this place or these people before, but something about the daguerreotype seemed strangely familiar. I let my eyes pass over it again. A man whose age could have been anything from mid-30s to mid-50s. A young, raven-haired woman next to him, smiling sweetly at the camera and holding the hand of a small boy of maybe four or five years old. Like his father, he was gazing sternly at the camera. The building in the background had to be Thornhill Mansion, and the man in the daguerreotype photograph could only be Algernon Thornhill, along with his wife Helen and their son.

I lifted my gaze to meet the eyes of the solicitor, perched on the edge of his seat across from me. He was watching me intensely, as if wanting to capture every nuance of my reaction to the images. "Algernon, Helen and Venedict, their son."

I picked up another daguerreotypes, this one of a little girl in a frilly Victorian dress and tiny embroidered shoes. Her hair fell in dark, glistening corkscrew curls to her elbows. She was standing next to a gilded cage holding two canaries, but she wasn't looking at them. She was looking directly, flatly at the camera, an ironic smirk on her small mouth.

"That is Octavia Thornhill, Algernon's second child. She was illegitimate, but Lord Thornhill acknowledged her and raised her as his own. He, in fact, doted on her. She was born to one of the servant girls not long before Helen fell from the balustrade and met her death."

I summed this up with the word, "Odd," and picked up the next faded image. This one showed Octavia Thornhill again, a few years older now, sitting in a velvet armchair. The boy from the first photograph, now grown into a young man, stood next to her with an arm on the chair. A third sibling, a small girl barely more than a toddler, was standing next to him, holding his trouser leg with one hand and peering out of the photograph with curiosity bordering on suspicion.

"Venedict, Octavia, and Dorothea Thornhill. Algernon Thornhill's three children. All born to different mothers," Gently narrated. "Venedict was Lord Thornhill's only legitimate child, his oldest child, and his only son. There was never any doubt that he was the heir to the Thornhill family fortune and estate."

I studied the three pale faces in the photograph. I was overcome by a sense of familiarity. Venedict, in particular, with his prominent cheekbones, small nose, and confident, direct stare, looked like he could be my younger brother, but I was imagining things. It was a coincidence. The daguerreotype was old and faded, my brain was overtired, and I was projecting things that weren't there. This was just a daguerreotypes of three Victorian strangers who'd died long ago.

I closed my eyes, then opened them again and squinted at the image, expecting any imagined familiarity to have evaporated. But no. The three faces in the photograph were still looking out at me with what now seemed to be knowing smiles.

I quickly slipped the aged daguerreotype back in the pile, replacing it in my hand with one of a beautiful young woman with delicate, aristocratic features and a waterfall of straight, jet-black hair. Helen Thornhill's younger sister, maybe.

"Keep these, if you'd like." Gently's voice seemed to reach me from somewhere far away. "They're yours. There are copies, as well as countless others."

"I can't accept them," I said immediately. "They must be priceless to Ms. Hartenbrook."

"She wants you to have them," Gently insisted. "She has so many more where these came from. Besides, she said to not accept a no from you on this."

Eli, who had been hovering in or near the doorway this entire time, had finally come fully into the room and had plonked his form into the incongruously dainty third wicker chair at the table. He was listening silently, not interrupting. I was glad to have him here. I handed him the photographs, and he studied them with alert eyes.

"The same goes for this." Gently reached back into his briefcase. His hand came out holding a set of large and somewhat rusty keys. They were oversized compared to modern keys, and he laid them down on the glass table with a satisfying jangle.

"The keys to Thornhill Mansion," I said it as a statement rather than a question.

"Indeed. And Lyrica Hartenbrook wants you to have your own set so you can let yourself in and out as you please during your stay. That being said, I'm afraid the mansion isn't in the best condition." Gently sounded saddened at this, as if he felt personally responsible. "There isn't any family fortune left to speak of, certainly not enough to restore Thornhill Mansion to its former glory."

"You still haven't told me precisely what she needs help with," I reminded him.

"I am afraid I don't have all the answers," Gently lifted both of his hands and spread his fingers apologetically. "My employer is very discreet. Secretive, even. She is afraid of not being believed."

"She knows what I do for a living, and she's sent you to

me. She must know that she can trust me with her vampire problem, as you said."

"Well, yes. That's it. She's worried that the Thornhill family has been followed by a shadow for centuries, or since the cemetery was built. She wants to bring an end to the haunting, the curse, whatever you might call it."

"Let me see," I said, "if I've understood this correctly, "The same... entity, vampire, whatever it is that killed Algernon Thornhill and his children is still stalking the Thornhill family to this day?"'

"That is my understanding of it, yes." Gently nodded, relieved that I'd picked up on all of his hints and had put them together in a coherent sentence.

"And Lyrica Hartenbrook is the only living member of the family left?" This time, it was my turn to lean in over the table.

"Yes, and she is willing to pay you thrice your retainer if you are simply willing to come to Thornhill Mansion and meet with her."

I exchanged a glance with Eli, who had finished studying the daguerreotypes and had put them back down in a neat little pile on the table without commenting on them. I was sure he'd do that later, or as soon as Jeremy Gently had left.

"Three times my retainer is fifteen thousand pounds." To be perfectly honest, I always changed my fee to fit the client. If I worked for someone who could afford it, I charged more, and if someone was in serious need of help but couldn't afford it, I charged much less. In my experience, it all evened out.

"I have the jurisdiction to transfer this to you instantly when you accept the assignment."

I felt the weight of Eli's hand on my shoulder. I knew

him well enough to know that he was cautioning me to think this through.

"What say you, Mr. Thorne?" Gently looked exceptionally hopeful, and of course I wanted to accept the invitation right then and there.

Eli cautioning me was an annoyance, but I thought it better to listen to what he had to say. Not in front of the solicitor, though. There was every chance he'd observed or thought of something I'd overlooked, and his instincts had saved my skin enough times for me to know that if his larm bells were ringing, I should at least hear him out.

"How long do I have to think about it?"

Gently's smile withered a little at the corners of his mouth. "There is no deadline, not as such. But I urge you to not think for too long. Poor Ms. Hartenbrook is worried out of her mind that this entity, this demon, this vampire, will soon have accomplished its goal, which seems to be to cut the entire Thornhill family tree off at the root. And what a tragedy that would be. I can only urge you, don't let the darkness triumph, Mr. Thorne. Don't think for too long."

"Thank you very much for your time, Mr. Gently," Eli said, rising from his chair, a clear signal to our guest that his visit was coming to an end.

"It has been my pleasure. Absolutely." Gently closed his briefcase with a small, precise click. He gathered up his hat. He'd never taken his coat off.

I followed him out through the hallway and bade him farewell on the doorstep. As we shook, he pressed his business card into the palm of my hand and urged me again to call him as soon as I'd taken whatever time I needed to digest his employer's proposal.

He had left the daguerreotypes and the rusty keys in the conservatory like a tangible, irrefutable, and irresistible invitation. And, of course, he'd left me with the desire to travel up to London, to the mysterious Mansion house in Highgate.

I stood watching on the steps as Gently climbed into his snub-nosed Beetle and drove off. Then I turned around and went back into the house, back into the conservatory where Eli was gathering the used china.

Even though I didn't want him to rain on my parade, I would at least listen to what Eli had to say.

"Harlan," he said the moment I stepped through the door, "I know you aren't going to want to hear this, but the full moon is tonight. My instincts are already dialled all the way up, and all of them are telling me this is a trap. And whoever has laid it seems to know you better than most."

FOUR

"Have you considered that the moon could be making you paranoid?"

Not even deigning to answer my question, Eli countered, "Have you considered that you're just stubborn and don't want what I said to be true?" He strode past me and called back over his shoulder, "Follow me to the kitchen."

The kitchen was at the front of the house, facing the driveway. It was decidedly cozy, with an old wood burning fireplace, a large battered stove and copper pots and pans dangling from the beamed ceiling. Shelves upon shelves were stacked with glass jars and bottles, many of them with handwritten notes and containing plants, seeds and tinctures.

Eli put the china down next to the sink and started washing the cups and plates with brisk movements. All the fine-boned, flower-patterned china cups and plates in this house always looked incongruously dainty in his big weathered hands.

Without even thinking about it I grabbed a kitchen

towel and started drying the dripping china. I'd long since stopped trying to convince Eli to get a dishwasher installed. He was famously averse to technology and preferred no-tech or metaphysical solutions whenever possible, like the powerful circle of lodestones laid down in the ground around the property to keep unwanted supernatural entities out, or like the herbal tincture in the cut-glass hip flask he now retrieved from his pocket and sipped from with a grimace.

We cleaned the dishes in silence and I put them away in the cupboard.

Eli, now seated at the table and sweating profusely, chucked back the contents of the cut-glass flask. He didn't take chances when it came to his beast and the tincture helped him keep it on a tight leash. The wolf in him was particularly strong on blood moons, though, so I expected to see him constantly swigging the tincture the rest of the afternoon and all through the evening.

He shrugged his coat off and draped it over the back of his chair. "That's better," he declared, licking his lips after consuming the tincture. I didn't know its exact components, but I knew he brewed it himself on herbs and extracts he collected from the surrounding woodland and from the carefully tended plants in the conservatory. It was the only thing that helped whenever the powerful tide of the moon rolled in. Of course, when the full moon actually came, there was no tincture or tonic powerful enough to keep him from shifting. But there was no need to let the beast take over the entire week.

Eli was good with herbs and tending to his greenhouse was, as far as I could tell, the only hobby he had apart from hunting monsters. Over the years, he had taught me the properties of at least half a dozen plants. I may not have received any formal education, but I knew how to heal wounds, set bones, and poison with plants. Among many other skills that were only useful in my particular line of work.

"Two bad things have happened to me today," I said, launching right into it now that the two of us were alone. "One of them is that Miranda Minerva has apparently suffered a stroke and is fighting for her life in a hospital. I don't even know which one."

Eli froze mid-motion, his hand holding the empty tincture bottle hovering near his pocket, where he was about to put it away.

"Well, I'll be damned." He shook his head in disbelief. "I've known Miranda for half a century. If there's any chance of her recovering, I know she'll pull through."

"The other thing," I said once the silence had gone on for too long, "is that I've had my license suspended."

Eli frowned. "Suspended? Why on earth would your license get suspended? In all of my years as a hunter, I've never heard of anyone's license getting suspended...unless there is a very, very grave reason." He shot me a questioning look from across the heavy wooden table. "What did you do?'"

"I swear I didn't do anything! You know me. You know how how thorough I am. Actually, I think that's the problem."

"Explain?"

"I don't want to say that I'm too good, but Ramsey Fairweather - you know, that obnoxious half-vampire, used to be a hunter, but now he does paperwork or something?"

Eli nodded.

"Well, he resents me. And today, this morning, when I rocked up after finishing my assignment, he told me to hand over my license. He wants to 'investigate' my conduct in the field. I have to attend a hearing, can you believe that? He clearly just wants to humiliate me, and if he can find a way to justify it, he'll take away my license for good."

Eli sat in silence, quietly chewing over the information I'd just flung at him.

"Hm," he said finally, "this all sounds... strange. The Society is changing, that's clear. That's been happening for a while, of course, but this is something else. This is unheard of."

"That's what I'm telling you! I swear, I did not step out of line or use what Ramsay called 'unnecessary violence' towards the supernatural community. That's how he put it. He just wants to get rid of me and any excuse will do."

"Ludicrous. The Society is short on hunters as it is, without them suspending one of their best."

I took a deep breath, inhaling the compliment. "Ramsay doesn't care about what's good for the Society, he just wants me gone. Honestly, I think he's been lying in wait, waiting for just a shadow of an opportunity to jump on. With Miranda in hospital and me slaying another vampire without an execution warrant - because I had no other choice - he finally had both, and he pounced. And now I don't know what's next."

"I'm beginning to see why you are so tempted by Lyrica Hartenbrook's offer."

I put my head down on the table. "It's so unfair. Ramsay doesn't have any reason to suspend me other than jealousy. He's only doing it to sabotage my rise as a hunter. All because he can't be one anymore."

"I'm getting a strange premonition." Eli had a feverish expression on his face, and combined with his pallor and the droplets of cold sweat crowning his brow, it was making him look slightly mad. "I'm not sure how the pieces fit together, and I can't say for sure that they do. But," he added, "you'll have to agree that this many coincidences in a day just don't happen every blue moon. Ramsay suspending your license and this solicitor, Gently, or whatever he said his name was, showing up here with an irresistible invitation."

"A bunch of unrelated unusual things *can* happen on the same day," I pointed out. I sounded defensive, even to myself.

"They can," Eli conceded, watching me closely to gauge my reaction, "but how often do they, exactly? I'll answer that. Almost never."

"I'll admit it's weird. But what if they are coincidences that just happen to align? This wouldn't be the first time I've taken on a private client."

"There are just too many tiny oddities about this that add up to something feeling off." Eli was insistent, wouldn't let it rest, "Don't tell me you don't see it, because I raised you to see right through bullshit. And your bullshit radar is excellent, unless there's something you don't want to see. And then you just don't see it at all."

All of this was true. My bullshit radar had saved me on more than one occasion. I still had the scars to remind me of a few close brushes with death, or worse, from the times I'd tried to override it.

"Is it pure coincidence, do you think, Gently showing up here just before you arrived?" Eli pressed on, raising one bushy eyebrow in a quizzical arch. "If you didn't invite him, how did he know where to find you? Not many people know about this place."

"You know, I don't have the answers."

"Then, is it really a good idea for you to travel up to

London to meet with this Lyrica Hartenbrook and get involved in her supernatural problems, the nature of which you still don't have the faintest clue about, other than what this man claiming to be her solicitor has told you?"

"If I don't go, I'm guaranteed not to find out."

"That's not a good reason for walking into something that I'm telling you looks like a well-rigged trap."

I sighed with frustration; I was getting irritable but tried to keep it under wraps. I wasn't about to let Eli corner me with logic and reason. If he did, I would have to admit that he was probably right.

"You know how much I value your intuition, Eli, but sometimes you're just too immortal to understand my point of view. Unlike you, I don't have unlimited time. I don't have the luxury of mulling things over for a decade before I make a move. Besides, Gently said this was urgent. You heard him."

"When did you hear me say you should mull things over for decades?" Eli folded his powerful arms across his chest. When my only response was flashing him a defiant glance, he added, "Let me just say this. If you're going up to London to pursue this, at least allow me to come with you. That'd be the only halfway sensible way to approach it."

"But aren't you going to be preoccupied this weekend?"

He drew a slow, deep breath through his nose. This weekend was not only the full moon but the anniversary of his wife and child's death at some unknown point before my arrival in Eli's life. He never spoke about them, but he kept photos of them around the house. Each year, on the anniversary, he would spend the night at their graveside in the nearby village cemetery.

"Well," he said. His eyes had grown distant. "You should wait at least until the weekend is over and then we can talk about it. My feeling is that you shouldn't go at all, but if you must, you shouldn't go alone. I'd come with you now, tonight, but you know I have to remain here until the moon has passed."

Eli had learned his lesson long ago, after what happened to his wife and son. Not that he had ever told me about how they died. The few times I'd tried to probe, he'd rebuffed me, leaving me without any clear answers, but still with the impression that their untimely deaths had something to do with his werewolf form and that feelings of guilt and shame were mixed in with his grief.

Out of respect for Eli's private pain, I'd resolved never to ask again, and whenever he visited their graves or brought fresh flowers in from the woods to place in front of the photos of them on the mantelpiece, I never interfered.

The yearly anniversary of their deaths was always a difficult time for him - and particularly when it coincided with a full moon. I knew I had to respect that, and if I wanted him to come with me to London, I'd have to wait for him to be ready.

Eli's dead family had always hung over us like a shadow. They were the reason why he had always refused to sign the adoption papers when I put them in front of him. Eli had raised me and he would readily admit that he loved me like a son. But the way he saw it, he had had his family and he'd blown it. He had sworn that he would never have another.

He took the same stance with women. All the time I'd known him, about twenty years, Eli had had some kind of relationship with one of the Society's occultist consultants, Margot, a witch. I was pretty certain she didn't even know where he lived.

Part of me was tempted to grab my bags from the chair

in the hallway and head straight for the airport on my own, but even I knew being in this much of a hurry could only be a bad idea.

As soon as I'd admitted this to myself, the realization of how bone-tired I was washed over me. I was also famished, and I definitely needed a shower. I suddenly had no fight left in me; I needed fuel.

I went over to the fridge and opened it. Its door swung open to reveal nothing but shelves stacked with packets of raw meat.

"You didn't announce your visit," Eli pointed out.

"I know. I'll manage." Scanning the shelves, my eyes settled on three large free-range eggs.

"You're welcome to any of it," said Eli. "Just leave those extra bloody steaks for me. The beast demands them."

I grabbed the eggs and a pack of bacon, determined to prepare a quick and simple but filling feast for myself. Carrying my selection over to the hob, I cracked the eggs on the countertop and poured their liquid contents into a large frying pan, along with the bacon. Within seconds, a delicious aroma filled the kitchen.

I watched over my shoulder as Eli got up from his chair and disappeared into the hallway, only to make an immediate return carrying my hunting kit.

"You know," he said, putting the kit down on the table, "I've told you what I think and what I sense, but something tells me you've already made up your mind to go. I can't stop you. But I can stop you from going without your kit being in order."

My bacon and eggs had reached visual perfection. I flipped the lot onto a plate and gobbled it all down hungrily, still standing next to the stove while Eli covered the dining table in torn-out sheets of newspaper so that my collection of stakes, many of them still covered in thick black vampire blood, wouldn't stain the table. Most people wouldn't be able to get a bite down while looking at this, but I guess you could say I'd become desensitized. For Eli and for me, this was normal.

"My whole life," I said between mouthfuls, "has been a history of stepping into unknown situations. Why should I draw the line at Lyrica Hartenbrook, of all places?"

"There's a world of difference," Eli insisted, opening the kit and laying the stakes, knives, crossbow and arrows out on the table, "between taking a calculated risk and stepping into something that is almost certainly a trap, rigged to corner you. But by all means, you're a grown man and can do what you want. And you will. I'm simply urging you to sleep on it and to look at it again in the cold light of day."

"It's day right now," I pointed out at the still sun-drenched driveway and grounds beyond the thick-paned windows.

"You know perfectly well what I mean," Eli sighed. He looked tired. Actually, his coloring wasn't good. He looked nearly ashen underneath his tan. The pull of the moon was clearly getting stronger.

We were at an impasse and we both knew it. Younger me would have pressed on and turned this into an argument - or simply rushed ahead into this mission, or trap, depending on who turned out to be right. Current me, however, was a little older and a little wiser.

"All right, I'll sleep on it," I promised, putting my empty plate in the sink and rinsing it off. "But I can't promise what I'll decide."

CHAPTER

FIVE

As soon as my head hit the pillow, the recurring nightmare that had haunted me for years returned.

As usual, I found myself standing in a burning house, its corridors consumed by fiery tongues, just like on the fateful night long ago when the family I didn't even really remember was taken from me by a vampire. Or vampires, I'm not sure.

This time, though, the dream took a different turn. The outlines of the burning corridor began to warp, shifting between what I presume were the walls of my childhood home and the arched structure of a chapel, engulfed in phosphorescent green flames.

A thin, vicious green mist crept along the floor, flowing over my boots. As the flames danced and writhed all around me, the contours of the chapel solidified. Its architectural details emerged, and the scenes and figures that adorned the stained glass windows seemed to come alive in the light of the unnatural flames. Beyond them I sensed that it was

43

night outside, a full moon hanging high and heavy in the sky.

Mocking, otherworldly laughter reverberated through the chapel. This laughter, or something like it, had followed me for what seemed like my entire life. Laughter like this was all I remembered clearly of my life before Eli.

I started running towards the heavy wooden doors that would take me to the cool fresh air outside, but then the sound of an infant crying stopped me in my tracks.

As if to confirm what I'd heard, the cries of the helpless infant grew louder, piercing through the cacophony of vampiric laughter that billowed with the flames.

Damn it. If there was a child trapped somewhere in the chapel, I couldn't leave without it.

The smoke hung thick in the air, obscuring my vision as I stumbled over the charred remnants of church benches and fallen icons, but I pressed on, my heart pounding.

Finally I spotted a flicker of white amidst the flames. Relief washed over me; there was the infant, swathed in delicate lace fabric and tucked behind the burning altar. The cries intensified, and I rushed toward the tiny figure.

As I neared the sunken altar, the entire thing collapsed in a heap of green-tongued flames and smoldering ashes. Reaching behind it, I got hold of a handful of the lace fabric and snatched up the infant. I frantically brushed flakes of burning ash from its face. The cries softened slightly, as if the baby sensed that we were leaving.

The vampiric laughter rose from the flames again, grating against my ears. But I had to ignore it.

Clasping the infant and using my body as a barrier to shield it, I made my way back toward the exit. The flames licked at my heels, hungry for flesh.

I reached the door, and miraculously it was open. Cool

early morning air came streaming in, filling my lungs with life.

But then a chilling realization hit me.

The infant's cries had stopped and been replaced by an eerie silence. I looked down at the bundle in my arms. It held only ashes.

Shock coursed through me like poison, turning my legs into rubber. My mind was reeling with disbelief as the ashes slipped through my fingers. Then, a gust of wind swept through the ravaged chapel and carried them away.

"Harlan," a velvety, haunting voice drifted down from somewhere above me.

Tilting my head back, I found myself face to face with something, or someone, floating in the air above me, a pale face inches from mine.

Like me, this creature was untouched by the flames. I wasn't able to make out any features clearly. They almost seemed to morph and ripple in front of my eyes, as if I were looking into a distorted fun-house mirror. Large honey coloured eyes, a short narrow nose and a pointy chin were the only constants.

"Harlan," the entity repeated my name. "We finally meet in this place where our nightmares and memories converge. I apologise for this rather unpleasant setting, and for the crying infant - they're all mine, I'm afraid. But at least they grabbed your attention."

"Who are you?" I rose to my feet, wiping my soot-stained face. "And what are you talking about?"

"You must listen to me," The voice was still soft, but the creature spoke with a sense of urgency. "You cannot imagine how hard it's been getting through to you. You have such defences, even in your sleep. It's been quite draining trying to find a way in. You have no idea what it has cost me, and I do not know for how much longer I can sustain my presence here."

"What do you want from me?" I demanded. I was now fully aware that this was a dream and I very much wanted it to end. We were still in the burning chapel, but I no longer feared the flames. Now they were just a setting, mere theatre props. As if they were responding to the lack of power they had over me now, they started waning and flickering out.

I was trying my damnedest to see the being I was speaking with clearly, to focus on his features, but somehow I wasn't able to. Everything kept fading in and out of focus, like a long-ago memory. I only managed to latch onto a few details: The burgundy velvet material of his coat, a pale hand, a gleaming cheekbone. Amber-colored eyes.

"Who are you and what do you want? Answer me that, or I don't think we have anything to talk about."

"I want you to come home. I've been waiting for a long, long time."

"You didn't tell me who you are."

"I'm your blood."

"You're lying."

"Blood never lies."

I awoke with a start, drenched in sweat, my heart racing out of my chest. The grey light of morning and the sounds of birds chirping in the peacefully swaying branches outside already filled my room.

I didn't foresee getting any more sleep tonight, so I got

out of bed, pulled on my robe and went out into the hallway, the dream still clinging to me like a dark aura.

I didn't know whether Eli would be back in the house yet or still roaming the woods in his werewolf form. I certainly hadn't sensed him return, or heard anything after I'd fallen asleep.

As I padded out into the hallway and looked down over the balustrade, nothing seemed out of the ordinary. But then I noticed what appeared to be a muddy trail leading from the open front door to somewhere deeper inside the house.

I descended the steps to the hallway quickly, the dark wooden floorboards creaking under my bare feet. The front door was flapping on its hinges, the grey light falling through it making the muddy paw prints on the floor all the more visible. And yes, now that I was close enough to see, they were unmistakably paw prints. Eli's, obviously.

Squinting down at the mess, it looked like there were little broken twigs and even a few feathers protruding from the puddle of mud.

As I pushed the front door closed, I saw that it was nearly torn off its hinges - there were even scratches on the outside. When Eli said this full moon was really getting to him last night, he clearly had not been kidding.

I followed the trail of paw prints. It continued down the hallway, accompanied here and there by claw marks raking the walls. A few landscape paintings hung askew. One hung from its frame in shreds.

Eli was a proud man and usually able to control his beast with the help of the tincture. This time, though, it didn't seem to have done him much good, despite the precipitous amounts of it I'd seen him guzzle down.

When he came to, he'd be mortified. He'd silently go

about fixing everything, but he wouldn't want any of it mentioned with a word.

The trail of wreckage continued past the kitchen - I eyed several broken plates and overturned chairs through the open door - before finally veering off into the library, a room covered floor to ceiling in bookcases and kept in bottle green and wooden tones.

Here, Eli himself had collapsed on the library's old chaise lounge, now drenched and caked in mud. I let out a sigh. At least he was here, and I wouldn't have to go looking for him somewhere outside in the woods.

He had clearly had a rough night and was draped on the couch with the complete abandon of a relapsed alcoholic after a bender. But instead of an empty bottle in his hand and reeking of alcohol, Eli was covered in mud, dry blood and feathers as he slept peacefully.

I picked up a throw that hung on an armchair and put it over him. Trying to wake him up now would be no use. He'd be sleeping like this for at least another 24 to 48 hours. I'd seen it before.

I felt a twinge of guilt knowing what I was about to do next. I knew Eli would be disappointed. But he'd forgive me, eventually, for going against his warning.

I went back upstairs, got dressed, and packed my bags. I hadn't really unpacked anything when I arrived here so all of this took me ten minutes or less.

I walked back down the stairs quietly with my duffel bag slung over my shoulder. It contained just about everything I needed for my trip. My hunting kit was in the kitchen, all clean, packed and ready to go.

There was no point in me staying here, hanging around waiting for Eli to give me his blessing to go. I wasn't going to get it, so I might as well go up to London and find out what secrets Thornhill Mansion held.

To be perfectly honest, I longed to see it for myself, to stand in that mysterious place and breathe in the atmosphere captured in those old daguerreotypes.

Or maybe it was just that I needed something to do with myself while I was exiled from the Van Helsing Society, and this was by far the most fruitful thing that I could pour my energy into. I'd be an idiot to say no.

Then again, Eli might be right and I might be an idiot to say yes. There was only one way of finding out. Right?

Back in the library, I rifled through the tightly packed shelves until I found what I was looking for. I scooped the few books Eli had on the Highgate Vampire phenomenon, ley lines, and Highgate's generally haunted history into my bag. There was no telling whether I was going to need any of these reference materials, but it was best to be prepared.

Then I wrote and placed a note on the coffee table where Eli was bound to see it when he woke up.

Well, the first thing he was going to see would be himself covered in blood and mud and feathers. But after that, my note would be waiting to convey my message; that I had gone up to London to meet with Lyrica Hartenbrook, that I hadn't made up my mind yet as to whether or not I was going to get involved in her vampire problem, and that if I did decide to get involved, he was welcome to join me or not join me as he wished.

I imagined him waking up, embarrassed to have lost control over his beast and at the state of the house. But there was nothing I could do about any of that.

Really, he wouldn't want me to see either him or the house like this. He wouldn't want me to tidy up the mess, either. Whenever he'd found me picking up broken china or scrubbing mud off the floor in the past, he'd admonished me to leave it to him. He seemed to think that picking up after his wolf was a necessary form of retribution. My going to London would actually be a relief to him. If I stuck around here, I'd be getting in his way.

"I'm sorry," I said out loud, "but I've got something I need to do."

Eli didn't stir in the slightest, but I thought that there was a catch in his breathing, as if he wanted to protest against my plans even in his deeply unconscious state.

~

A few hours later, I was riding in the back of an Uber up Swain's Lane in London. The lane is steep and narrow and runs down the middle of Highgate Cemetery, dividing it in two uneven halves.

It was early afternoon, and the sun was gleaming golden through the branches reaching over the lane, forming a sort of canopy overhead.

The memory of the dream, which had followed me to the airport like a persistent shadow, was finally starting to fade, but the ghost of it still lingered. The mysterious creature's words still bothered me. I didn't like the way it, or he, had talked about building a bridge and gaining entry into my mind, I mean what the fuck? And what had he meant when he had told me to 'come home'?

The hum of the car's engine created a soothing backdrop as I looked out over the sun-dotted Victorian cemetery, trying to ignore the unease that clung to the edges of my mind. The truth was that I didn't have time to be consumed by cryptic messages from my subconscious. It's what I loved the most about my job, actually - helping others get rid of the darkness that stalked their lives usually meant I didn't have time to dwell on my own.

I'd been in this area of London before, but I'd never paid it the kind of attention I was paying it now. I asked the driver to drive uphill as slowly as he could so I could take in the view. He didn't seem to think this was an eccentric request, and why would he? Highgate Cemetery is perhaps the crown jewel among the Magnificent Seven Cemeteries that were built to accommodate the capital's dead in the late Victorian era. Today it is a Grade 1 listed nature reserve, at least according to Wikipedia.

Highgate Cemetery West is also where the entity known as the Highgate Vampire allegedly roamed and attacked people back in the early '70s. Back then, it would have been both easy to see and access the cemetery from the road, but now it was nearly hidden from view behind tall walls and heavy fencing. These things had been put in place, not as much to keep the entity in as to keep would-be vampire hunters out.

Driving up Swain's Lane, it is much easier to get a good look at the East Side. Looking in, it seemed to be a perfect balance between decay and order. Here and there, lone visitors and small groups of tourists were visible through the fence and branches, walking around among tumbling tombstones and moss-covered stone angels.

I'd skimmed through Eli's books on the plane between Edinburgh and London Stansted, brushing up on my knowledge about Highgate and its mysteries, ley lines, entities and hauntings. A couple of the books had his own notes and theories scrawled in the margin, revealing that Eli had been one of the Society hunters sent to investigate the alleged vampire phenomenon. But apparently, Eli had never set foot in Thornhill Mansion, despite its proximity to the cemetery and its apparent connection to it.

As I looked up now, Thornhill Mansion came into view, looming above the West side of the cemetery.

Hadn't Jeremy Gently said that the mansion was as old as the cemetery, and that the grounds now housing the cemetery had once been part of the Thornhill estate?

While both sides of the cemetery were well kept and looked after, the crumbling plasterwork, broken windows and unkempt grounds of Thornhill Mansion suggested that it was decades past its glory days.

I reached into my pocket, my fingers brushing against the rusty set of keys that the solicitor had given me as the car pulled up in front of an old but impressive wrought-iron gate. In front of it stood Jeremy Gently dressed in a neat, pale blue pin-striped linen suit. With him was a tall, slim younger man dressed in black. I'd called ahead, of course, and knew that my arrival was expected.

"This is it," I assured the driver, who was giving me a doubtful look in the rearview mirror. He hesitated momentarily before killing the engine and stepping out to open the trunk for me. I stepped out of the car too, the payment already settled through the app.

As I stood there on the warm pavement of Swain's Lane, looking up at the mansion, it seemed to have an almost otherworldly quality about it. It reminded me faintly of a fairytale castle, forgotten by time and covered in vine and the snaking stalks of thorny roses. All that was missing was a sleeping beauty in a glass coffin inside. Or was I mixing up my fairytales here?

I retrieved my duffel bag filled with clothes and my hunting kit from the Uber's trunk. Who knew if Lyrica Hartenbrook's vampire problem was going to require the stakes, the thin, sharp Japanese steel blades or perhaps even the crossbow?

Then again, there was always the possibility that Lyrica Hartenbrook would turn out to be one of those clients that have deluded themselves into thinking they're haunted or plagued by some supernatural entity when really they're just depressed, traumatized or otherwise disturbed.

My gut told me that this wasn't the case, though. I took a step forward; I was ready to find out.

CHAPTER
SIX

The sprawling city beyond the unkempt grounds of Thornhill Mansion must have changed countless times since the days when horse-drawn carriages used to travel the narrow passage of Swain's Lane. But the mansion, lost in time, had only faded.

Cracked, arched windows framed by weather-worn shutters peered out onto the world with a melancholic gaze, as if the mansion had a consciousness and was perfectly, painfully aware of this.

My attention was so consumed by the grandeur of the building that I momentarily forgot all about the solicitor and the younger man standing with him by the gate.

My trance was broken when Jeremy Gently cleared his throat politely and extended his hand towards me for a shake. "It's good to see you again, Mr. Thorne. I wasn't sure you'd come."

I blinked at him a few times, then shook his hand. "Neither was I, to be honest. But I've decided to at least meet with Lyrica Hartenbrook, hear what she has to say."

"I know she'll appreciate it. Now, before we go in,"

Gently said, turning to his black-clad companion, "let me introduce you to Sebastian Rose."

The young man standing beside the solicitor, arms crossed, seemed to relax slightly, extending his hand to shake mine. He eyed me with a sense of suspicion that I can tell you right now was entirely mutual.

"Sebastian Rose," he said his name with a slight but unimpressed smile. "Pleasure to meet you."

"Sebastian Rose is here working on a photography book." A note of approval was evident in Gently's tone. "With Ms. Hartenbrook's permission, of course."

I eyed the photographer with even greater suspicion now. I hadn't expected this. Why bring a vampire hunter and a photographer here at the same time? Having a guy with a camera traipsing around the place, capturing images of my activities, and probably asking probing questions, was not what I needed.

"Harlan Thorne," I introduced myself, reluctantly shaking Sebastian's outstretched hand. His fingers were bony, but his palm was warm. His eyes were deep pools of dark blue when he removed his sunglasses. His skin was fair, and his hair, falling nearly to his shoulders, was pitch black. His features were all sharp and narrow.

"Young Mr. Rose here," Gently elaborated, apparently enthused that we had made each other's acquaintance, "is rather famous. He has a tremendous following online. He's here to capture material for a book he's working on, his latest and greatest, as I understand it?"

Gently glanced over at the apparently famous photographer as if seeking confirmation.

"That's right," Sebastian nodded. "I've been struggling with inspiration lately, but this place," he gestured towards the crumbling mansion, "really refills my creative well. I think I'll feature it on the front cover of 'Haunted Halls,' my book? It's all about haunted UK houses, mansions, pubs, castles. And you, I hear you're some kind of a paranormal investigator?" He asked this with a hint of genuine interest dancing in his eyes.

"Something like that," I mumbled, hoping I wouldn't have to elaborate on the white lie Gently must have told him.

"I'm glad to see the two of you getting on," Gently commented with a note of relief that I, for one, didn't share. The weekend had barely begun, and I was already worried about Sebastian getting in the way of the work that I was here to do. I hoped Lyrica Hartenbrook had thought this through.

Where was she, anyway, the mysterious owner of this place? Shouldn't she be here to meet me and clue me in on her vampire problem?

As if reacting to my thoughts, the next words out of Jeremy Gently's mouth were, "Ms. Hartenbrook is on her way. She's given me permission to show the two of you around before she arrives."

"That would be great," Sebastian said, eyes gleaming with the thrill of anticipation. Turning to me he added, "You know, I don't mind you being here. As long as your equipment doesn't obstruct my scenes, we should be fine."

"Likewise," I responded, the word falling from my lips clipped and dry.

"Are you familiar with my work?" Sebastian asked testily. "'Fairgrounds of Doom', or perhaps 'Mountains of Despair?'"

"Can't say that I am."

He frowned, as if my ignorance was hard to wrap his head around. "I'll show you later if you're still around."

I left his offer hanging in the air without a response.

Gently interjected, breaking the tension, "Why don't we step inside, gentlemen? Let me give you the grand tour. And I'm sure," he added, "that both of you can pursue your respective endeavours without getting in each other's way."

Looking at the sceptical expression on Sebastian's face, it was clear that neither of us were as optimistic as the solicitor, who now dropped his voice low and said, "Before we enter, let me just say this as clearly as I can. I'll show you around the place, but only until Ms. Hartenbrook arrives and takes over as your guide and hostess. When she does, that will be the end of my involvement here."

Sebastian shrugged, but I acknowledged the solicitor's words with a nod. "Sure. I won't bother you if the plumbing doesn't work."

Gently smiled but did not laugh. "Shall we go in?"

"Please, after you," I said before realizing that I, too, held the keys.

Retrieving them from my pocket, I selected the largest one, adorned with a lion's head at the top. Slipping it into the lock, I turned it with a satisfying click. The ornate gate swung open as if a set of hidden springs had been released.

I stepped through the gate, Sebastian following close behind. Gently lingered for a moment, as if waiting for someone else to take the first step off a plank. Then he followed us, looking anxiously over his shoulder as if to reassure himself that the gate was still open.

The grass, tall and vibrant, reached up to my knees, a vivid emerald shade of green. It felt like an untamed wilderness. Gnarled trees, their branches bending like witches' fingers toward the golden glow of the sky, created a haunting ambiance. Butterflies and bees fluttered lazily amidst the wildflowers that speckled the lawn. Here and there, statues with mournful faces peeked up through the tall grass.

The entire grounds seemed on edge, as if holding their collective breath, waiting for something to happen.

Then again, maybe it was just me. I exhaled, realizing I had been holding my breath.

"Isn't it, for want of a better word, magnificent?" Gently's voice brimmed with anxious awe. I could only nod. No word of a lie. There was something about the rambling beauty of this place that made my eyes water.

The mansion itself perched upon a vast terrace facing the cemetery. The large windows that punctuated its exterior overlooked both the cemetery and Swain's Lane. Rising three stories tall, the architectural style fluctuated between Gothic and Rococo. Whoever the architect had been, he had been fond of majestic columns, turrets and delicate curlicues.

"Thornhill Mansion has been abandoned, more or less, since the mid 1800s," Gently narrated as Sebastian and I took in the mansion and its grounds. "In its day, it was a symbol of the Thornhill family's magnificent wealth."

I nodded silently.

"Why was it ever abandoned?" asked Sebastian. "And why, if she lacks the means to restore it, hasn't Lyrica Hartenbrook sold it? Can't be hard to get rid of a house in this postcode."

"Oh, she could never bear to part with the family seat," Gently dismissed the possibility, "even if it comes with certain challenges. But you're quite right. Although some repair work was carried out in the '70s, there weren't the means to complete the restoration. That would require millions."

"It seems almost sinful to let a beautiful place like this sink into ruin," Sebastian murmured, and for the first time he'd said something I agreed with. He crouched down and snapped a few photos of the mansion seen through the tall swaying grass.

"Unfortunately, it happens all the time. Beautiful historic places, left to decay. Now," Gently gestured to indicate the right side of the mansion, "let us first explore the gardens. See the well over there? Records found in the attic indicate that one of Algernon Thornhill's scullery maids tragically drowned in it, as did several servants' children over the years. It could have been seeing one or more of these child ghosts that triggered Helen Thornhill's descent into mental illness, ultimately leading to her fatal fall from the balustrade inside the house."

Of course. It seemed inevitable that a place like this would have more than a few ghost in its haunted history.

"Do you still have those records from the attic?" I asked, my curiosity piqued. "I don't know, but they could turn out to be helpful."

Gently nodded. "I have them in my office. Helen Thornhill's diaries and a few other documents. I saw it fit to remove them from the building to protect them from the rain and such, which could have destroyed them long ago. I've kept them safe, but you're welcome to read through them. If you wish, I'll have them sent tomorrow by taxi. But," he added, "just a heads up. Helen was already descending into madness when she penned her last diary entries. It appears she experienced sudden delusions."

"In the Victorian era, weren't most women deemed delusional?"

"In this case, I believe she truly was," Gently said solemnly. "But it's not for me to draw conclusions."

While talking, we had gravitated toward the well, our footsteps leading us near the muddy ground surrounding it. It looked ancient, far older than the building itself, its copper lid a rusty green, firmly affixed.

"Of course, they covered it after what happened," Gently observed. "It was said that the ghost of an ill-fated servant child haunted this area, seen playing around the well. Numerous family members, guests, and staff witnessed such spectacles. Shall we move inside?"

Gently turned around and started leading us towards the mansion's front steps. "I'm eager to show you the rest. But keep your wits about you when we step inside - I've been unable to maintain the upkeep of this place, to the point of it being uninhabitable, at least in the conventional sense. Squatters took refuge here in the late '60s - hippies, of course. They caused some damage, in addition to the damage already been wreaked by decades of winds and rains."

We ascended the stairs to the front doors. Only a few were cracked but all of them were covered in ivy and the enthusiastically overgrown roots of trees. Gently skillfully navigated around the treacherous roots and branches in a way that was so familiar as to suggest he would have known where to put his feet in his sleep.

"Please, open it," he insisted, stepping aside. I retrieved the keys from my pocket and inserted the smaller of the two into the lock. The door yielded with a soft click and then it opened, its weathered wood emitting a groan.

Stepping across the threshold, I found myself in a magnificent hallway, Sebastian squeezing in behind me with his camera lifted and his finger on its trigger.

Somehow, the mansion was much larger on the inside than it had appeared from the outside. The ceiling soared to a height of perhaps eighteen feet, topped by a shattered stained glass cupola.

Several of the great hall's windows were shattered and the branches of trees extended through them, some of them bearing fruit - red apples and plums, nearly ripe. Dusty sunlight filtered through the stained glass and blended with the shadows of the branches. Dust and leaves covered the black and white marble-tiled floor. From the hallway, several doors beckoned, leading to other rooms. And a dark wooden staircase ascended up into the gloom, disappearing from view on the first landing.

I audibly released a breath. Gently remained silent, clasping his hands in front him as if deliberately refraining from interrupting the moment. Even Sebastian was momentarily frozen in awe, the camera dropping from his hands and dangling from its strap around his neck.

Finally, the solicitor spoke, breaking the silence. "Welcome," he said emphatically, "to Thornhill Mansion."

CHAPTER

SEVEN

L eaving our bags in a pile in the hallway for now, Gently
proceeded to give us the grand tour he had promised.

I was conscious of leaving my kit behind, but I
took comfort in the two short blades I always carried,
tucked into hidden sheaths in the backs of my boots.
Besides, if Lyrica Hartenbrook was really troubled by
vampires, the force or entity that haunted her wouldn't
show up for at least another hour.

The first room Gently showed us was a large drawing
room. Its faded walls were covered in gilded paintings,
swords, and bayonets.

Ancient wicker chairs and a table still stood in its
center, giving the impression that the mansion's inhabi-
tants had just stepped away. The delicate bone china on the
table added to the impression that someone had recently
savored a cup of tea and might return at any moment.

The only thing that contradicted this illusion was the
dust that had settled on everything in the room, including
the ivy creeping across the floor.

In the next room we entered, also a drawing room or living room of sorts, a fallen chandelier glistened with fragmented crystals. A majestic white marble fireplace dominated one wall, stretching almost its entire length.

Gently led us through this room to smaller rooms that had once served as servants' quarters. In its heyday, he explained, the Thornhill family had employed not only chefs and scullery maids but also a coach driver and a gardener in addition to all the crew members who worked aboard the family's ships.

On the other side of the servants' quarters was a large kitchen, its beautifully crafted sturdy wood cupboards and surfaces covered in cobwebs and dust. Gently pulled out an empty drawer with a sigh, "Regrettably, the squatters made off with what was left of the silver."

Adjacent to the kitchen was a dim dining room with a very long dining table. "This is where the family would gather for meals and entertain guests and business acquaintances. And there," Gently paused in front of a strikingly lifelike painting, "we have a portrait of a young Algernon Thornhill."

Although twenty years younger, the square-jawed man staring out of the canvas with steely determination was easily recognizable as the proud lord I'd seen in the daguerreotypes. Sebastian snapped several photos of the portrait.

"Oh dear, time's slipping away," Gently interrupted, glancing at his wristwatch. "We must get on. Follow me, gentlemen."

Stepping through the door on the other side of the dining room brought us back to the entrance hall.

"Should we bring up our bags?" asked Sebastian.

Gently hesitated, as if he wanted to say one thing but was obliged to say another.

"If you wish to stay here overnight. It is entirely up to you. Two rooms have been prepared upstairs, with new mattresses, fresh bedding, and towels. The plumbing in the corner bathroom works, but there is no hot water, I'm afraid. And of course, as you've just seen, the kitchen is entirely defunct. Miss Hartenbrook has instructed me to stay that although the arrangements are humble, you are both more than welcome to stay. She is, however, also willing to cover more comfortable lodgings at a hotel."

"Oh, I'm staying here," Sebastian declared, gathering up his bags. "I want the full haunted house experience. It's all creative fodder." He turned and shot me a glance, silently daring me.

"I'm still undecided," I said honestly. "I'll let you know once I've met and spoken with Lyrica."

"Very well." Gently gestured uneasily towards the staircase. "Shall we?"

Each step seemed to groan beneath my weight, making me wonder if they could bear the burden of all three of us.

Turned out that it could. Against the odds, we arrived on the first landing, where several more portraits adorned the walls. The largest one depicted Algernon again, a man in his prime this time, captured at around the age forty to forty-five. Lord Thornhill appeared more robust in this painting than in the one downstairs, and he was dressed as befitting a prosperous merchant of the era.

A beautiful ebony-haired woman sat beside him in a wingback chair. Two small children, a fiery-haired girl with vibrant curls, and a stern-faced boy stood on either side. Both children seemed somewhat petulant, their gazes challenging.

"The family gathered," Gently announced, pointing out Algernon, Helen, Venedict, and Octavia. "This is the only painting we have of the entire family together. It was painted right down there in the front parlor. Just a few short years before it all went... awry."

We continued our ascent, the creaking floorboards accompanying us to the first floor. Up here, a dim hallway seemed to stretch endlessly in both directions. To one side, doors led to individual rooms, while on the other side, a grand set of doors beckoned us into the library.

"This way," Gently said, pushing the half-open doors fully open with a screech of rusty hinges. "This is one of my favorite rooms in this house, if I may say so."

The library was bathed in the soft glow of tall, slender Gothic windows overlooking the garden. Instead of a conventional ceiling, a stained glass dome covered the room, reminiscent of the shattered one covering the hallway below.

Floor-to-ceiling wooden bookcases lined every inch of wall space, all of them close to overflowing with ocean-blue and green leather-bound books, hues that mirrored the dark, swirling patterns of the carpet.

Most of the books were intact, as far as I could tell. "These are probably pretty valuable," I remarked, and Gently gave a slight nod. "This room seems to have been remarkably spared by the weather. That's why I left them here instead of moving them elsewhere, although perhaps I should have."

I pulled out an old copy of 'Frankenstein' from one of the shelves and flipped through the yellowed pages. It was a first edition, but despite its age, it seemed to be in pretty good condition. I imagined curling up in one of the moth-eaten armchairs and reading it like a true Victorian in the dim light of flickering candles or oil lamps.

"Well then, let's get this tour wrapped up," Gently suggested, casting a glance towards the windows where the sun was already setting, and shadows from the nearby cemetery were extending through the fence.

We exited through another set of creaky doors and passed through a recital room before returning to the corridor where Gently continued to lead the way, opening doors here and there, revealing the rooms beyond. Most appeared to be guest rooms or private quarters, occupied by four-poster beds and a variety of canopy styles, some accompanied by dust-covered writing desks, cracked mirrors, or empty wardrobes. Dust and cobwebs were the two most prevalent features.

The two best-kept second-floor bedrooms - Venedict and Octavia Thornhill's, apparently - had been made up for me and Sebastian. Just as Gently had promised, each was equipped with a new mattress and made up with fluffy, inviting bedding. At the foot ends were neatly folded towels, and between the two rooms, connecting them, was a marble-tiled bathroom that seemed to have been recently cleaned.

Sebastian immediately claimed Venedict's red-lacquered room overlooking both the darkening garden and the cemetery by offloading his bags on the bed. This left me with Octavia's room, no less ostentatious but facing the other way, towards Highgate Village and away from the cemetery.

Gently ushered us along to the second and third floors, which revealed more of the same, except that up here many of the old rooms had been sealed off due to, he explained, the extensive damage caused by decades of rain and fallen branches. Finally, we came to a stop at the end of the third-floor hallway. Gently pointed to a winding and rather rusty wrought-iron staircase.

"Up here," he said, "is the last thing I'm bound to show you."

Gripping the rusty handrail, the elderly solicitor started climbing. I was vaguely worried that he'd trip and fall, but he seemed surefooted. Sebastian and I followed, and soon the three of us stepped out into a vast attic space with sloping walls.

The attic seemed to stretch across the entire house without any dividing walls. There were few windows in this expansive space, but they allowed enough dim light to filter through, reflecting dusty squares on the floorboards. Old trunks were scattered and in some cases stacked throughout the space. In one of the squares of twilight falling through an overhead window stood a dollhouse, an intricately crafted replica of the mansion.

"This place," Gently explained from his lingering position on the stairs behind us, "still contains many of the Thornhill family's possessions - clothes, diaries, daguerreotypes. You're both more than welcome to explore it all, in your own time. But now, I must be on my way or I'll be running late for my granddaughter's piano recital. Ms. Hartenbrook really shouldn't be long now."

Jeremy Gently was glancing at his watch again, and for some reason he suddenly reminded me of the White Rabbit from Alice in Wonderland. He was clearly anxious to be on his way.

"I don't think we have any reason to keep you," I said, hoping to reassure him and ease his nerves. "I don't mind if you leave now. Thanks for the tour."

Sebastian didn't respond one way or the other, his

attention fully concentrated on getting a shot of the dollhouse.

I hesitated, but then I reluctantly tore myself away from the attic and its secrets, deciding to see Gently out.

I accompanied him all the way out to the wrought-iron gate where he and Sebastian had been waiting for me earlier. Leaning against it I watched him climb into his Beetle and speed off down Swain's Lane while the setting sun cast its last rays over the garden.

I turned to go back to the house, but the sight that met me froze me in place.

Sebastian, who I thought I had left behind, happily occupied in the attic, was standing over near the fence separating the garden from the cemetery. His back was to me, and he was gesturing animatedly.

He wasn't alone.

I started hurrying over to where Sebastian and his mysterious conversation partner were standing engrossed in their exchange. The overgrown garden seemed to conspire to keep them both hidden from view as I approached, their figures partially obscured by tangled foliage and creeping shadows.

Finally, I was close enough to see them both clearly. Standing halfway between Sebastian and the wrought-iron fence, facing me, was an ethereal beauty who could only be Lyrica Hartenbrook.

CHAPTER

EIGHT

O ur eyes locked, hers burning with a cool, blue fire. Time stood still as we both stood frozen, the world around us echoing with a deafening silence. The entire grounds held its breath, waiting for the momentary enchantment to rupture.

Lyrica Hartenbrook stood at around 5'5. She was dressed in a long, deep blue velvet dress, old-fashioned high-heeled leather boots peeking out beneath it. She had straight, obsidian-black hair that cascaded down her back and gleamed like a midnight sky. It framed her slim-boned, elegant face and large, luminous eyes. Her porcelain skin was as flawless as the moonlight's reflection on a still lake and completely without pores.

But it wasn't just her porcelain skin or the fact that she seemed frozen in eternal youth that gave it away. It was her undeniable aura, a primal sort of magnetism that humans just don't possess.

Yes, you guessed it; Lyrica Hartenbrook was a vampire.

I blinked, looked away, and broke our eye contact. I

knew better than to look a vampire in the eyes for long. Eye contact is a key component in how they hypnotize you, although some of the older ones have mastered additional ways of taking control of their victims' minds, like using hand gestures or even just their voices.

"Sebastian, get back!"

I didn't wait for him to react but stepped out in front of him while reaching for the blades in my boots. I was careful not to look Lyrica in the eye, but I didn't take my eyes off of her.

"What the hell are you doing?" Notes of outrage and shock were vying for dominance in Sebastian's tone, and I could understand why. He was blissfully unaware of what Lyrica was, and oblivious to the danger she posed.

"I didn't think you were a thug! Gently already showed us around, and there's nothing really of value in the mansion!"

"Look down, Sebastian. I don't have time to explain, but our hostess here could be extremely dangerous."

"What are you on about?"

Sebastian was reluctant, but he hung back, not wanting to get anywhere near my gleaming blades.

I knew that Lyrica Hartenbrook would have strength and speed that far surpassed my own. And to make matters worse, my crossbow, stakes, and gun were all still inside in the hall.

I also knew that I had Sebastian to contend with. He was a regular civilian and it was going to be up to me to protect him against Lyrica's attack, if she decided to go down that route.

There were also the more mundane risk that he might call the police and get me arrested for armed robbery or whatever he thought I was up to. Thankfully, he didn't seem to have his phone on him, only his camera. Behind me, I could hear him cursing under his breath while patting his pockets.

I hadn't been prepared for this and now I was cursing myself internally. In the blink of an eye, Lyrica could close the distance between us and sink her teeth into my artery, or Sebastian's.

Thankfully, she remained frozen in place. She only opened her mouth slightly, revealing glistening fangs. My concentration was split between her face and her hands, searching for the faintest twitch or sign of aggression.

"Stay right there," I commanded her through clenched teeth, infusing my voice with as much authority as I could summon. "I know what you are. And I know how to use these." Indicating the knives I held aimed at her heart, I hoped to make it clear that underestimating me would be a mistake, and it would be.

Silence hung heavily in the air, her lips still not moving. It was as if she retreated into herself. If I didn't know any better, I'd say she seemed embarrassed to have been immediately recognized as a vampire.

"I know who you are." When she finally spoke, her voice was deceptively soft and gentle, almost vulnerable. "And I am so delighted to see you. To see you both."

In a decidedly inhuman gesture, she sniffed the air, her pearlescent nostrils flaring. There was a pause, a hesitation, before she said, "You're of my blood, yes, I was not mistaken."

My eyes widened.

She took a step forward and I tightened my grip on both knife handles.

"Don't come any closer," I warned. "I won't hesitate to harm you."

Just like you probably won't hesitate to harm us, I added silently.

"I mean you no harm," she reassured me, her voice like a ribbon made of midnight blue silk. "I merely wish to speak with you and, well..." She hesitated again. "You're of my blood, the two of you. I know it as surely as I know anything, and that is why I have summoned you here. You, of course, already know that I am Lyrica Hartenbrook. And as you have clearly already sensed, the vampire problem that I called you here to resolve is very... personal."

"This is all getting more and more confusing by the minute," Sebastian cut in from somewhere behind me. His words mirrored my own feelings about how the evening was going. "Isn't someone going to explain what is going on?"

"I think Lyrica here is the one who owes us both an explanation," I said, backing up a little in a way that also forced Sebastian to step away from Lyrica's reach. "She's brought us both here under false pretenses. She's not what she seems."

"But she just said she's Lyrica Hartenbrook," Sebastian protested.

"I had to lure you here. What other options did I have?" Lyrica's tone was melancholy. "If I'd stated clearly what I am and that I would like to meet with you and speak with you because you are my descendants, neither of you would have come."

"Wait, are you saying we're related?" Sebastian's tone hovered somewhere between skeptical and hopeful. "If you'd just said that, I would absolutely have come. I grew up in foster homes and have longed to connect with my real family my entire freaking life! Any invitation would have done it for me, honestly."

"I understand your confusion, and I can sense your doubts," Lyrica's eyes flickered from me to Sebastian and back again. She held up her palms in a gesture to show that she meant no harm. Her intention fell somewhat short thanks to her long, translucent fingernails that tapered into talon-like points and the pale, marble-like flesh of her hands. "But I know, in the depths of my bones and my soul, that the two of you are the last of my bloodline, and that I had to meet you."

I looked from her to Sebastian. Despite the obvious differences that set them apart, I had to admit there were also echoes of familiarity in their faces. The contrasting coloring of their skin and hair, and particularly the deep cerulean color of their eyes.

My own coloring, of course, was different, but it didn't seem impossible that my features might have been carved by the same DNA as both of theirs. What to make of that?

"I swear on my soul," Lyrica spoke again, "and as far as I know I still possess one, I am Lyrica Hartenbrook, and this house, these grounds, they belong to my long-lost family. You, Harlan Thorne and Sebastian Rose, belong to them as well. I would not even dream of hurting you. If I simply wanted your blood, I would have made my move, would I not? Now, please, let us talk. Allow me to tell you my story. That's all I ask. If, after hearing me out you don't believe me, then you may plunge your blades through my heart."

She nodded toward the blades in my hands, their twin points still aimed at her chest.

"I have no fear of dying," she added calmly. "In fact, I

believe I may have already lived for far too long. I have a vampire problem, indeed. But please, let us continue this conversation inside, in the library. It will be more comfortable there. I will keep my distance, I promise. I'll sit on the other side of the room, if you wish. If I make any false move, you will have ample time to retrieve your weapons. All I ask for is a little of your time."

"What is all this crazy talk about blood and having lived for too long?" Sebastian demanded, stepping forward again, stopping only when his chest bumped against my raised arm still holding the knife. "And of course, we'll hear your story - well, I can't really speak for Harlan, but I want to hear every last bit of it. I want to know everything about the Thornhill family and how we're, as you say, connected."

"There is so much I have to explain, so much I have to share," said Lyrica. "Please come with me."

"I'm coming with you," Sebastian started walking in an arch to get around me so he could follow Lyrica back into the shadow-filled mansion. "Harlan, if you're coming with us, you better put those knives away. Or I'll call the police once we're inside. Can't believe you'd actually threaten an unarmed woman." He walked over and stood beside Lyrica, fixing me with a disapproving glare.

"Harlan is quite right to want to protect you from me," Lyrica said, as if trying to smooth things over between us. "It is true, I could be very dangerous. It just happens that I am not dangerous to you. Like I said, you are my flesh and blood, even if the link that connects us is very old."

I weighed my options while Sebastian, in the background, was asking more questions. On one hand, we could stand out here until sunrise. And on the other hand, by offering to tell us her story, Lyrica had offered something that was likely better than the tense standoff we were currently engaged in.

I also had to admit that her claims about our supposed blood connection had piqued my curiosity. I mean, how could it not? Like Sebastian, I barely knew anything about my roots. I'd always longed for anything at all that might connect me to a history, a place, a family.

"Before we go any further in any direction you've got to answer me this. How did you find us?" I challenged her.

Lyrica sighed. "I never willingly let you out of my sight. I've always, as far as possible, kept an eye on the last mortal branches of the family tree. From a respectful distance, of course."

Unexpected. Had Lyrica, had this vampire been aware of me and kept an eye on me all my life? And if so - my mind immediately went there - what did she know about my parents, about who they'd been and how they had lost their lives? Despite the infuriating lack of detail that defined my own memory of them, I knew this much: my parents had died at the hands of a vampire. A male vampire, though. I remembered him - or at least, I remembered the outline of his shoulders and the cast of his chin, silhouetted against flames. It couldn't have been Lyrica.

My mind was brimming with questions, but this was the one that came out of my mouth. "If you've known about me for 27 years, why contact me now? Why not sooner or not at all?"

"Well, to be honest, both of your parents got away from me. I've only known about you, Sebastian, from the time you entered the foster care system. And you, Harlan, flew under my radar for even longer than that. I only found you when I started haring whispers on the grapevine, whispers of a phenomenal hunter of my kind."

Lyrica lowered her voice to almost a whisper, as if the words had sharp edges that made them difficult to get them out.

"Once I found you, I never wanted to interfere with either of your lives. I wanted you to live untouched by the darkness that engulfed me long ago. I am sorry it didn't quite work out that way, for either of you. I've contacted you now because, well, you deserve to know the family history. And perhaps I deserve to finally confess my story to someone."

I lowered my knives.

"All right. We'll talk, have a civil conversation - but make a false move, and our truce will be over just like that."

"Of course."

Lyrica fearlessly turned her back to us and started swiftly gliding through the tall grass, with Sebastian and me following her.

"Is it just me," Sebastian whispered in my ear, but I had no doubt Lyrica's refined hearing was also picking it up, "or are you and she both rambling mad?"

I let his question go unanswered, but my shoulders relaxed a little as we followed the vampire back into the mansion, up the dark staircase, and into the library. As Lyrica had pointed out, if all she wanted was our blood, she would have already attacked. Besides, why go through the effort of having her solicitor track me down and draw me in with an elaborate ploy if she simply wanted a meal? London was heaving with potential prey. No, it seemed plausible enough that she wanted both myself and Sebastian here, alive.

With twilight falling through the tall arched garden-facing windows and filtering through the stained-glass dome far above our heads, there was more natural light in here than there was outside.

Lyrica's supernatural senses meant she had no trouble seeing in the dark, but she turned on all the green banker's lamps, a few of them flickering reluctantly as they sprung to life. I hadn't expected the mansion to have any electricity - it was a nice surprise that it did.

Cast in the soft glow of the lamps, I noticed a vintage record player on a table in the corner, and next to it a tall stack of vinyl: Black Sabbath, The Carpenters, Alice Cooper. A lot of stuff from the '70s and '80s.

Lyrica selected a moth-eaten Victorian loveseat for herself, and Sebastian and I sat down on the worn blue velvet sofa across from her. Between us was an ornately carved dark wooden coffee table. Expressive cherubic faces formed a border around its oblong edge and seemed to be peering out of the wood. They, too, were waiting to hear Lyrica's story.

I maintained my composure, but I couldn't help but shift uncomfortably in the vampire's presence. Sebastian shifted uneasily too, but in his case, the reason seemed to be a rusty spring protruding through the ancient upholstery.

"You must promise to hear me out with open minds."

Lyrica's clear cerulean eyes brimmed with something like longing. She let her gaze glide from me to Sebastian and back again.

"Of course," Sebastian promised easily.

"I'll try," I said, not wanting to make any promises I couldn't keep.

Through the tall windows, the view of the garden and the soft drizzle that had started as soon as we were inside were the only reminders that there was still a world outside.

"You already know who I am," Lyrica began. "And you know that I preside over Thornhill Mansion in the absence of any other heirs. But there is so much more to know. In order to fully explain why the three of us have come to be here tonight, you must allow me to take us all the way back to the beginning. Or more specifically, to my beginning."

CHAPTER
NINE

"I was born," Lyrica began, shifting a little in her chair as if settling in for a long journey, "in 1839."

I didn't bat an eyelid, but Sebastian lifted both of his hands as if in protest against what he was hearing.

"Wait, hold on! You said eighteen-thirty-nine. That would make you - that's impossible." He laughed nervously. "If you want me to listen with an open mind, you've got to keep to the facts."

"The year of my birth is a fact," Lyrica said firmly. "And yes, I am 184 years old."

Sebastian looked crestfallen. Now it was his turn to get up in arms. "Is this some kind of joke?"

"Not at all," Lyrica assured him. "I am truly that old. I know I don't look it, but my appearance has been frozen in time since All Hallow's Eve, 1861. I was 22 years and 9 months old when I was turned."

"Turned?"

Lyrica's eyes twinkled - she clearly sensed Sebastian's disbelief, which now hung in the air like a spirit demanding an exorcism.

With a graceful movement, she rose from the loveseat and stepped back to create a small distance between herself and the carved table. The moonlight fell on her porcelain skin, intensifying her ethereal aura.

"I understand that you are sceptical, but I have walked this world for nearly two centuries, Sebastian," she said softly. "And I possess immortal strength. Allow me to show you just a glimpse of it."

As the words left her lips, an air of concentration enveloped her. In the blink of an eye, her figure blurred with rapid movement, and when it solidified again, she stood by the window several feet away.

Sebastian's eyes widened as his mind struggled to wrap around what he had just seen. His expression as he gawped at Lyrica was a mix of awe and complete bewilderment. She moved easily back toward us, but at a normal pace this time. She rearranged herself in the threadbare loveseat. She'd proven her point.

"I am what you would call a vampire, but please do not let that frighten you." Lyrica was addressing this to us both, but her eyes flickered to Sebastian. "The two of you are completely safe in my presence. You are the last unspoilt fruit on the family tree."

She flashed us a smile that would have been reassuring if it weren't for the pearlescent gleam of her fangs.

Sebastian had turned almost as pale as Lyrica and was pressing himself back against the sofa's backrest, now completely heedless of all the rusty springs. His mouth was working, but no words were coming out. He looked to me, as if for my reassurance.

"She isn't lying, at least not about being a vampire."

Lyrica folded her hands in her lap. "Shall we get on with my story?"

"Absolutely," I said, but Sebastian could barely nod his head.

~

As I was saying, I was born in 1839, not far from here. A leisurely half-hour walk would take you to my childhood home in Kentish Town. Alas, the building where I grew up has been replaced by so-called luxury flats and no longer exists.

Back then, the population density was much lower. London's boroughs resembled separate towns loosely connected. In other words, growing up in Kentish Town was quite like growing up in a different town from Highgate Village, where we are now.

One of the mysteries of vampirism is that you don't exactly cease to grow or change as a person when you become one. But your essence is permanently shaped by your human life, regardless of how short it might have been. In my case, of course, I grew up in London in what is now known as the Victorian Era. On some level, I suppose, I'll always be a Victorian.

My immediate family consisted of my parents, Harold and Emma Hartenbrook, as well as myself and my older brother, Clyde. He and I were the only two out of five Hartenbrook children to survive infancy.

We weren't wealthy, nor were we impoverished.

My parents owned their own shop, Hartenbrook Trade. We resided in the two floors above it, and I practically grew up within those walls.

I loved helping out in the shop and whenever I conjure it in my thoughts, even now, it immediately appears, replete with the rich scents of wax used to clean the floors, the aroma of coffees, teas, and spices sourced from far-off lands like India and China.

Formal schooling was scarce back then, but Clyde and I were fortunate. We received tutoring from some of the best teachers that money could buy, for the simple reason that they were already employed by my uncle Algernon, who had hired them for his own children.

My connection to Thornhill Mansion played a significant role in the education and relative privilege I enjoyed growing up. I'm well aware that Thornhill Mansion is not what it used to be, but I'm asking you to imagine it as it was in its heyday, during my childhood visits, when it seemed like a palace.

But let us return to my parents, for now. I hold fond memories of them both, but they're all accompanied by a deep sense of longing and loss.

My father, Harold, a tall and lean man with thinning black hair peppered with salt above his ears, was always engrossed in his work. In most of the memories I have of him, he is in the Hartenbrook Trade shop, surrounded by bags of flour and coffee, donning a striped apron, completely in his element. Though his personality and interests were more academic than business-oriented, he took his merchant role seriously and found great pride in it.

And he was great with the customers - he'd remember all their names and birthdays and preferences, and his conversation would always soothe them or make them laugh, no matter what they were going through. Whenever a customer would come into the shop to buy groceries - or sometimes, it would seem to me, simply to vent - my father would listen empathetically with the patience of a saint. That was his gift.

It was a gift much in demand. Between high childhood mortality rates, arranged marriages, ill-understood diseases, and the always looming threats of the workhouse and the madhouse, the average Victorian Londoner had a lot on his or her mind.

My mother, Emma, was the one with a keen business sense and a knack for numbers. She operated behind the scenes, ensuring the gears of our family's affairs turned smoothly. She was petite and delicate, but she possessed a very astute mind. She ran both our little household and handled the practical side of the business with equal flair. And it was her blood that connected us to the rich and powerful Thornhill family.

Before I was born, my mother's younger sister, Helen, had married the much older Algernon Thornhill. Enabled by his wealth, Lord Thornhill had a reputation for getting whatever he desired, including my, at the time, 16-year-old aunt. Today, such a union would be frowned upon, but back then a middle-aged man marrying a teenager was not uncommon.

It has to be said that Algernon Thornhill was not a particularly pleasant man, but also that he was generous, at least when it came to family. And undoubtedly, he sought to impress his young bride by incorporating her family into his prosperous empire.

The wealth of the Thornhills was built upon trade, with Algernon owning a fleet of approximately nine boats - a significant expansion from his father's initial share in just one vessel. Algernon was the family's visionary entrepreneur, transforming their modest merchant fortunes into something extraordinary.

My father hailed from a once wealthy landowning

family, but by the time it fell into his hands, along with his twin brother's, there was little remaining. All that was left, really, was a dilapidated country house nestled in the Cornish countryside. It was my father's brother who took charge of it, and in return, we received fresh dairy products and vegetables for our own table, as well as some to sell in the shop.

Everything else sold at Hartenbrook Trade arrived on imposing black ships owned by my uncle, laden with goods from far-off lands. Sugar cane from Jamaica and the plantations of the Caribbean, silks and spices from China, and teas of exquisite flavors were brought to us. Coffee, a prized treasure, arrived in batches on three ships that sailed like synchronized timepieces.

What I really want to convey is the deep connection I felt to the shop and its endeavors, and also the deep connection that existed between the Hartenbrooks and the Thornhills. Growing up, I was acutely aware that Algernon Thornhill held the reins and was in control of any fortune, comfort, and privilege my own family enjoyed. Without his favor, it is uncertain where we would find ourselves.

Algernon and Helen only had one child before Helen met her tragic and mysterious end, falling to her death from the balustrade that overlooks the internal hallway downstairs.

My cousin Venedict would be the first of many to insinuate that his mother's death had been no accident.

What he claimed to have seen, at six years old, was his father picking up his mother by the throat and dangling her over the edge of the balustrade while she kicked and screamed and tried to get hold of the handrailing. Then, Algernon had let Helen go, and she'd fallen some twenty feet until she hit the marble floor, her skull, neck, and spine breaking instantly. We walked over the very spot where Helen fell earlier, on our way up here.

Of course, the official story was that Helen had flung herself from the balustrade during an argument with her husband - who had immediately rushed to the hallway and lovingly gathered her lifeless body into his arms.

In both versions of the story, six-year-old Venedict had also run to the hallway, where he, wild with grief, had attempted to pry his dead mother from his father's arms. Infuriated by this, Algernon had swatted the boy away and ordered the servants who had been attracted by the commotion to take him to his room.

I've read extensively on psychology and psychiatry, and I've concluded that witnessing his mother's death and possible murder at the hands of his father, and at such a young age, must have had some influence in shaping my cousin's psyche.

Venedict was always quite the character. How much of that comes down to trauma, I cannot say. But I've come to think that it might have been a decisive factor in what eventually drove him to attract a curse. A curse that would destroy the family.

LYRICA STOPPED and looked out the window at the ink-black branches gently swaying outside and the glowing orb of the moon.

"Ah, but this story is so long and convoluted," she said. "I can't see how I'll be able to unspool this entire yarn in a single night."

In the silence that followed, I heard myself saying, "If

the story is too long, let's save the other half for tomorrow night. I want to hear all of it."

"Oh yeah, me too!" Sebastian agreed. "This is all completely fascinating. I'm still reeling from your... demonstration earlier. I think I'd actually prefer having more time to process everything you're telling us."

Lyrica's features subtly lit up, as if illuminated not only by the moonlight but also from within.

"I would not have insisted on it, but I am glad you suggested it. When sunrise draws near, I'll pause wherever we happen to be.'

Honestly, I was finding Lyrica's mannerisms pretty disarming. Despite knowing what she was, she gave off an impression of something like calm benevolence. Or maybe it was a sense of familiarity.

Or maybe sitting here across from her in the dim library created the illusion that we were just people sharing a conversation.

I reminded myself that it would be all too easy, and potentially deadly, to forget about her superior strength and any unknown intentions that she had yet to reveal.

She seemed to be sinking into herself again, her eyes nearly closed, as if she were reaching for something deep down and far away.

WITH AUNT HELEN dead and gone, Uncle Algernon began to... unravel, I suppose you could call it. It was as though she had been his glue, the thing that kept him from spinning out of control. A mismatched pair they may well have been, but her gentle presence and beauty had inspired at least some restraint in beastly Algernon.

With her out of the picture, all of his bad ways and bad habits returned tenfold. The drinking, the partying, the prostitutes, the violent outbursts. His capriciousness and foul moods had everyone around him fearing him, truly afraid of him. I had been only eight or nine when we laid Aunt Helen to rest in Highgate Cemetery, so I'd barely known Algernon during his 'good years' when he had Helen by his side.

Even before Helen's death, Algernon had picked a beautiful redheaded Scottish scullery maid to be his mistress. Their relationship was a very ill-kept secret, and it was this union that produced my cousin Octavia.

Algernon acknowledged Octavia as his child, even though she was illegitimate and he refused to marry her mother - whose name, regrettably, eludes me. I am also unclear on what happened to Octavia's mother - one day, she was simply gone, never to be seen or spoken of again at Thornhill Mansion.

Her replacement, another scullery maid, barely a teenager, became the mother of Algernon's third and final child, Dorothea.

Allegedly in the grips of what we would now call post-partum depression, Dorothea's young mother drowned herself in the pond outside, mere weeks after giving birth. Unlike her older siblings, Dorothea only really knew their father during his 'bad years.'

Venedict, the eldest, found his own outlets. He entered the family business as soon as he was able and helped his father hold the reins of the growing empire.

Venedict was creative at heart, but he had a good head for business, too. He took what his father had built and accepted the responsibility of carrying it on. Perhaps because he handled his filial responsibility with such finesse, Algernon never once, to my knowledge, spoke about disowning Venedict or sending him packing, despite my cousin's eccentricities and suspected proclivities.

One exemplary manifestation of my cousin's character was that he used to dye his hair with eggplant leaves that turned his original strawberry caramel into a deep dark purple that made him impossible to overlook in a Victorian crowd. He also pierced his ears like a pirate and would occasionally wear makeup like a stage actor. He was deeply fascinated by and showed me illustrations of Louis XIV and his palace. The unbridled extravagance and theatricality of it were what Venedict admired and wanted to emulate.

Naturally, my cousin's unusual appearance and demeanor sparked many rumors, but his wealth protected him, just like it had always protected my uncle.

And scoff and whisper as they might, no one could deny that underneath Venedict's flamboyant exterior was a determined, steel-clad spirit with the ability to grasp and control the family business.

Strangely, Algernon, who had succeeded in elevating the Thornhill family to the higher echelons of the nouveau riche, took his continued wealth and success for granted in a way that his son never did. For whatever reason, Venedict always seemed to think that the family fortune could be destroyed or snatched away at any moment, and he was obsessed with finding ever-new vehicles to pour the profits into to make them continue to grow.

Perhaps, seeing his father act out the way he did and still not get taken to jail, Venedict understood that wealth and power are the only protection against the consequences of your actions.

But I digress. In his teen years, Venedict gradually took over managing the family business completely. I suppose he sensed the need for growing up and becoming responsible fast, lest Algernon's actions and addictions derail the Thornhill empire.

By the time he was fifteen and I was eighteen, he and I were both more or less running the businesses for our respective parents.

In my case, it wasn't because my parents were irresponsible, but they both contracted tuberculosis and neither of them ever made a full recovery. They were still able to work in the shop on most days, but neither had as much energy as they should have had, and some days they even had to stay in bed. It was painful to see my parents grow old and frail before their time, but at least I was mostly too busy to dwell on it.

Whenever I did have time to dwell on anything, I would dwell on books. I've always been a big reader, and no memory of my mortal life is more dear to me than that of sitting in the windowsill above the shop on a rainy day, just reading and letting the words and the stories transport me to a different world.

And where was my brother Clyde in all of this? Despite being the son of a grocer, Clyde had always had a much more scientific mind than anyone else in the family tree, and his dream was to go to medical school and become a surgeon.

Most Victorian parents would have said no, would have demanded that he take over their business, but not ours. Ours encouraged him and applauded his dream, and so Clyde attended the Royal College of Surgeons and helped me in the shop whenever he could.

We spent many mornings and afternoons in the shop together; me writing lists for the shop or even reading, and him flicking through his medical textbooks and notes.

When it got busy, we both put down our papers and focused on the customers.

I also had my dreams, but they were much more private. As a girl, I wasn't expected to do much of anything except find a relatively well-off husband. But as I believe I've already conveyed, my family was progressive for the time, and so I managed the shop and was free to do as I pleased with whatever time I had left over.

Deep within the pit of my mind, a desire grew to expand Hartenbrook Trade into the next building and to turn that section into a bookstore. I imagined filling the shelves with poetry, books on history and science, and of course, literature. The Victorian era was a hotbed for English Literature and I imagined myself becoming a renowned bookseller, always the first to spot a future phenomenon.

If things went well, I might even start a printing press in a backroom of the shop and expand the business into publishing. I particularly wanted to publish works by female writers, who often struggled to get their works acknowledged.

Mary Shelley was my biggest idol. You probably find it hard to imagine, but she was a controversial figure back then. More than one critic downright refused to believe that her seminal work, Frankenstein, could have come from a woman's imagination.

Modern men like yourselves would find this idea preposterous, but the Victorian era was not a different time so much as an entirely different world. Ah, it is hard to explain to someone who hasn't lived it.

Either way, Clyde and I both loved Mary Shelley's Frankenstein. I loved the words, and he loved the forbidden science it contained. And of course, we both pitied Franken-stein's monster.

Neither of us could have imagined how much our own fates would come to resemble the tragic story found within the dog-eared pages of our favorite book.

CHAPTER
TEN

It was while I was working in the shop one rainy afternoon in the spring of my 20th year that my uncle Algernon walked in and seemed to notice me for the first time.

I remember it vividly. It was no longer pouring down, as it had been earlier. The rain outside had turned to a fine mist, and I remember the raindrops like a glittering mist caught on the fur collar of Uncle Algernon's coat. He was also wearing a top hat and cape, and pointy boots that had gathered mud.

Algernon, never one to make a quiet entry, burst into the shop, huffing and puffing, and wiping droplets from his collar with a gloved hand while removing his hat with the other. Underneath it, his lank caramel colored hair was thinning.

There was no one else in the shop.

"Hello, uncle," I greeted him. "You're not expected, but let me take your coat."

By the time I'd made my way around the desk and over to him, he'd already removed it himself. He shoved it into my arms, along with his hat, cane, and gloves. I turned to hang his rain-heavy clothes on the rack above the door leading to the back room.

It startled me when I heard him say my name very close to my ear, and I spun around.

He was standing less than a foot behind me.

"Lyrica," he said again. I smelt alcohol on his breath. His expression was both startled and searching. "Lyrica, you look so much like your darling aunt, like my beloved Helen. How come I have never noticed this before?"

He reached out a large hand and picked up a strand of wayward hair from my cheek. He brushed it behind my ear, his fingers lingering there for a few uncomfortable moments while I stood frozen in place.

"Thank you, uncle."

I took a step backwards, wanting to put more space between us without seeming rude. I had always been afraid of my uncle, but as long as I'd lived I'd also known he was to thank for my family's continued livelihood and the relative material comfort we enjoyed. I'm sure you understand when I say that my overall feelings towards Algernon Thornhill were ambivalent.

"How are you, my dear Lyrica?"

Algernon had never asked me this before. He reached into one of the large glass dispensers containing cashew nuts in the casual manner befitting the true owner of Hartenbrook Trade. He poured the nuts directly into his mouth and chewed while watching me expectantly.

"Do you study?"

"I used to have more time to study, mostly literature, but since my parents took ill, I've been too busy taking care of this." I made a vague gesture to indicate the shop surrounding us.

"I see," Algernon raised his hand to his chin and stroked it thoughtfully, his eyes gleaming. "I must say, this is rather impressive. How long exactly have you been taking care of the business?"

"It has been about a year. Mother and father contracted the illness around mid-February last year. I remember them being bedridden on Valentine's Day."

"Oh, that is most tragic," Algernon observed, in a tone of voice that implied the opposite. "But it is fortunate that they have such a bright daughter to help them run things and not fall behind on their responsibilities. You must have a good head on your shoulders, and not just a remarkably pretty one."

Not sure how to respond, I opted for silence.

"No doubt taking care of the shop is a heavy responsibility. Does your brother help?"

"When he can. He's enrolled in medical school - The Royal College of Surgeons." I said it with pride. "He has a fine head, too. It seems to run in the family."

Algernon made an impatient wave with his hand, as if to signal his lack of interest in hearing another word about his nephew. Instead, he cut in with a question. "Tell me, Lyrica, how old are you now?"

"Twenty."

"You look much younger. Hm...twenty and still not married?"

"I have no marriage plans. Perhaps one day, but for now, I have other responsibilities. My parents agree that there is no haste."

"Well, well, well."

Again Algernon sunk his hand into the glass dispenser before crunching his loot loudly between his teeth.

"A real shame. Such a lovely young creature, in full

bloom, yet not even betrothed. Of course, Herbert and Emma only have one daughter. They should pick your husband wisely. Just in case your brother's surgeon career doesn't go as planned."

Algernon went quiet after that, eating the last few nuts from his palm and chewing pensively.

You can probably imagine what this encounter was the beginning of. From that pivotal, cursed moment, Algernon Thornhill, my uncle and my beloved aunt's widower, began courting me.

I felt like a deer that had unwittingly stepped into the headlights of an oncoming freight train. This is one of those metaphors of this century that I have really come to appreciate. It truly captures the feeling that washed over me in continuous waves over the following months.

When Algernon walked out of the shop that day, he left me with a tight knot in my stomach. I couldn't honestly tell you whether it was fear or disgust, but I can tell you that it was there. Something invisible had passed between us, and I'd clearly sensed myself getting caught in the searchlight without any means of escape.

Algernon went all in on courting me. Looking back, I think he knew all along that I wouldn't be able to refuse his advances and his eventual marriage proposal. He was a wealthy and influential man; I was a young woman whose entire economical past, present, and future depended on him.

Of course, I was reluctant. My parents, wanting to see me happy, did not like it much either. And yet, my feeling of duty towards them was so strong that it didn't occur to me to put their livelihoods at risk by refuting Algernon's advances.

Flowers started arriving at the shop - enormous

bouquets of roses and lilies. They would have handwritten letters, at least some of which were clearly penned by literate servants rather than by Algernon himself. There were also gifts: expensive dresses, jewelry, even a litter of baby bunnies. I always responded to his letters and gifts, briefly and gratefully, but without a hint of sentiment. I wasn't in love with my uncle, and I didn't pretend to be.

That didn't bother him. The flowers, letters, and gifts were soon followed up with invitations to go to the theatre, to concerts, and expensive dinners.

Algernon insisted, for the sake of my spotless reputation and my parents' peace of mind, that I must always have a chaperone for these occasions.

More often than not, he would bring his daughter, my cousin Octavia, who was a few years younger than me, along so she could keep an eye on us. On other occasions, he would bring his elderly mother, who was mostly deaf and entirely blind.

Hilda was originally from Germany and would frequently mumble to herself in her mother tongue, of which I understood nothing. The only thing I was able to grasp very clearly was that she didn't like me much. It is possible she thought I wasn't good enough for her son.

It didn't take many months before Algernon asked the dreaded question and presented me with an ostentatious silver ring set with sapphires.

I must remind you again that it was a different time. How different you cannot truly comprehend. From the outside looking in, it might seem as if I had other options, but truly, I was trapped. Every alternative avenue I pursued, if only in my secret thoughts, led me to a dead end. I could see no way out.

This was when my mortal life began to collapse in on

itself.

The wedding preparations were soon in full swing. If I had imagined that Algernon Thornhill, a widower, would want a small, discreet second wedding, I imagined wrong. Algernon engaged several extra staff alone to help prepare the wedding banquet, which was to take place at Thornhill Mansion, my new home. The ceremony itself was to take place at Highgate Chapel, only a few minutes by foot or horse-drawn carriage from the mansion.

I had no say in any of it. All I had to do was show up for wedding dress fittings and to sample different flavors of wedding cake, all of which tasted like ashes to me.

Because of the wedding preparations, I had occasion to visit Thornhill Mansion more often than I had in recent years.

I cannot possibly describe the strange and eerie feeling that beset me the first time I stepped through the grand doors after Helen's funeral. Knowing that I was soon to marry her widower put a lump of guilt in my throat.

Everything looked much the same as it had then, nearly a year prior. And yet, something was very different.

At Helen's funeral banquet, the air had been heavy and swirling with sorrow and secrets. Strangely, instead of lessening over the intervening months, the heaviness seemed to have intensified. There was latent electricity in the air.

I was far from the only one to pick up on it. All the servants seemed ill at ease. All of them were refusing to meet my gaze. All except Venedict's personal butler, Nathanael.

It was he who stepped forward to take my coat and my steel-boned umbrella, and he who held that same umbrella over my head and asked me how I was doing as he escorted me up the front steps.

"I am as well as I could be." I replied curtly. It was difficult to speak around the lump sitting in my throat, threatening to block off my airways.

Nathanael nodded as if he had heard my silent addition of "under the circumstances."

"Both now and once you are the Lady of this house, I will be here to assist you with anything you might need," he assured me, without averting his gaze. Nathanael was the perfect servant in every way, except this. He would look you in the eye even if you were his master. I liked that about him.

"Thank you, Nathanael. I may need it."

"You can trust me with anything," he replied, just as we reached the front doors, which were held open by two other servants.

Tailors and seamstresses had set up shop in the front parlor, as had a florist and a baker. Each had their own station, and each had brought samples of their wares for me to peruse.

Lord Thornhill, I was told in hushed tones by one of the older maids, had left the mansion on unknown yet urgent business. In his absence he had appointed his son to assist me with the choosing of flowers, wines, cakes and fabrics.

"Lyrica, it has been such a long time!" Venedict exclaimed, standing in front of the unlit fireplace while a mustachioed tailor was pinning an unfinished collar onto the equally unfinished waistcoat he was wearing. We had not seen each other in months.

"You'll have to excuse me if I am late in expressing my joy at yours and my father's looming union. I've got something important to share with you in private, but first duty calls."

Venedict gestured towards the baker's table, which was

laden with decadent-looking cakes on silver plates.

Dutifully, I went over every sample and mouthful I was offered, with as much patience as I could muster. The entire experience did nothing to make me feel any less disconnected from the wedding plans.

Finally, Venedict and I found our chance to talk in something resembling privacy. Most of the vendors had left and taken their silks, wines, and flower arrangements with them. Only the tailor and his little army of seamstresses were still working at the far end of the room.

Venedict plopped down on the plump red velvet sofa across from me and said without preamble, "My mother has been appearing to me lately, Lyrica. Well, not just to me, but to Octavia, Dorothea, and the servants too. I don't think she's very happy about your and father's plans to marry."

I didn't know how to respond - how could I? I swallowed, cleared my throat. "If Aunt Helen is upset with me, why hasn't she appeared to me?"

Venedict shook his head as if denying an accusation.

"My mother isn't upset with you - she's upset with my father, positively furious! More furious than I've ever seen her when she was alive. She reappeared yesterday in my study. It was a sight to behold! She kept moaning soundlessly and wringing her hands. She tried to lead me somewhere, I believe, to show me something. But when I got up and followed her out into the hallway as she was beckoning for me to do, she disappeared." He leaned in, lowering his voice, "It seems to me that she cannot sustain her apparition long enough to get her point across. Imagine the frustration! I truly want to listen to what my mother has to say, but she keeps dissolving."

Venedict made a swirling motion in the air with his

fingers, as if to demonstrate how the ghost of his mother had dematerialized.

At this point, Nathanael came back into the parlor, pushing in front of him a wrought metal and glass serving tray on wheels. It was laden with tea, strawberries, a pitcher of cream. He poured tea into two china cups and added cream and sugar. He wore white gloves as he handled the china without making a sound.

"If I may?"

He placed my steaming cup in front of me, and I nodded.

"Lady Thornhill - the former Lady Thornhill, I should say - has been appearing to me too. It seems her apparition is stronger and more vivid during thunderstorms, of which we happen to have many right now. I also believe the proximity of the wedding is inspiring in her a sense of urgency. And if you don't mind, young Master Thornhill, I'll make one more observation."

Venedict gestured for the butler to go ahead.

"Helen is not enraged at you, Miss Hartenbrook." Nathanael looked straight at me again, holding my gaze. "When she appears, I would say she seems worried, distraught."

Venedict sighed. "We cannot work out the details of why she is in such turmoil, and neither can any of the mediums I've consulted with so far."

"Gentlemen," I said, "you are not exactly putting me at ease. I already have a guilty conscience over marrying my aunt's husband. What if I have... incurred Aunt Helen's wrath?"

Venedict placed a slim-fingered hand on my arm. "Never. My mother adored you - why would she haunt you? My father might, but *you* have nothing to fear."

CHAPTER

ELEVEN

Venedict was wrong. From that night onwards, Aunt Helen started haunting me relentlessly.

Until then, I had always believed that ghosts were bound to a specific location. And let me assure you, Helen has visited me on multiple occasions since then, always within the confines of this house.

However, during that particular period, she made a point of appearing in my narrow bedroom above Hartenbrook Trade.

I would wake in the middle of the night to find her standing at the foot of my bed, her hair in disarray, her face contorted with grimaces. She would scream silently into the air. It was a distressing sight, and I felt utterly powerless to assist or soothe her.

My attempts to ask her about her troubles were fruitless; she was unable to respond. All she seemed able to do was point out of my window, towards Highgate, Thornhill Mansion and the chapel where my wedding to her husband was slated to take place.

Whenever Helen appeared in my home, just like Venedict had said, she could never sustain her presence for very long. She could only manifest during dramatic weather when the storm raged outside, rain pouring and thunder crackling in the air. Even then, her appearances lasted only a few fleeting seconds.

Initially, I must admit, I was terrified whenever Helen suddenly materialized at the foot of my bed, her silent screams reverberating in the room. But gradually, I grew less fearful of her. I reminded myself that, living or dead, this was my dear aunt, who would never do me harm.

Sometimes when I saw her at Thornhill Mansion she would turn and start moving - gliding or floating, rather - down a hallway or up a staircase, I would follow her. Most of the time, she would vanish or dissolve into thin air before we could reach any destination. But on one occasion she led me to the attic.

Outside the wind howled and rain cascaded down, falling against the roof like knuckles rapping.

My palms grew damp with sweat as I followed her into the dust-filled space. Old suitcases and wooden crates overflowed with clothes, books, artifacts, piles of daguerreotypes.

There, in the corner, stood Helen beside a large wooden chest. She appeared more vibrant than I had ever seen her, no longer wispy and translucent, but almost solid.

Her face bore an imploring expression as she gestured toward the chest.

Her lips moved without sound, but the message was unmistakable. She wanted me to uncover something within that chest, and uncover something I did.

As it turned out, my aunt had diligently kept diaries throughout her life. The chest contained years upon years of memories and thoughts, neatly bound and labeled with their respective dates.

Under ghostly Helen's watchful eyes, I swiftly rifled through the trunk, painfully aware that I couldn't possibly carry all the diaries with me without drawing attention. I also knew I didn't have much time. Someone was bound to interrupt me, and Helen's time was limited - it always was whenever she manifested. Thunderstorm or no thunderstorm.

It didn't take me long to locate the last few volumes she had ever penned. I slipped the most recent one into my corseted waistcoat to take with me.

I vowed to Helen that I would read it as soon as I could, and hopefully find some clues as to her unsolved death.

As I prepared to leave, I realized Helen had already vanished.

Lyrica stopped speaking, and a meaningful silence settled over the room.

She was the one to break it again by noting, "Daylight is just behind the horizon now. I will have to continue my story tomorrow night." She hadn't looked out the window or consulted a watch - she didn't have to. Vampires always know when sunrise is approaching. "If that is agreeable with both of you."

Sebastian and I both nodded reluctantly. Admittedly I'd been completely drawn into her story and was loath for her to stop.

"Do you still have Helen's last diary?"

Jeremy Gently had mentioned that he had stored several of Helen's diaries at his office, but did he have the last diary, the one Lyrica had been guided by Helen to retrieve from the attic?

"I thought you might ask, and yes, I have it here," Lyrica pointed to a small leather-bound book that I hadn't even noticed laying on the table between us.

Not waiting for my response, she lifted it from the table. Gingerly, she unwrapped the binding string that held it closed. And with both Sebastian and I leaning forward in anticipation, she opened it to a random page.

"Reading my aunt's diaries," she said, "seemed to support Venedict's claims and my own suspicions - that my aunt Helen was in fact murdered, and Algernon was her killer. The truth was either that, or she had indeed succumbed to madness like Algernon claimed. Either way, she grew increasingly fearful of him in the months leading up to her death."

Lyrica let me take the diary from her. Scanning the pages, I was drawn to the last entries. The handwriting was delicate and slanted, and not all that easy to read. Water had smudged some of the ink, but certain sentences stood out clearly amidst the blur. One paragraph struck me with remarkable force:

I see no love in his eyes anymore - not even embers. What I see instead is something within him tightening taut like a wire, ready to snap. Something within him yearns to burst free through his skin. That something wants to tear me limb from limb.

Some pages had come loose, and I delicately picked one up between my fingers. I held it out to Lyrica.

"Mind if I have this one tested to confirm its age?"

"By all means," she extended her palms in permission. "Do whatever you wish with the diary and anything in this place if it helps you understand and believe my story.

It is vital to me that you know that everything I've said is true."

"If you really mean that, you'll let me have a hair from your head for DNA testing. Sebastian, I'm also asking you." I fixed both of them with a challenging stare. "If we're actually related by blood, a single strand of hair from each of you should be enough to confirm it."

Vampires are usually, understandably, unwilling to provide DNA samples for any reason, but immediately Lyrica plucked a single obsidian black strand of hair from her head. Sebastian followed suit.

"Now, I really must leave you," Lyrica rose from the loveseat. "Please resist any temptation to search for me during the daylight hours. You won't find me. But I will return to this very spot tomorrow night to continue and conclude my tale."

She left the library.

As soon as she stepped out of the door into the hallway, she seemed to vanish into thin air. There was no sound of footsteps, no creaking floorboards as she left. No indication of where she had gone.

SOFT, gray morning light filtered through the curtains, casting a soft glow across Octavia Thornhill's old bedroom.

Sebastian poked his head around the doorframe. "Knock knock. Harlan, can I come in?"

I hesitated. I really just wanted to enjoy a moment of solitude before catching a few hours' sleep.

"There's something I want to ask you." Sebastian pressed on, undeterred by my lack of enthusiasm.

"All right. Come in."

He stepped into the room, hesitantly closing the door behind him. The warm glow of the ancient bedside lamp illuminated his face and cast gentle shadows in the dimly lit room. He was wearing silky pyjamas with an exuberant pattern of birds and branches. He walked over and stood near the broad windowsill where I was sitting, and for a moment the only sound was that of the branches softly tapping against the window.

There was a vulnerability in his voice as he said, "Harlan, I couldn't help but notice that you've seemed completely unfazed by anything Lyrica has told us, and by what she is. Unlike me." Here, he laughed nervously, "It's as if you, I don't know, already knew about all of this, or as if you expected it somehow. I'm not sure exactly how to ask this, but who are you? What are you? I mean really. You're not a paranormal investigator. Lyrica said something about a hunter of her kind."

I sighed. Sebastian had already had more fantastical truths hurled at him in one night than most human psyches can take without breaking. I didn't want to add what might be a final straw, but I also didn't want to lie to him.

Sebastian wasn't stupid. And given that we were apparently related, trying to bamboozle him my usual spiel about being an antiques dealer or working for a private security firm would be downright insulting, wouldn't it?

Maybe the truth was best for a change.

I motioned for him to join me where I was sitting on the windowsill.

He settled next to me, eyes full of curiosity and just a touch of apprehension. Leaning against the window's cool glass, I spilled my best-kept secret.

"So I'm probably not what you imagine when you think of a paranormal investigator. I don't investigate supernatural entities so much as hunt them and kill them. Mostly vampires."

"Oh."

Disbelief, curiosity, and a trace of fear danced in his eyes. He opened his mouth to speak, but I raised my hand to stop him.

"When I was five, a vampire killed my parents, and nearly killed me." My voice was neutral, despite the weight of those distant, murky memories. "I can't actually remember much about the night it happened, but it shaped the course of my life. I was raised by the hunter who saved me. So no, the existence of vampires and other strange phenomena doesn't faze me. They're my job."

I could see the wheels turning in Sebastian's mind.

"What has fazed me tonight, though, is meeting a vampire who claims to be related to me," I continued, "That one is new. And meeting you, a potential relative, is also new. If Lyrica isn't lying to us, you and I are distant cousins, or something like that. And in my world, that's really something, because I have no one else, no other family at all."

"Me either." Sebastian's eyes clouded over as if he were straining to reach for some half-remembered piece of information. "But my memories of my family are completely nonexistent. If I try to recall anything before roughly the age of five or six, there just isn't anything there. I draw a blank. I grew up being bounced around between different foster homes, without any memories of having any family before that."

Silence settled over us until Sebastian broke it.

"Know what? I think we've been brought together by fate to discover the truth about our roots."

"Maybe. And maybe we've been brought together by a vampire whose motives may not be as clear or as noble as they seem. I know Lyrica seems sincere, but we have to be careful - especially you, because you're unfamiliar with... all of this. Vampires tend to be deceptive. They're like people, only most of them have been undead for so long that their sense of humanity, empathy and all of that jazz has begun to slip. Lyrica hasn't been human for a long, long time."

Sebastian leaned back a little, nodding, contemplating this.

"But her story rings true to me. Crazy, sure, but true. Promise you won't go hunting for her as soon as the sun is up." He squinted, eying me suspiciously. "You can't slay the only person who may know about our ancestral history."

CHAPTER

TWELVE

I took a deep breath, trying to clear my mind as I descended the creaking stairs of Thornhill Mansion.

I'd only slept a few hours. What I needed now more than anything was the moment of alone time I hadn't managed to squeeze into last night, a chance to gather my thoughts undisturbed by unexpected cousins or centuries-old vampires. Was this so much to ask?

Stepping out onto the patio, I was greeted by the soft whisper of a gentle breeze. A wrought-iron table and chair set that I'd spotted yesterday beckoned me now, promising a perfect spot to sit and think.

I settled into one of the ornate chairs, angling myself towards Swain's Lane so I could soak in the view of both the garden and the cemetery beyond the fence. The silent tombs in there provided a perfect contrast to the buzzing bees and colorful butterflies circulating among the garden's wildflowers.

Knowing that I would have to confront it eventually, I slipped my phone out of my pocket. It was only 08:37 but I already had a missed call from Eli. He hadn't bothered leaving me a voicemail or sending a text, clear signs of his annoyance.

I slipped the phone back in my pocket, determined to shove the missed call to the back of my mind for now.

The events of the past 24 hours had turned just about everything on its head, but how would I even begin to explain any of it to Eli, and in a way that wouldn't make him insist on either joining me or me leaving the mansion immediately? Lyrica's revelations and the potential existence of an ancestral connection between me and the Thornhill family were bombshells I needed time to digest, on my own.

My heart skipped a beat. I'd caught sight of two familiar figures moving inside the cemetery.

The familiar outlines belonged to Jed and Carmen, and they were walking along the path on the other side of the fence, coming closer. What were they doing here - and how would I explain to them what *I* was doing here?

I hesitated, but then I called out to them. They were going to see me sitting here in the garden, anyway, weren't they? I might as well make myself known.

Besides, I could use their help to get the DNA samples and the diary page I'd collected last night tested. Being suspended from the Van Helsing Society meant I didn't have access to the Society's lab facilities under my name. It wasn't noble, sure, but I would have to use my friends as a Trojan horse to get the items to the lab.

My mind raced, trying to come up with a plausible explanation for my presence in the garden of Thornhill Mansion. I wasn't ready to reveal the real reason for my visit, couldn't risk them interfering with my experience, or with the personal discoveries I was making. Or with Lyrica.

The sense of protectiveness welling up in me surprised

me. I didn't like it, but it was there, making my shoulders tense up.

Jed and Carmen were now very close to the fence, their eyes scanning the spaces between the wrought-iron bars until Carmen's eyes settled on me.

"Harlan!" Carmen called out.

"Harlan, what the hell?" Jed's eyes lit up.

They made their way up to the fence. Carmen, small but fierce, looked up at me through the peeling iron bars. She was both startled and curious.

Jed leaned in, nearly as tall as the fence. "What are you doing here?" He put his hand through the bars, demanding a fist-bump.

"I'm here on a job."

My tone was deliberately nonchalant as I nodded in the direction of the imposing structure behind me. Just casually visiting a crumbly mansion in this famous haunted location. So what?

"What are the chances! You're not here to try to get involved in our investigation, are you?" Carmen head was tilted to the side, her eyes narrow, her skepticism palpable.

I gave her my most affable smile. I'd always liked her directness and lack of a British filter, but it was kind of inconvenient right now.

Carmen's parents had immigrated to the UK from a small town in Spain when Carmen was just a toddler, and she had three older brothers who now all worked for the London Metropolitan Police. She'd grown up sparring with them and had learned not to take any prisoners.

"Not at all," I assured them.

I was determined that this was all they were going to get out of me. I found it difficult to lie to my friends, but leaving things unspoken, that I could do.

"You don't need to worry about my being here," I promised. "I'm not here to interfere with anything. I actually didn't know there was something to interfere with - but thanks for cluing me in."

Jed and Carmen exchanged a glance, unsure of whether they had revealed anything they shouldn't have.

"You being here has nothing to do with the Highgate Vampire?"

Carmen's question hung in the air. I shook my head in zealous denial.

"Nothing at all."

I didn't know whether I was telling them the truth or not - Lyrica was technically a Highgate Vampire, but was she *the* Highgate Vampire? Were my two friends actually here to hunt her down? Had they been sent to slay her for one of the many transgressions she would inevitably have committed during her prolonged undead existence?

If so, I had to throw them off her scent, at least until she'd told me her story in full.

Carmen's piercing gaze was still fixed on me, her hazel eyes searching mine. I hadn't convinced her. But I'd convinced Jed, who was breaking into a broad smile.

"Well, that's a relief, because we're under strict instructions not to share any information or accept any help from you."

I shrugged. "You can tell Ramsay - who I'm sure you're obliged to report back to - that's perfectly fine by me. I have my own reasons for being here, and they've got nothing to do with yours."

"Have you signed an NDA or something?" Carmen asked, the note of skepticism in her voice still there. "You're being all mysterious. It's making me wonder what you're really up to."

"I can be as mysterious as I want to be on my own time," I countered. "If the Society isn't willing to share information with me, I have to be cautious about what I reveal, too. I mean, who knows what you're obliged to report back to Ramsay?"

"We only owe him information on the case." Jed winked at me, his defences having fallen completely by the wayside.

"Speaking of the devil," I said, "don't mention to him that you've seen me here. That could land me in even more trouble. He definitely won't believe that my being here in Highgate is a coincidence. He's going to leap right to the conclusion that I'm here to meddle in the Society's affairs."

"Sure," Jed agreed. "Whatever you need."

Carmen had fallen silent next to him, and going by her expression, she was still weighing up my words.

"So you're here investigating the Highgate vampire?"

I was eager to turn the conversation back to them and away from me, away from all potential questions about what was unfolding within the walls of Thornhill Mansion.

"We can't tell you anything about it," Jed pointed out, shielding his eyes against the morning sun and looking up to really take in the grandeur of the mansion behind me. "But maybe you could share a little something about what you're doing here? Even if it isn't about the Highgate vampire, whatever you're dealing with in there has got to be something interesting. I mean, what a house! And what a vantage point, right here next to the cemetery. Place must be haunted, at least."

I shook my head slowly. "I can't tell you anything. The owner of the place has asked for absolute discretion, and I have to honor her wishes."

"So you're not going to invite us in?" Jed was half playful and half disappointed.

A surprised chuckle escaped my throat and I realized how much I missed our usual banter.

"No way. Don't get me wrong, I would, but I can't bring you into this right now." I hesitated for a beat before deciding to just plainly ask. "I need you to do something for me though. I don't ask favors often."

Carmen rolled her eyes at me, as if she disagreed.

I looked from her to Jed, hoping they would understand the importance of my request, and without asking too many questions. "I need to test a document forensically to determine its age, and I also need a couple of DNA samples looked at."

"Harlan, you know this could get us in a lot of trouble," Carmen's brow furrowed. "It wouldn't help you if Jed and I also get our licenses suspended."

"I understand that it could be risky, Carmen. But I don't have access to the Society's lab. I wouldn't ask you if it wasn't important, or if there was another way. If you say yes, I'll owe you one, big time. Anytime you need anything from me, I'll be there for you."

"You already are, so this isn't really a great bargain," Carmen pointed out.

But Jed's expression had already softened. "Of course we'll do it. If this is important to you, then it's important to us. Right, Carmen?" He nudged her gently in the ribs. "Did Ramsay accuse us of being the Three Musketeers for nothing?"

Carmen had folded her arms across her chest, and she was actually pouting. But a smile was tugging at the corner of her mouth and I knew that she was caving in.

"We'll get it done all right. But only this one thing," she said with a sigh.

Just as a sense of relief was coursing through me, Sebastian's voice called my name from somewhere behind me.

Great, now I would have to explain his presence to the others.

Sebastian, clad in his luxurious silk pajamas and a flowing night robe that trailed in the dewy grass, came strolling through the garden. His air of easy confidence suggested that he owned the place. Carmen raised an eyebrow, her curiosity piqued.

"And who's this?"

"This is Sebastian," I introduced him. "He's a... distant relative. Sebastian, come meet my friends, Jed, Carmen."

I gestured toward them. Sebastian raised his camera in response and began snapping photos of the three of us, huddled together conspiratorially with the ancient fence separating us.

"He's a photographer," I offered.

"That part of it is true." Sebastian lowered the camera and extended his hand through the fence. Jed immediately took it and shook it warmly. "Sebastian Rose. Google me. But I wouldn't describe myself as a *distant* relative. I'm Harlan's cousin."

"I never knew he had one." Carmen accepted Sebastian's outstretched hand, apparently intrigued. "Very nice to meet you, Sebastian."

"We've got a long day ahead of us, don't we, Sebastian?"

I was hoping that he would catch my drift so I could get him away from my colleagues before he spilled something to them that I wouldn't be able to explain away. After a beat of hesitation, Sebastian sighed.

"Yeah, you're right. We do have a lot to do. Carmen, Jed, it was great meeting you both, but Harlan and I have got to skedaddle. I'm absolutely ravenous and I need to make the most of the daylight." He lifted his camera, rattling it slightly.

As soon as Sebastian's back was turned and he was strolling away through the grass and wildflowers, Carmen motioned for me to come back to the fence.

"About those items you need tested," she whispered. "Swing by the cemetery later and bring them. I'll make sure they're sent to the lab, along with a few things we've found."

Jed leaned in, a mischievous glint in his dark eyes. "After all, nobody can stop you from taking a walk in the cemetery. You could even visit the mesmerizing Circle of Lebanon, particularly the Julius Beer Mausoleum. You know, the one that was infamously opened by black magicians in the '70s and used for necromantic rituals?"

"Read about it," I confirmed. "I'll find you there later."

"Neat, this place, isn't it?" Sebastian looked around appreciatively. We were standing in line for coffee and pastries at a café in Highgate Village. The contrast between its cozy ambiance and the dilapidated grandeur of the mansion just a few minutes down the road could not have been more glaring.

Instead of waiting for an answer, Sebastian lifted his Canon and captured a snapshot of me, grumpily waiting for my caffeine boost.

"By the way, why did you refer to me as a distant relative earlier? If we're each other's only relative, I wouldn't say we're distant."

"You're forgetting about Lyrica."

"Yeah, that's a bit of a mind fuck, isn't it? I mean, what exactly is she to us - a great-great-great-great-gandcousin?"

As we approached the counter, a gangly, spotty-faced barista took our orders - a black coffee and two plain croissants for me, an almond milk latte with all the trimmings, a large Cornish pasty and a blueberry muffin for Sebastian.

"Let me let you in on something," Sebastian said while another barista prepared our coffees. "I've been eager to photograph and explore Thornhill Mansion for years, but contacting the owner always proved, well, totally impossible."

Shocker. I'd had no idea, not even an inkling, that Sebastian already had a history with Thornhill Mansion. I could feel my eyebrows rising high onto my forehead.

"Really?"

"Oh, yeah. Even while I was working on my other projects, I knew I'd one day be working on one about haunted houses, and that I wanted Thornhill Mansion to be the centerpiece. I always knew in my gut that that place was haunted, but I had no idea about all the rest."

"How long have you known about Thornhill Mansion? And how long has Lyrica known about you wanting to photograph it?"

"About three years," Sebastian shrugged. "Well, it's been three years since I first reached out to her through letters. It's not like Lyrica can be found in any phonebook or directory, so physical letters seemed to be the only way. I'd handwrite them and slip them under the door. Of course, I didn't know who I was addressing them to and I have no idea whether she's read them."

He hesitated, as if trying to decide whether to add the next bit or not. In the end he did. "Once I even broke a window and tried to get in, but I saw something that scared the living crap out of me."

"What did you see?"

I was holding my breath now. Leaving the coffee shop with our orders in hand, I scanned our surroundings, gauging whether anyone paid us any attention. But, like us, everyone else seemed preoccupied with their own errands and conversations, oblivious to ours.

"I don't really know what I saw, or thought I saw." Sebastian shook his head, as if trying to shake a memory loose. "It might have been Helen Thornhill. At any rate, it was a glowing and nearly transparent figure, definitely female. She was warning me not to go in."

"She spoke to you?" "

"No, not exactly, but her body language was clear. She materialized in the empty frame of the window I'd just broken and she motioned for me to leave. It seemed urgent that I leave, and I ran. I guess I panicked. Then I tried to forget about the damned mansion for a while, but it didn't work. It just kept reappearing in my thoughts. Every time I'd try to come up with a new concept, all I could think about was Thornhill Mansion. All roads seemed to lead me back to it. I was blocked, and I was haunted, and I knew I couldn't finish 'Haunted Halls' without including Thornhill Mansion in it. I drove my girlfriend, Irene, away because I was so obsessed. We were engaged, actually, not that that matters now." His voice trailed off, wistful. Then he took a large sip of his coffee, as if to steel himself before continuing, "I tried to focus on other work, but it was unfulfilling. I tried to forget about Thornhill Mansion, but it worked its way into my dreams! I just couldn't escape it. I'd dream about wandering those hallways, looking for something or someone."

As Sebastian spoke, I was reminded of my own recent dream of a burning chapel and a shadowy being urging me to come home. I pushed it down and drew a dark, heavy curtain of forgetfulness over it. This was my go-to way of dealing with troubling thoughts.

Sebastian's voice lowered as he peered at me over the rim of his round sunglasses.

"Isn't it strange that I have access to Thornhill Mansion now, after feeling drawn to it for so long? And it's stranger still that I've met Lyrica, and you. I must have known on some deep subconscious level that I was connected to the place."

A comfortable silence settled over us as we walked through the village, across the old square and then turned back down onto Swain's Lane. The green treetops inside the cemetery stirred peacefully in the gentle summer breeze.

Sebastian broke the silence with a question that caught me off guard. "Your friends, do you think they were looking for Lyrica? I mean, she's the real Highgate Vampire, she has to be."

I tensed up a little. "What makes you think they were looking for the Highgate Vampire?"

"Oh, come on," He punched me playfully on the shoulder. "They were obviously vampire hunters like you. The way they were dressed, the way the three of you huddled together and whispered. Their *auras*, Harlan! It was too obvious."

"Okay, well. Now you see why I didn't want them to hang around."

"You want to protect Lyrica?"

"For now." I admitted it reluctantly to myself as much as to Sebastian. "Until and unless it turns out that she's been lying to us. I've never met a single vampire that could be trusted, but Lyrica might be different. That's why I'm giving her the benefit of the doubt. Besides, if anyone is going to have to slay her, it's going to be me. Hopefully, though, it won't come to that."

CHAPTER

THIRTEEN

Walking through the temple-like gateway and up the sloping path of the Egyptian Avenue in Highgate Cemetery, I was struck by the beauty of the place. The Ancient Egypt-inspired structure with its tall columns and carvings was clearly deserving of its fame.

The sun filtered through the thick branches overhead, casting shifting patterns on the gravelly Avenue. The scent of blooming flowers filled the air, mingling with the deeper notes of grave dirt. And despite the grand Victorian tombs and mausoleums rising out of the ground on either side of me, it was difficult to imagine that anything dark could be stalking these hallowed grounds.

The cemetery was officially closed to visitors today, so I knew only Jed, Carmen and whichever other entities might dwell in this place were going to be in here with me.

In the satchel bag I carried slung over my shoulder were the page I'd taken from Helen Thornhill's diary, and three carefully labelled test tubes with their three DNA hair samples - mine, Sebastian's and Lyrica's. These tiny tubes held the key to unravelling the truth of my lineage.

Well, hopefully. The prospect of potentially being this close to uncovering something, anything pertaining to my lost past had my pulse racing. The results, when they came, would either cement my trust in Lyrica or undermine it completely.

At the apex of the Avenue, I stepped into the Circle of Lebanon. The atmosphere here was hushed yet infused with a palpable energy, as if the spirits of those buried here were still lingering, whispering the tales of their lives just below earshot. I'd nearly reached the cemetery's center-piece: a circular set of tombs, and on top of them, crowning them, an ancient cedar tree.

A golden plaque above the door of the central tomb proclaimed THORNHILL. I reached out and touched the letters which had been warmed by the sun.

"Harlan, up here!"

Carmen was standing on the plain above the Circle, waving me up. Her voice startled me. I took a quick step back and withdrew my hand, conscious of how weird my wistful gesture had to look to her.

Jed and Carmen had set up their base of operations inside the Julius Beer Mausoleum, originally built as a somber tribute to a merchant's beloved daughter. From the books I'd borrowed from Eli's shelves, I knew that its tran-quility had been shattered in the late '60s and early '70s when aspiring black magicians had broken in to perform necromantic rituals. According to Eli, this was actually what had stirred up the minor dark entity that had sparked the Highgate Vampire rumours.

As I stepped through the door, I was struck by both the

grandeur of the tomb and the many gadgets and contraptions that my friends had filled it with.

In the middle of the space stood a clapboard table, heaped with an assortment of gear. Jed was bent over an instrument that resembled a Geiger counter, but probably wasn't.

"Harlan," He motioned for me to step closer. "We can talk freely. I changed the frequency of one of the spectral analyzers to repel Ramsay's ravens, and it seems to be working. We're not being surveilled in here."

"That's a relief - but it sucks that it's necessary," I said, raising an eyebrow. I hadn't seen any of the trained ravens circling the skies above the cemetery yet, but that didn't necessarily mean they had not seen me.

"Yeah," Jed agreed, "but it is now, after what happened to you."

I let my eyes sweep over the equipment-laden table. There were several EMF meters with flickering digital displays, an infrared camera, voice recorders. Two hunting kits stood over by the wall, open and ready to reach into.

Jed turned his attention from his instrument.

"I know, lots of equipment. To be honest, it kind of seems to me like we've been saddled with a lot of excess gadgets as a form of distraction. Carmen agrees."

Carmen had walked over and was now standing next to me. She nodded. "Oh, yeah. I'm pretty sure we're chasing shadows here. The infamous Highgate Vampire case was put to bed ages ago, so either something new has emerged, or Ramsay just wants us out of the way for whatever reason. My gut feeling is that he's keeping us distracted while he is looking for grounds to dismiss us. Anything he can find."

"But there's nothing we can do except verify that there

is really nothing supernatural at play here," Jed added. "If you ask me, within the Society is where something unusual is going on."

"I agree," I said, intrigued. "But what do *you* mean? Do you know anything I don't?"

Jed shook his head with frustration. "Don't think so. Not yet, at least."

"Ramsay is keeping us in the dark about Minerva," Carmen added. "Apparently, she's still incommunicado, but that's all we know despite specifically requesting updates on her condition. Ramsay is either lazy or deliberate. I don't think he's lazy."

"And all I know," I said, "is what you've just told me. No one else has spoken to me - I suppose no one else has had the guts, or the opportunity."

I left the cemetery after entrusting the DNA samples and the diary page to Jed and Carmen, having made them promise to call me as soon as they had the results back - day or night.

"Harlan, you've got to come see this!"

Sebastian's voice echoed from inside the mansion. He practically tore the front door open from the inside, just as I was about to open it. Intrigued and more than a little apprehensive about what he could have discovered, I quickly stepped inside.

"You won't believe what I've found," Sebastian was bursting with enthusiasm. "They're all in the basement, or really it's more like a crypt. I mistook it for a wine cellar at first, but I was dead wrong. By the way, Gently dropped off some boxes of papers for you."

"Who exactly is in the basement?"

An indeterminate feeling, something between excitement and pure dread coiled in my stomach.

"You wouldn't believe me, so I have to show you."

Sebastian motioned for me to follow him to what I'd assumed was an old broom cupboard - but when he pushed the door open with a slow creak, it swung inward to reveal a winding staircase going down. He shot me a sheepish glance, as if he knew I would disapprove of his blatant ignorance going into the basement of a haunted, vampire-riddled mansion on his own, even if it was broad daylight outside.

"I didn't go looking for this, but it's not exactly well hidden. When I found a secret staircase, I obviously had to see where it went. For the sake of art."

I skewered him with a piercing gaze, not really buying his excuses. He hesitated, then confessed, "Okay, yes, I did go looking. I'm sorry, but 'Haunted Halls' is my magnum opus. It's the pinnacle of my career, and I need it to be perfect, all right?"

"You should have waited for me instead of going down there on your own. Lyrica may be incapacitated during the day, but not all entities are."

Sebastian looked disturbed.

"What'd you mean, not all entities?"

"You might have been closer to finding out than you know. Now are you going to show me what you found down there?"

We descended together, and when I insisted on leading the way, Sebastian accepted it without protest. Actually, he hung back and let me walk ahead of him with a palpable sense of relief.

The air grew colder around us as we descended the

rickety old stairs, and a vaguely musty scent rose into my nostrils.

At the base of the stairs, we entered a narrow hallway, its walls lined with old candelabras bolted in place, their candlesticks partially used and dripping with wax. The floor was littered with discarded matchsticks.

The air down here felt heavy and tense as we navigated the corridor using the torches from our phones. Several doors lined the passage, but Sebastian pointed to the one at the far end.

I pushed the heavy wooden door open with a Hammer Horror-worthy creak and we stepped into a circular room without windows. Not a chance of even the faintest glimmer of daylight making its way down here.

The walls were draped in thick red velvet, and six caskets were arranged in a perfect circle along the wall, each one distinct from the others. One was noticeably smaller than the rest - a child's casket.

"You know what this means, don't you?" I half turned to look at Sebastian.

He nodded, his eyes as big as saucers. "Vampires. If they were just regular caskets, they wouldn't be down here, right? Besides," he added, "One of them has Lyrica's name on it. And the others, well..."

I approached the casket nearest the entrance, reading the plaque affixed to it: *Clyde Hartenbrook*. So these weren't just the caskets of a more or less random coven of vampires - they were Lyrica's family, or at least this one was.

"There's no one in that one," Sebastian pointed out, motioning towards Clyde Hartenbroook's dark wooden casket. I shot him a glare as he admitted, "I tried to take a peek. I lifted the lid."

It took all my willpower to not snap at Sebastian.

Inhaling a deep breath through my nose, I repeated to myself, like a mantra, that he lacked the experience and knowledge that I took for granted as a hunter. He didn't know any better. I made a mental note to keep a more watchful eye on him.

"Never," I emphasized, my voice clipped but calm as I pushed the words out through gritted teeth, "open a vampire's casket. Even in broad daylight. Under any circumstances. Just always assume it's a bad idea."

Sebastian nodded, apparently remorseful. "I was just hoping to catch a glimpse. I was curious. Besides, I didn't open any of the others."

"Right," I said, "Did you read all the other plagues?"

In response he pointed to each casket in turn, "Clyde Hartenbrook, Octavia Thornhill, Dorothea Thornhill, Venedict Thornhill, Nathanael Hall, Lyrica Hartenbrook."

The caskets were all beautiful and intricate to look at, but my attention snagged on the one that stood at the far end of the room. Venedict's casket. It was crafted from what looked like mahogany with ivory inlays.

But what really set it apart from the rest were the heavy, rusty chains wrapped around it. The chains were secured with padlocks so old they appeared to have rusted in place, their various parts fusing with each other.

"We should leave without disturbing anything, but give me just a moment." I turned and walked over to the chain wrapped casket. "This is strange. I mean, even in context."

"Yeah, that one spooked me," Sebastian admitted, hovering near the door. "What do you think the chains are for?"

"To keep something in or to keep something out."

I looked down at the casket again and, for some reason I couldn't have explained, I let my hand hover in the air above it. It might have been my mind playing tricks on me, but I thought I sensed a faint prickle of energy. I retracted my hand as if I'd been stung by an electric current.

"Okay, really, let's go. Or rather, you go ahead. I need to check whether Lyrica or any of the others are here. If there are vampires in the house we're staying in, we need to know."

"But didn't you just say to never open a vampire's casket under any circumstances?"

Sebastian frowned.

"I said you shouldn't, but I can. I'm a professional. Just go upstairs and I'll join you in a few."

"You aren't going to kill them, are you?"

He was still standing in the door, reluctant to go and leave me alone with the sleeping vampires, presumably our distant relatives.

"I don't kill without reason. Our relatives here, or whatever they are," I used my knuckles to rap on the lid of the coffin nearest me and Sebastian winced at the hollow sound it made, "have probably eaten quite a few people between them. But I can't just go ahead and assume. This isn't Dracula and I'm not Van Helsing. Now get out of here. I'll see you upstairs."

CHAPTER

FOURTEEN

N ight had fallen, and as agreed, Lyrica, Sebastian and I gathered in the library. Without needing to discuss it, we each took the same seats as before. The only difference between last night and now were the little bowls of nuts and chocolate-covered raisins that Sebastian had set out on the table.

And, of course, the fact we now knew about the caskets in the basement.

They had all turned out to be empty, with the possible exception of Venedict's which I'd decided to leave alone because of the chains. At least, if he was actually in there, the chains were working as they were meant to. Rusted in place and covered with a thick layer of dust, it was clear they had not been disturbed for a very long time.

In other words, it looked as if we didn't have any other vampires to worry about for now, besides Lyrica.

$\sim$

JUST WEEKS BEFORE THE WEDDING, an unexpected event unfolded, which, had it not been followed by a series of tragedies, I might actually have considered a stroke of good fortune. I was among the first to receive the news.

It was very early when the sound of the brass doorbell for the apartment above Hartenbrook Trade alerted me to an early morning visitor. Hurriedly, I threw on a coat to be decently dressed and then I descended the stairs.

Venedict stood at the door, panting as if he'd run, and wearing a rather unhinged expression, eyes wide, pupils like pin pricks. Behind him in the street stood one of Lord Thornhill's horse-drawn carriages, barely visible through the drizzle. I couldn't make out a driver and guessed that he had driven it here himself.

"Lyrica," Venedict spoke as soon as his eyes met mine, "Something unthinkable has occurred. May I come in?"

Before receiving an answer, he brushed past me and went up the wooden staircase leading to the apartment where I still lived with my brother and my parents. He burst into our humble kitchen with me in tow.

My parents and Clyde were gathered around breakfast. My mother, sensing that something unusual was afoot, swiftly rose to prepare another round of steaming hot coffee.

Venedict was soaked after his ride here, but he seemed oblivious to it. When I fetched a towel from the bathroom, he left it draped over his shoulder as he relayed his shocking news.

Apparently, my uncle's headless body had been found by a terrified scullery maid in the wee hours of the morning, prone on the stairs outside the mansion. The front doors had been ajar, as if Algernon had opened it for someone he knew.

By the time the maid made her grim discovery, Algernon's blood had already drenched the once-white marble steps with crimson. He had been dead for hours.

"And this is truly strange," Venedict elaborated, "My father's head was nowhere to be found. London Metropolitan Police detectives have already snooped around for well over an hour, but they haven't recovered it."

As Venedict spilled the tea, as you call it nowadays, I glanced around at my family, their faces pale with shock. None of them particularly cherished Algernon, but he was my intended husband and a crucial pillar of support in our lives. Now he was gone.

"Do they know who the murderer is?" my father inquired after a deep silence.

Venedict shrugged.

"I don't believe they ever will. The detectives have asked only irrelevant questions. What's more, they've audaciously taken my father's body away with them for an examination, which I'm sure will yield nothing but the obvious, namely that he is dead because his head is gone."

Clearly, Venedict's encounter with the London Metropolitan Police's newly established detective unit had left much to be desired. Waving his hand as if to dismiss the matter of his father's brutal slaying, my cousin moved the conversation on to the wedding.

"Of course my father cannot marry Lyrica now," he sighed. "But it is a shame, considering all the preparations that have been made. It would be a tragic waste if there were to be no wedding."

My parents nodded in silent agreement, and Venedict finally noticed the steaming cup of coffee that my mother had placed in front of him. He took a slow sip while the rest of us awaited his next sentence with bated breath.

"My suggestion," he said, slowly replacing the cup in the saucer, "is that the wedding goes ahead. First, I must arrange for my father's funeral. But afterward, it will delight me to announce the engagement between my cherished sister, Octavia Thornhill, and our very own Clyde Hartenbrook. Their secret romance is no secret to me. And now that I am Lord Thornhill, they can marry with my blessing."

My eyes widened. Clyde's and Octavia's secret affair was news to me.

My brother and I were usually close, but I guess there were things he didn't tell me. As for our parents, they both visibly relaxed their shoulders. Our family's future was secure after all.

Algernon Thornhill's funeral took place at Highgate Cemetery West about a week hence, after the London Metropolitan Police had released my uncle's headless body back to the family.

The Thornhills already owned several of the grand tombs in the very center of the Circle of Lebanon. My aunt Helen was already buried there, and now her husband, minus a head, was due to join her.

I had expected Aunt Helen's haunting to cease now that there was no longer a threat of me marrying her husband. But after a brief respite, her spectral visits not only picked up again but increased with alarming frequency.

I came to expect waking up in the middle of the night to find her standing at the foot of my bed. Hunched over, silently screaming and pointing toward Highgate, towards the cemetery and the mansion perched behind it. It was as if Helen were caught in a repetitive loop, or perhaps she was alarmed about something new, some strand of information I couldn't grasp.

Not even her last diary had yielded anything definitive. There was nothing for me to hold on to.

A SUDDEN RATTLING sound caught all three of us by surprise.

I looked up sharply, reaching for the blades in my boots. The old chandelier suspended from the ceiling was swaying as if moved by an invisible force. Faint flashes of blue light danced among its empty arms and its stripped crystals.

"Whoa!" Sebastian shouted. "I've got to capture this." He reached for his Canon, which had been sitting on the sofa beside him.

"She's here," Lyrica said, "It's Helen. Please, don't be alarmed. She still visits me from time to time, but she means no harm. Her appearances are much less tangible these days. I think she knows that whatever she was trying to save us from way back when has already happened."

Lyrica lowered her head before slowly lifting her gaze again to meet mine and Sebastian's. "I also think Aunt Helen is glad that, despite everything, a few branches of our family tree survived the darkness and evil that consumed the rest of us. And of course, so am I."

The pale ethereal light flashed once more, illuminating the faded crystals, and then it disappeared.

"I think I captured it, her," Sebastian's tone was reverent.

"There are still lots of unanswered questions," I pointed out, my mind practically feverish with curiosity. "And the most pressing ones are probably how you became a vampire, and how Sebastian and I come into the picture. What branch of the tree do we come from?"

As if on cue, my phone started vibrating in my pocket.

I took it out and saw Carmen's name flashing on the screen.

"I have to take this. I'll only be a minute," I told the others before stepping out into the hallway and putting the phone to my ear.

I didn't go far down the hallway; I wanted to keep Lyrica in my line of sight. Her story and seeming sincerity had done quite a lot to disarm me, but I wasn't ready to lower my guard completely. Not yet.

"Carmen. You have the results?"

My heart was threatening to race out of my chest.

Carmen cleared her throat. "Yes. Those three DNA samples you provided, they all match. Whoever these individuals are, they're related."

I could feel my blood drain from my face and the ground threatening to swallow me whole. I swallowed audibly, my throat suddenly dry like desert sand.

"Harlan, are you still there?" Carmen's voice came through distantly. I realized I had lowered my hand holding the phone and quickly brought it back up.

"I'm here," I responded, attempting to sound composed. I don't think it was working very well. "Anything else?"

"One of them is a vampire."

"Thank you, thank you so much, Carmen."

My words were coming out in a rush, and then I broke off the call. As for the document I had been waiting for, it was now forgotten. It didn't matter.

I walked back into the library on legs that felt like overcooked strings of spaghetti.

Sebastian and Lyrica were sitting together on the sofa. Both looked up with surprise painted on their all too similar faces. I hadn't seen any daguerreotypes of Clyde

Hartenbrook, but he must have looked a lot like Sebastian.

"You look like you've seen a ghost," Sebastian commented. "I mean, another ghost."

"It's worse than that." I let myself sink into the loveseat Lyrica had been sitting in earlier.

I should be kicking myself for forgetting to keep her in my sights while I was on the phone, but then again, was it really necessary? The fact that we were related changed everything, didn't it? It confirmed the truth of her narrative, at least the central part of it.

"What was that phone call about?" Sebastian wanted to know. "Was it bad news?"

I shook my head.

Lyrica looked at me intently. With her preternatural hearing she would have caught every word of my conversation with Carmen. Of course, none of this was news to her. She'd known all along. Sebastian was the only one left in the dark.

"It was the DNA test results," I revealed. "They were positive. Lyrica has been telling us the truth, at least on that score. You and I are related. She and I are related. We're all part of the same family tree."

The three of us sat there in silence, allowing the weight of this new reality to settle on us.

"I won't ask you to believe my every word now," Lyrica finally spoke, breaking the silence. "But I hope you are beginning to see that I am sincere and not out to deceive you. Now, shall I conclude my story?" There was a glimmer of determination in her eyes. "I would like to finish it tonight. We're approaching some of the most crucial parts."

Sebastian and I both nodded in agreement.

"Yes, of course. And this time, I'll turn off my phone."

I felt a tinge of guilt over the now several missed calls and messages from Eli. Taking just a few seconds, I sent a brief message intended to keep his questions at bay. "I'm okay. Don't disturb. I'll call later."

Turning my attention back to Lyrica, I noticed how the moonlight outside illuminated her skin, underscoring its pearlescent glow. She was ready to dive back in, and both Sebastian and I were ready to follow her.

MY UNCLE ALGERNON was laid to rest from Highgate Cemetery's dedicated chapel. You've probably seen it as you drove up here - it's on the West side, facing Swain's Lane. Of course, most of the chapel today is a rebuild of the original chapel, which was badly damaged in a fire. And as you may have noticed, it's quite small.

Despite that, there was no shortage of guests in attendance at my uncle's funeral. I couldn't say for certain how many, but it seemed like hundreds showed up. Many were left standing outside on the road, while the chapel doors remained open, allowing the sounds and sights to reach those gathered in the street and cemetery grounds.

Clyde, my parents, and I had front-row seats to the proceedings.

As we entered the chapel, the haunting melodies of the organ already filled the air. The place was practically heaving with black roses and white lilies. It was nearing the end of August and the evening was mild, much like tonight. A soft rain fell outside, blending with the scents of the flowers and of the hundreds of flickering candles.

I almost hesitate to describe the atmosphere as somber.

It felt more like we were an audience gathered in a grand theater, eagerly anticipating the start of a show.

Everyone was seated in the chapel before the arrival of the casket. It appeared not through the front doors, as one would expect, but rather through a secret tunnel beneath the floor. A large flagstone had been removed at the front of the chapel, and the pallbearers, dressed in black satin and starched white linen, lifted the casket through this opening.

Though we knew of the underground tunnel connecting the two sides of the cemetery, witnessing a casket being brought in in this manner was unprecedented. It was very theatrical and elicited several gasps from the pews. One big-bosomed woman fainted, folding over like a modern folding chair and collapsing at the back of the chapel.

Observers standing at the open doorway turned to shout and inform the outside spectators, those in the metaphorical cheap seats, of what was transpiring.

The organ music swelled as the casket was lifted and placed in front of the altar. The customary hymns were sung, but instead of the priest, it was Venedict, wearing a suit of heavily embroidered black velvet, who rose to speak before the congregation.

My cousin spoke animatedly of his father's accomplishments and virtues, and he emotionally recounted how Algernon had single-handedly raised his three motherless children to the best of his abilities. My uncle's violent temper, alcohol dependence and opium binges were all left out. At various points when speaking of his father's generosity, Venedict gestured towards Clyde, my parents, and myself in the front pew.

Towards the end of the ceremony, Venedict called on his two sisters who, both wearing black lace dresses and with ribbons in their hair, rose to place roses on the glistening lid of their father's casket. There were no tears from either of them.

I couldn't shake off a feeling of unease - it was like a subtle nudge at the back of my mind.

When the crowd dispersed into the cemetery grounds it had just stopped raining. The air was fresh and the ground muddy. And that's when I first laid eyes on him.

Gabriel Graves cut a striking figure amid the gathering of mourners. He was tall and slender, with an ethereal complexion and hair nearly white as pearls with a faint golden hue.

My eyes were magnetically drawn to him as he directed the pallbearers toward the Circle of Lebanon and the Thornhill family tomb. He himself didn't actively partici-pate in the funeral proceedings, no, but his presence exerted a silent, magnetic force that seemed to guide the event toward its conclusion.

As the procession reached the Thornhill tomb and we all fanned out in a semicircle, I saw him standing behind Venedict, his marble-like hand resting gently on my cousin's shoulder.

Instinctively, a sense of fear welled up from somewhere in the pit of my stomach, though I couldn't, at the time, justify the reason for it. I was blessedly unaware that his pale skin, luminous eyes, and captivating aura were the signs of his, you guessed it, vampiric nature.

Someone - the woman who had both fainted and been revived with smelling salts in the chapel - whispered to me with a sense of awe that the pale stranger was the funeral director, Gabriel Graves.

At the time, the name meant nothing to me.

While we all stood watching, the Thornhill tomb was

opened by two of Gabriel's assistants, and then Algernon's casket was carefully placed on a designated marble shelf. Flowers from the chapel were heaped onto the lid in a big, fragrant pile.

After the funeral followed a grand dinner in the spacious dining hall at Thornhill Mansion. There were so many guests that the doors to the patio had been opened and more tables and chairs were set up outside.

Servants milled between the tables, refilling glasses and offering refreshments. I couldn't help but pick up a distinct sense of quiet jubilation among them, or at the very least a sense of relief. They finally had a new Lord to contend with, and eccentric as his reputation was, Venedict wasn't known for random eruptions of violence.

I wasn't grieving for Algernon, but I still found it difficult to get a single bite down the entire evening.

My attention remained captivated by the funeral director. Despite his pleasant and graceful demeanor, there was simply something about him, a feeling of something lurking or slithering beneath the surface, that set all of my animal instincts ringing in alarm.

I observed him silently as he moved through the party. Everyone he interacted with seemed to respond positively to him, or to even be enchanted by his attentions. Women smiled at him, blushing, and men looked at him with appreciative respect.

Was I the only one that felt a cold sense of dread whenever his pale green eyes glided in my direction?

I wish I had understood or known, back then, how deep Gabriel had already gotten his hooks into Venedict's mind, clouding it with dark and impossible promises. If I had seen Gabriel for what he was, perhaps I could have done something to stop him.

FIFTEEN

I 'd studied Helen's diary fervently for clues, and when it had yielded no certain answers, I'd returned to Thornhill Mansion for the preceding volumes.

For a while, I made a point of returning the volume of Helen's diary I'd most recently read and replacing it with another from the trunk in the attic. But although my aunt's diaries were rich in detail about her life, none of them helped me understand why she might be haunting me. Algernon was dead - surely any threat he had posed had followed him into the grave?

Only on one occasion did I come close to grasping the truth, and from Helen's own mouth. Venedict, equally eager to commune with his mother and to cause a stir, decided to host a seance so that we might encourage Helen to speak.

On the eve of the seance, the grand doors of Thornhill Mansion swung open and sucked me and Clyde into an atmosphere which seemed to crackle with equal parts excitement and apprehension. Other guests dressed in their finest attire already filled the entrance hall and the opulent parlour with an electric energy.

A couple of servants, Nathanael among them, were serving fruit and wine. A harpsichord had been brought into the hallway and a long-limbed man with salt-and-pepper hair was curved over it, filling the air with rippling, haunting melodies.

I glanced around nervously, but Gabriel Graves was nowhere to be seen. That was a relief - his presence would have really set me on edge.

Through the open doors I could make out a sliver of the dining room where the stage had been set for the medium to appear. The long oval table had been covered in black velvet, and although night had already fallen beyond the arched windows, all curtains had been carefully drawn. Wax candles flickered in tall silver candelabras, their flames swaying faintly in the breeze from the doors. It was a muggy and oppressive Indian summer evening.

Clyde left me to go find Octavia in the crowd, and I stood at the heart of the entrance hall, dressed in a blue velvet gown that matched the color of my anxious eyes. In my hands, secreted beneath a gossamer shawl, I clutched Helen's diary. I had shown it to Clyde, but no one else. I hoped that the diary would help draw Helen's spirit near, that her own words inscribed on the pages would help steer her towards us.

Venedict appeared from the crowd, placing a hand on my elbow.

"Lyrica, are you prepared? This will amaze you - I have engaged for the evening the most powerful medium in all of London, Csilla Zichy. Do tell me you have heard of her? If anyone is capable of summoning my mother and making her speak, she is."

I'd heard of Csilla Zichy, of course. Any Victorian Londoner worth their salt had at that point. Through whispers and fragmented tales, I had a rather good idea of the medium's background. She was said to have been born in Hungary, an orphan of unknown origins. Adopted by a British aristocratic couple, the Fairweathers, Csilla's psychic gifts began to reveal themselves even before she reached puberty.

~

"HOLD ON, BACK UP, WAIT!" I had to interject into Lyrica's story. "Did you say the Fairweathers?"

"Oh yes, the Fairweathers." Lyrica nodded. "Maximilian and Forthilda. They lived in Hampstead and were very well known, both to my family and in general. They were aristocrats and philanthropists - but they had their shortcomings, at least where their adoptive daughter was concerned."

"Did you know that the Fairweathers were founding members of the... organization I work for?"

Lyrica shook her head. "I wasn't aware, no. But given what I know of them, it really isn't surprising."

~

THE FAIRWEATHERS DIDN'T much like what they did not understand. When Csilla's unusual powers began to manifest, they initially tried to hide and suppress what was going on with their perfect daughter. And when this didn't work, they eventually disowned her for what they saw as the inconvenient evidence of her "gypsy blood."

Desperate to maintain their societal standing, Maximillian and Forthilda dissolved their adoptive papers, leaving Csilla to navigate the bustling streets of London alone.

But Csilla was resilient, and by then not only had her psychic powers blossomed, she had also acquired a taste for the finer things in life. And so she began honing her skills, captivating audiences with her seances held in the back rooms of tea houses, dimly lit bars, and eventually the grand theaters of London.

Whispers of her phenomenal gift spread like wildfire among the Victorian elite, as you can probably easily imagine, and her reputation soared. Far from being ostracized from polite society, Csilla became quite the celebrity.

Of course, at this time, her former parents attempted to reconnect with her and pick up their familial connection where they had cut it off. Csilla, however, had no interest in reconciliation. She needed neither their acceptance nor their love or their money. Even their last name she left in the dust, shedding it in favor of her original Hungarian surname, Zichy.

Within a remarkably short time, Csilla Zichy had amassed a fortune. The wealth she accumulated through her seances and other appearances allowed her to purchase a grand house in the prestigious neighborhood of Bloomsbury - still a highly desirable postcode today. There, surrounded by opulence and wealth, she became perhaps the dominant figure in London's spiritualist community. And all of this she accomplished before her twentieth birthday.

I had never witnessed one of Csilla's seances before, but the prospect filled me with excitement and not a small amount of trepidation. She was only a few years older than me at this point, but she had already accomplished more than anyone I had ever known - apart, of course, from Algernon.

"I met her at her seance at the Millford residence last

month," Venedict interrupted my train of thought. "What I saw her do rattled me to the core; I left there utterly shaken." He hesitated as if searching for the right words to follow this with. "I think I may be in love with her. This is a very confusing time for me. I have so many things to get to grips with in the wake of my father's death, so many important decisions to make. And now my judgment is clouded by this most unwelcome infatuation. I have a lot going on in my life right now."

He heaved a sigh. I had never seen my cousin this nervous before and found it quite disarming. I nodded sympathetically.

"Still, if she can summon my mother we will at least finally have some clarity on that front, and wouldn't that be something? I don't know about you, but I for one am tired of being haunted."

Minutes later, we had all filtered into the dining room, now the seance room, and taken our seats around the table. On top of it, scattered among the candelabras, were some of Helen's most prized belongings - pieces of jewelry, framed daguerreotypes of her with Venedict as a toddler in her arms.

I sat between the two eldest Thornhill siblings, balancing Helen's diary on my knees. Even little Dorothea, dressed in an emerald green lace dress, had a seat at the table. Not how anyone would raise a child in this day and age, I'm sure.

The music had stopped playing from the hallway and a moment of hushed silence fell over the room as the medium made her entrance.

Clad in a black ensemble that shrouded her from head to toe, even her face was hidden behind a delicate veil. She was small and lithe, but she emanated a powerful, electric aura. Her graceful, silk-gloved hands hinted at the rare abilities we all knew her to be in possession of.

Csilla's two assistants followed closely, their faces pale and serious. Agitated whispers swirled in the air.

My heart fluttered anxiously as the medium drew nearer, her veiled face a beautiful and impassive mask. All of a sudden, I was painfully aware of the dreadful weight of the hauntings pressing against my chest. It was an oppressive feeling and I was desperate to be free of it. I hoped with every fibre of my being that Csilla had the power to amplify Helen's silent warnings so that I might finally hear them.

With a collective breath held, the guests leaned forward, their eyes fixed on Csilla and her assistants, who had taken up their positions behind her. They appeared to be twins, distorted mirror images of each other; a young man and a young woman, both red-headed, green-eyed and with pale, freckled skin.

The room fell into a reverent silence, broken only by the soft rustling of Csilla's veil and the faint ticking of the ornate grandfather clock in the corner of the room.

"Ladies and gentlemen," Csilla's voice filled the space easily, despite being soft and melodious. Her English accent was nearly perfect, but there was a hint of something that had to be her Hungarian roots. "Tonight, we gather to summon forth the spirit of Helen Thornhill! Tonight is her chance to speak and to share any long-held secrets with her family. We are ready to begin."

Csilla rolled her slight shoulders, and everyone in the room inhaled sharply, even though nothing had actually happened yet.

"Is anyone here faint of heart?" Csilla scanned those gathered at the table, daring us one by one. "If so, you should leave now. Once the circle has been formed, breaking it could easily disturb my trance and cause the spirit to flee. If you begin to feel unwell once the spirit has come through, do not break the circle, but hold up a hand and one or both of my assistants will help you. Those who remain must quickly close the gap. And unless I say otherwise, the seance must continue to the end. Questions?"

No one got up to leave and no one asked any questions. Presumable, everyone here had already had to reassure Venedict of their spiritual strength and courage.

Apparently satisfied, Csilla removed her gloves and laid them neatly on the table. Then she reached out and took one of Venedict's hands, and with the other she reached out to Nathanael, who had come to join the table.

"Let us join hands."

I took Venedict's and Octavia's hands and closed my eyes. Through the veil of my lashes, I could sense that the rest of the guests, twenty or so in total, were also linking their hands.

A collective shiver ran through the room. The seance had begun.

"Helen! Helen Thornhill, come to us!" Csilla called out. Her words were like a command, rather than a request. "Helen, manifest through me! I invite you to use my body as your instrument."

The candles flickered, their flames dancing as a current of energy surged through the room, sending shivers down my spine. The air was practically crackling.

As Csilla chanted and called out to Helen in a hypnotic and repetitive manner, the atmosphere grew more and more heavy with an otherworldly, whispered presence.

Eyes closed, I felt a tingling sensation crawling up my arms, as if invisible fingers were brushing against my skin. If the few startled gasps from others at the table were anything to go by, I wasn't the only one starting to feel that something had already joined us in the room.

Slowly, I opened my eyes. Csilla was leaning forward in her chair, her delicate form almost slumped over the table. The black veil covered and obscured her features completely and she went silent. Then, a powerful spasm wrought its way through her. She shook violently, an uncanny sight accompanied by a guttural retching sound.

The unearthly wind that had caressed my skin now lifted Csilla's veil, revealing her half open mouth and eyes whose pupils had rolled back into her skull. Several people gasped with shock.

"My god!" Venedict exclaimed admiringly.

An otherworldly wind whipped around the room, rustling the curtains and causing the flames of the candles to dance madly.

Ectoplasm, ethereal and glowing, slowly started to emerge from Csilla's mouth, glistening tendrils coiling and extending into the air above the long table. There were murmurs, more gasps and even one high-pitched scream, but so far, everyone remained in their seats and the oblong circle was unbroken.

My heart raced as the ectoplasmic mist solidified more and more, taking on the unmistakable form of Helen, her features traced in the luminous substance.

Helen's outline shimmered as she stood before us, right in the middle of the table. She was looking around, as if she was surprised to find herself in this situation and was wondering what we were all doing here. She spoke, her attention inevitably drawn to the most familiar face that greeted her.

"Venedict, my son, how you have grown. Where is your father?"

Her voice sent shivers down my spine as I listened intently, completely unable to take my eyes off her. Venedict cleared his throat and spoke, leaning forward in his chair as if restraining himself from breaking the circle by reaching out towards her.

"Mother! Father is with you now, or at any rate, he is no longer among the living."

"He is not with me, but I am pleased he is no longer with you."

Venedict shifted anxiously in his chair.

"Mother, tell us why you are haunting Lyrica. And if you can, settle this for me. It plagues me. Tell me how you died."

The spectral, silvery form of Helen froze and was completely still. For a brief moment, I was worried that she would begin to dematerialize, but then she responded, "You were there. You remember. Despite the story you were told, you never forgot what you saw with your own eyes."

Venedict nodded slowly, his teeth gritted. A lone tear ran down his cheek.

"Mother, have I failed you or disappointed you?"

Ghostly Helen reached out a silvery, shimmering hand and, astonishingly, caught the tear as it fell from her son's chin. "You have never disappointed me, and in my eyes, you are without guilt. I love you, regardless of the mistakes that you might make."

"Mistakes?"

"I have witnessed the darkness that seeks to engulf our family," Helen's words flowed now with a sense of urgency. "There are secrets that threaten to tear the family apart - the Thornhills and the Hartenbrooks alike. Beware who you let into your life, whose promises you listen to." Helen's form wavered, her essence suddenly as fragile as a wisp of smoke. "I have been trying to warn Lyrica. She, too, shares my blood."

"Aunt Helen, what are you warning me about?"

The silvery form slowly turned towards me, a look of bewilderment on her face.

"Where am I?" Helens' voice trembled. "Why are you all staring at me? It is as if you have all seen a ghost."

"Never mind that, aunt Helen." I said, rushing my words. "What have you been trying to tell me? You have my full attention - I am listening now."

"My own flesh and blood!" Helen shivered as if suddenly terrified. "The vision I have seen of our family tree, forever suspended in darkness beyond redemption. Torn up by the roots, all the fruit tainted. No longer a tree of life, but a tree of death."

As Helen's spectral form began to dissipate, the ectoplasm retreated back into Cilla's mouth, and as it snapped shut, her hazel pupils rolled back down into her eyes. I wanted to call out to Helen and beg her to stay, but it was already too late.

Languidly, while the rest of us sat stunned, Csilla stretched her limbs. "Could someone fetch me a cup of tea, please?"

A LOUD CRASH brough an abrupt end to Lyrica's description of the seance.

The ancient chandelier had come loose from the ceiling and lay shattered on the floor, mere feet away from where we sat. And from its twisted wreckage emerged a ghostly figure, her semi-transparent, raven-black hair cascading around her and her face distorted.

SIXTEEN

Helen, clad in a gown that resembled billowing translucent smoke, floated away from the fallen chandelier and towards us. Her ethereal form seemed almost tangible, as if I would be able to reach out and touch flesh as solid as my own.

A sorrowful expression was painted on her face as she hovered, positioned right where the table stood so that it was cutting her off just below the knees. A slight chill radiated from her, as if she were an open door to the evening outside.

Sebastian's face had turned ashen while Lyrica remained unruffled. Helen's ghostly apparition was nothing new to her.

"Aunt Helen," she addressed the ghost, "You're welcome to join us. We'll be here for a while longer. I'm finally telling our story." She leaned forward in her chair. "These two young men," she gestured towards Sebastian and me, "are your descendants. That frightening vision you had long ago only almost came true."

In response, the ghostly figure of Helen raised a semi-transparent arm and pointed towards the hallway, her spectral features etched with what looked like alarm. Perhaps the ghost of Helen was still trapped in the same spectral loop, endlessly returning to deliver silent warnings of long-past events.

Then again, she seemed completely aware of Sebastian and me and of the present moment.

I rose from the sofa and automatically reached for the blades concealed in my boots. I went out into the hallway, casting my eyes in both directions. There was nothing to see but the empty, shadowy hallway.

I returned to the library, shaking my head. "Nothing to see."

Sebastian wiped his brow nervously and shot me a sideways glance.

"Helen is the apparition I saw that day when I... when I tried to break in years ago. The one I told you about."

Lyrica raised one eyebrow slightly but didn't comment on Sebastian's admission. Had she already known? If everything Sebastian had been telling me earlier was true, and it probably was, Lyrica was well aware that he had been trying to contact her for years.

Sebastian's hand trembled as he reached behind him to grab his camera. He offered up a pale smile. "I'm dying to take her portrait... a family portrait, I suppose. I only got a blue shimmer earlier."

Lyrica splayed her hands in an inviting gesture.

"Take as many photographs as you like, of Helen and of me. I've long since stopped believing that getting photographed would rob me of my soul."

Helen remained silent as she drifted gracefully to the

side of the sofa, closer to where Sebastian was fumbling with his Canon.

"I'm not sure she's up for this," he stammered, the barest note of panic in his voice as the ghost floated very close to him and stood at the edge of the sofa.

I was still feeling on edge, but not because of Helen. Leaving the others to it, I went back into the hallway, compelled to check one more time. I even went down the stairs to ensure the front door remained securely locked, as I knew it would be. Something had made my skin pimple into gooseflesh, but what?

When I got back upstairs, Helen had vanished.

Sebastian and Lyrica had apparently decided to continue the photoshoot, Lyrica standing by one of the bookcases, her posture upright and her expression solemn, as if she was posing for a Victorian daguerreotype. At Sebastian's request, she obligingly bared her fangs for the camera.

"These are phenomenal!" Sebastian declared. "I just hate that I won't be able to use them in the book. No one will believe they're real."

"You can do whatever you'd like with them," Lyrica assured him. "They're yours. And speaking of which, both of you are truly welcome to anything within these walls, even the walls themselves. I have no need for this mansion. I never did. But we'll get into that later. My story is nearly at its end. Let us sit down again so I can wrap it up."

"First, though," Sebastian insisted, "I've got to snap one of Harlan."

"Do we have to?" I protested, but Sebastian was already herding me towards Lyrica and the bookcase. He swiftly captured a few photos of us side by side, Lyrica looking stately and serious, me probably looking uneasy and annoyed, and then a couple of me alone, despite my refusal to fetch my crossbow from upstairs to pose with.

Sebastian's artistic inclination finally satiated, we all settled back into our respective seats, anticipation thick in the air. But before Lyrica could delve back into her narrative, Sebastian asked a question that had been burning in both our minds.

"What happens after you finish telling your story?"

"Well, that is entirely up to you. As I've hinted, I would like to bequeath the mansion to you. It rightfully belongs to the last living members of the Thornhill family. And if the family business empire still existed, I would pass it on to you as well. I should not have any part in these matters. I have long been detached from the world. All I truly need is a place to hide during the day, and I already have that inside the cemetery."

Sebastian and I exchanged a knowing look. She still hadn't mentioned the caskets hidden in the depths of the mansion's basement.

I wanted to let Lyrica give us this particular piece of information, and a good explanation for it, of her own volition, without backing her into a corner.

If she told us about the caskets, it would be one more strong reason to keep building on the fragile trust that had been established between us. If, on the other hand, she concluded her narrative without giving them a mention, it'd tell me that she was still keeping secrets.

$\approx$

THE SEANCE LEFT me feeling equally frustrated and unsettled. Helen's warning had been dire, but unclear. I was dying to discuss it with Venedict, but he had suddenly become very elusive.

The imminent wedding between my brother and his sister, set to coincide with All Hallow's Eve, occupied my family's collective attention.

Most of the preparations were already in place. The only significant change - aside from the replacement of the bride and groom - was the wedding dress.

As it turned out, the gown originally intended for me would not fit Octavia, whose burgeoning pregnancy was becoming apparent. An unwed Victorian woman with child would be tainted by scandal, her reputation irreparably damaged. Even if she was as wealthy as my cousin Octavia.

The identity of the child's father was shrouded in mystery.

The child was probably Clyde's. Yet, I silently entertained the notion that it could be Algernon's. As I've already explained, my uncle was a man with insatiable appetites and questionable ethics. Such thoughts were the whispers of my mind, but I never dared to speak them aloud.

As for myself, I have to say that I was relieved. I was no longer bound by the impending marriage. Instead I envisioned a future where I would continue my life as a shopkeeper and eventually also a printer of books. I imagined myself caring for my aging parents. All in all, the fate I foresaw was one I would have been utterly content with.

And so, the plans proceeded as scheduled.

The wedding was to take place under the shroud of night. Only Dorothea, Nathanael, and I were invited to the ceremony, which was to be held at Highgate chapel.

These various departures from tradition piqued curiosity, as did Venedict's insistence on personally officiating the wedding instead of involving a priest. He did, however, reassure my worried parents that a priest would later sign all the necessary documents to validate the marital union.

I have to mention here that in the months following Algernon's funeral and leading up to Clyde's and Octavia's wedding, an extensive investigation unfolded under the watchful eye of the London Metropolitan Police.

Every lead was diligently pursued in an effort to uncover the truth behind Lord Thornhill's demise. But each lead fizzled out without yielding any significant breakthrough. And my uncle's head never surfaced.

I was among those subjected to questioning by the detectives, but if there were any dark secrets to be divulged, I wasn't privy to them. In all honesty, I wasn't all that interested in discovering the identity of Lord Thornhill's murderer. Some mysteries are better left unsolved.

On All Hallow's Eve, Clyde and I, both wearing clothes tailored for the occasion, were whisked away in a horse-drawn carriage. The driver, silent and glum, escorted us to the carriage and held my hand while I climbed in. With a wave goodbye to our parents, we embarked on the journey uphill, traversing the narrow streets of Kentish Town that eventually feed into Swain's Lane.

We passed the cemetery before arriving at the illuminated chapel. Neither of us had set foot here since our uncle's funeral.

This time, the interior was decorated with beautifully dyed blue and red flowers - apparently symbolic of our two families uniting. Jack-o'-lanterns dotted the ends of each empty pew. And instead of the gloomy tones of the organ, the ethereal sounds of a solo violinist filled the air.

Startled, I realized that it was Nathanael, the butler, who was playing the violin so skilfully and with such feeling. He stood in the shadows at the end of the isle, swaying to the music as if in a self-induced trance.

Octavia, as expected, was nowhere to be seen just yet, but Venedict stood resplendent near the altar, dressed in crimson, the same deep shade as the roses that represented the Thornhills.

Once again, I found myself seated in the front pew, only this time on the right. Across from me, Dorothea sat alone in her own pew, while Clyde went and stood nervously beside Venedict at the altar, awaiting his bride.

She soon emerged from the back of the chapel, a stunning vision in her vibrant red wedding gown. The crimson lace fabric accentuated both her porcelain complexion, her delicate frame, and the incongruous evidence of her pregnancy.

"Welcome, all of my dearest ones! We're here to celebrate the union of two precious souls," Venedict's opened the ceremony. "But also the truly everlasting merging of our two families." His gaze shifted between Clyde and Octavia as they exchanged rings.

Then something very strange happened. Still standing before the altar, Venedict enveloped both the bride and groom in a tight embrace. Clyde and Octavia seemed to lean into him, their bodies collapsing against his, as if he effortlessly held them upright.

I wasn't able to see clearly was was happening, but Venedict's face appeared to be buried in the napes of their necks as the violin music swelled and swelled. The embrace lingered, the seconds stretching on forever.

A sense of unease had been lapping at the edges of my consciousness from the moment I'd set foot in the chapel, but now it was rapidly escalating into dread.

Venedict's face was still hidden from my view, buried

against Clyde and Octavia's necks. His shoulders rose and fell with the rhythm of his breathing. As the last strains of the violin drifted into the air and broke, Venedict finally released his hold on them.

Looking back, it seems pretty darn obvious that what Venedict was doing was draining the bride and groom of their life's essence. But back then, I had no idea. I only knew that adrenaline was singing in my veins and that my heart was pounding with fear.

I darted a glance across the pew at Dorothea, her petite legs barely reaching the edge of the bench. The serene expression on her cherubic little face told me that she didn't sense anything amiss.

Returning my attention to the altar, I saw that both Clyde and Octavia had slumped to the floor and that Venedict was kneeling over Clyde, clutching his wrists to my brother's mouth.

I finally managed to rise from the bench and rush toward them, a scream of protest tearing from my throat.

I attempted to shove Venedict aside, but of course it was futile - unbeknownst to me, Venedict had already been a vampire for weeks at this point, and his strength now far surpassed that of a mere mortal. I pulled and tugged at his arm to separate it from my brother's lips, but my cousin was as immovable as if he had been carved out of living marble. He laughed, amazed by his own strength.

"Patience, Lyrica, patience. I promise your turn will come."

It sounded like a threat.

"What are you talking about?" I demanded, panic reverberating through every fiber of my being. My cousin's words weren't making any sense, and now Clyde's lifeless form lay sprawled and completely motionless on the cold flagstone.

"What have you done to him? What have you done?"

I was wild with fear and anger, my own blood rushing in my ears.

"Can't you see that I am helping him, awakening him to immortality? Just as I will soon awaken you. Then you will understand."

I pushed Venedict forcefully in the chest, but he didn't budge an inch. Helpless to pry Venedict away from my brother, I turned my attention to Octavia, who was lying curled up on her side next to him.

"Oh no, I haven't taken their lives - I have given them new ones!" Venedict defended himself against my unspoken accusations. "Just wait and see. Soon they'll be reborn, just as I have been reborn."

His eyes were wide and shimmering like backlit glass. Clearly, he had lost his mind.

Finally realizing the futility of my attempts to help my brother and Octavia, or to reason with Venedict, I rushed back to the pew. I had to at least rescue Dorothea from her deranged brother's clutches.

But as I reached out to grab her small hand and pull her with me towards safety, I discovered that she, too, was immovable. She giggled, amused by my efforts.

"I have already been turned!"

The peal of laughter that followed echoed through the chapel like silver bells.

Turned?

I had no idea what that meant, but Dorothea had clearly been gripped by the same madness as her brother.

Only I and Nathanael were left, or so I thought. He stood at the back of the chapel near the doors, still playing the violin, his dark auburn hair falling around his shoulders. He paused only briefly when I reached the chapel door. It was locked.

"Nathanael, we must find a way out," I pleaded. I was gesturing wildly towards the altar and the ground in front of it which was now soaked with blood. But Nathanael shook his head slowly, his eyes calm and reflective, like the surface of a lake.

"Oh no, dearest Lyrica. Through the door is not how we'll make our escape - only the blood can provide us with a true alternative to the reality we've occupied until now. I too was fearful of the transformation, Lyrica. But then I came to understand that the dark blood is the rarest, greatest gift."

He stopped playing the violin, lowering it slowly from his shoulder. Then he reached out and rested his hands on my arms as if to reassure and steady me. His fingers were cool to the touch - cool like marble or stone.

"What are you all?" I demanded, my voice faint with fear. I was fighting a wave of dizziness as my mind struggled to understand what was happening.

"Venedict will explain everything," Nathanael replied calmly. "For now, we must conclude the ceremony. I believe it is nearly your turn."

Across the chapel, my eyes caught sight of Venedict, now tending to his sister, apparently feeding her blood from his wrist, just like he had done with Clyde.

Clyde.

My eyes drifted to him. He was still lying in a pool of his own blood, convulsing on the floor while black fluids seeped from his mouth, nose, ears and eyes onto the flagstones, like puss seeping from a wound.

I couldn't let him die like this, abandoned and terrified.

I went to him, attempted to lift him, called his name, but he was lost in a delirium and didn't seem to recognize me. His eyes rolled back into his head as I held his trembling body close, whispering, "I'm here with you, I'm here with you," over and over.

I still didn't know what was happening to him, but I knew that I needed to be there for him, to see him through this.

Venedict's voice cut through my despair, "Admittedly, this part of the turning is far from pleasant. Clyde will soon emerge stronger and more formidable than you have ever seen him, but first he has to endure this. There simply is no other way."

"He's dying," I sobbed as Clyde kept convulsing despite my efforts to hold him still.

"He's not dying at all." Nathanael was suddenly at my side. "Allow me to aid his transformation, make it more bearable, through music."

With a fluid motion, he lifted the violin to his shoulder again, allowing its tones to fill the air. Amidst this mad symphony, Octavia also started convulsing, mirroring Clyde's ordeal.

It was then that realization washed over me - Clyde's jerky movements had ceased. Instead, he lay motionless in my arms, his bright blue eyes suddenly looking up at me. They were shimmering with an otherworldly glow, like starlit skies.

He was alive!

But how?

"Lyrica," he spoke softly, but his voice somehow carried above the music. "What are these tears for?"

He reached up and brushed them away with his hand. Then, with unsteady movements, he rose to his feet. Something about it reminded me of a newborn deer finding its balance. He spun around and looked at the chapel, then spun around again to look at me. I was still kneeling on the cold, blood-drenched flagstone behind him, in shock.

"Oh, this is exquisite," Clyde breathed, looking around at the decorated chapel. "I have never witnessed such beauty before, or perhaps I have never *seen* before. Not like this."

His face was suddenly glistening with crimson tears. Although I didn't know it at the time, his turning was complete.

Beside me Octavia was groaning and unleashing piercing, tormented screams.

"It's merely a rite of passage," Venedict murmured, caressing his sister's hair and patting her trembling hands.

In the next moment, a stillness enveloped him, and his gaze locked with mine.

"It is your turn now, Lyrica."

"No," I said firmly, as if he were a wild animal poised to attack.

But there would be no bargaining. Venedict leapt on me, sinking sharp teeth into my neck, rupturing an artery. I knew instinctively that I was mortally wounded and in a fragment of a second my consciousness was slipping away from me. I had the distinct sensation of falling.

Then, for what seemed like an eternity, I floated upon a vast, abyssal sea. It was perfectly tranquil, and not altogether unpleasant.

Gradually, Venedict's voice wound into my awareness, beckoning for me to "Drink, Lyrica, drink!"

An indescribable elixir poured into my mouth. Coursing through my veins, it seemed to animate every last cell in my body.

Next thing I knew I was drinking with an urgency I'd never known, spurred on by an unfamiliar and desperate thirst.

Then the world began to materialize once more, but it was not the same world as before. It never would be again. This is how I became a vampire.

CHAPTER
SEVENTEEN

As I opened my eyes, a bewildering sight greeted me. Clyde and Dorothea were dancing, swirling through the chapel while the notes of Nathanael's violin floated in the air.

Clyde had to hunch and bend forward quite a bit to be able to hold Dorothea's small hands. Venedict, too, swayed to the music, but his gaze was fixed on me, as if he'd sensed it the second my consciousness returned to my body.

"Welcometo your new life!"

He was watching me expectantly, as if awaiting praise. He would be waiting a while.

Octavia was still lying motionless on the floor beside me. A plaintive whimper rose from her blood-stained gown. Lifting the lace, I discovered a small infant nestled between her ankles, still connected by the umbilical cord.

Acting on instinct, I lifted the infant, and with unfamiliar sharp teeth, bit down and severed it. I somehow knew that I had to break their connection before the cursed blood could flow from mother to child.

Octavia was lost in a distant realm, her eyes rolling back into her skull when I tried to rouse her.

Fortunately, it seemed that I had acted swiftly enough to prevent what I later learned was vampire blood from reaching my newborn nephew. Tearing a fragment from Octavia's red lace skirt, I used this to swathe the youngest member of the clan. The last human heir.

I cannot describe how difficult it was to concentrate. All my senses were completely overwhelmed by the beauty of the chapel, and of everyone in it. The vibrant hues, the interplay of light reflected through stained glass windows, the painted altarpiece depicting Jesus' resurrection, the flowers, the music, and even the walls and floors - it was all a spectacle to my newborn vampire eyes.

I willed myself to focus on the fragile human life in my arms.

"If we transform him now," Venedict mused, following the direction of my gaze, "he will remain an infant. You did the right thing by severing the cord, I believe. Truth be told, I did not think this aspect of tonight's ceremony through. Let us grant him a few years before we bring him over - a playmate for Dorothea, don't you think?"

Suddenly a heavy crash reverberated through the chapel. A fiery projectile, a stone wrapped in gasoline-soaked linen, shattered one of the stained glass windows. Flames engulfed the wooden panels where it landed.

"What is happening?" Clyde bellowed. He had been helping his bride to her feet, but now he froze mid-motion.

"Damn it, somebody must have discovered our secret!" For the first time tonight, Venedict sounded uncertain. "We must leave, come gather round!"

He was already standing over the flagstone that had been removed to accommodate his father's casket when that was brought into the chapel. Now he crouched down and in one swift motion lifted it, a task that would normally demand the strength of several burly men.

Venedict stumbled backward, stunned. When I saw what had rattled him, my heart sank.

The secret tunnel had been sabotaged, filled with pebbles and stones, by someone who must have foreseen our potential escape route.

"Get to the windows!" Nathanael's urgent voice pierced through the chaos as several more heavy stones wrapped in burning linen came raining down on us like cannonballs.

Flames were soon spreading through the pews and consuming the flowers and Jack-o'-lanterns as they withered and blackened.

"Careful of the flames!" Venedict's voice was taut with alarm. "Fire can still harm us."

At that moment, I was still grappling with the finer details of my transformation. Uncertain of what I had become, I knew only that I was otherworldly, unnatural, something steeped in darkness. Something both connected to blood, and reliant on blood.

Clutching my infant nephew tightly, I was desperate to protect him - in the first instance from the flames, but also from the rest of us.

Just then, another torrent of flaming rocks hurtled into the chapel from both sides. The roof was bombarded, too.

Gradually, flames began to dance along the interior edges of the ceiling. With both the door and the underground passage barricaded, the windows were the only way out. We all realized this soon enough, so we divided ourselves up, each making our way out through a different window.

We didn't know how many our assailants were, or really which side of the chapel they were on.

I emerged through one of the crushed stained glass windows on the cemetery side, still holding the infant boy. I had to cover his mouth to prevent him from crying out, and I was terrified of accidentally choking him.

At least none of our attackers were paying this side of the chapel much attention, and as I landed softly on the ground, agile as a cat, no one noticed. I could see angry and distorted pearlescent faces through the branches that obscured me from view.

Our assailants were all vampires, and Gabriel Graves, who I later learned was Venedict's maker, was among them. He hadn't sanctioned the creation of any more vampires through his bloodline. I believe he was the one who rallied the others against Venedict - and because of Venedict, against the rest of us who had had no choice in any of it.

"I KNOW THE TIMING'S TERRIBLE," Sebastian cut in, "but I really need the loo."

I shot him an incredulous glance. "Seriously? Right now?"

"Yes, seriously. I've been holding it in for the past hour. I really need to go." If his tone was anything to go by, he wasn't kidding.

"When you come back," Lyrica said, "I'll wrap up my story. As you can probably tell, we're near the end."

Sebastian left the room and vanished down the corridor, leaving me alone with Lyrica. She sighed into the silence, a wistful sound.

"We were all so young when our lives were cut short. Sometimes I wonder if there was any way I could have prevented these events from happening. You have a lot of time to think when you no longer have a life expectancy." She chuckled to herself, but the sound was bitter.

"Maybe there wasn't," I surprised myself by saying. "It sounds like Venedict took you all by surprise. It sounds like he decided to turn the entire family, without bothering to ask if any of you wanted your humanity stripped away and replaced by, well..."

"You can call me a vampire. It's okay. It's what I am." Lyrica met my gaze. I'd noticed both tonight and last night that, when she spoke, she would look either me or Sebastian in the eyes, but never for long. If she had been human, I might think she was shy, but knowing what she was made it seem like a gesture of politeness, a way for her to demonstrate that she wasn't trying to hypnotize us. A considerate gesture.

"Do you know what happened to the others - and what happened to Octavia's son, the last living Thornhill?"

"I know what became of some of my companions, but not others. I'll tell you what I know."

As I stood hidden behind the dark swaying branches of a tree in the cemetery, Venedict abruptly appeared, dragging Octavia behind him. With a swift motion, he grabbed me, too, and forcefully pulled me along, deeper into the cemetery.

I demanded to know what had become of Clyde, Dorothea and Nathanael.

"I didn't see where they went," he hissed, his gleaming

teeth clenched. "There might be nothing we can do for them now. We need to get ourselves to safety before we can afford to think of the others."

Octavia trailed behind, disoriented, probably in a state of shock. Venedict had her arm in an iron grip so she didn't stumble.

We followed a familiar path, guided by Venedict, leading us to the circle of Lebanon and up to the front gate of the Thornhill family tomb. With a key retrieved from somewhere on his person, Venedict unlocked its door.

Stepping inside, I immediately realized that my vampiric senses granted me perfect vision even in the pitch darkness of the tomb. Several new caskets had been placed on the marble shelves along the walls. The new caskets were side by side with the two existing caskets belonging to Algernon and Helen.

I suppressed a shiver.

In a rushed whisper, Venedict explained that we had to sleep in these caskets during the day. To demonstrate, he went over to a beautifully crafted ebony casket and lifted its lid. It opened to reveal a plush pale blue satin interior.

"This one," he turned to me, "is yours. Of course, we have other caskets scattered throughout various locations, but I will show you those some other night."

"Can I hold him?" Octavia asked me suddenly, meaning the infant. Her voice, transformed by the dark blood, had an ethereal timbre. Until now, she had shown little interest in her son, but now she reached out for the little bundle in my arms. "I can smell his blood. Let me hold him. He is, after all, mine."

I reluctantly handed her her son, but I kept an eye on her every move. "What shall we do with him?" she asked, looking at him with great curiosity. "Feed on him?"

Feed? The expression disgusted me.

"Absolutely not. Tomorrow night I'll bring him to my parents for them to raise. We can provide them with abundant wealth, make sure he has every material comfort."

I glanced over at Venedict, who to my great relief nodded in agreement.

"Yes, that is what we shall do. Then, after a few years, we can reclaim him and usher him into the realm of darkness to live with us. Now," he proceeded to lift the lids of the other caskets, "it is best if we rest. Daylight is so near now that we cannot risk going back out there. Nathanael knows of this hiding place, and many others. If he can, he will lead Clyde and Dorothea to safety."

Venedict clambered into his casket (A white, polished, ostentatious one adorned with his name in golden lettering) announcing, "I must now retreat to solitude to reflect and mourn."

Then he closed the lid, leaving me alone with Octavia and the infant, alone to ponder the terrifying and tragic events of the past few hours.

"Not so quick - don't you think you owe me an explanation?" I pounded on his casket lid. "Why have you done this? And why can't we go back out there? I need to know what fate has befallen my brother."

"We cannot go out in the light of day anymore, and alas," Venedict's voice rose muffled from within the casket. "I do not know what has become of Clyde, Dorothea, or Nathanael. They must fend for themselves."

"If there's even a sliver of hope that Clyde still breathes, I have to go back out there to try to find him."

Venedict threw the lid back and fixed me with a stern look. "Not a chance! This place is locked from within, and I cannot jeopardize losing you. Let us hope that the others have made it to a secure refuge, but we cannot risk our own lives to ensure it."

"How do you know we are safer in here than out there?" I demanded.

"Because I've put a circle of protection around this place. Powerful lodestones charged with my own immortal blood are buried in the Circle of Lebanon which surrounds us. No supernatural blood can cross it against my will."

I didn't believe a word of it, but what could I do?

In the end, I retreated to my casket to welcome the death sleep that would fall over me every morning from then on. As it turned out, it was sweet oblivion.

When I ventured out of the tomb and wearily picked my way through the cemetery the following night, the vampires that had hounded us were nowhere to be seen.

I could have left the infant on my parents' doorstep, accompanied by a note explaining his parentage. But I needed to see my mother and my father one last time.

They greeted me with a mix of confusion and relief when I stepped into the drawing room of their narrow apartment. Hartenbook Trade had closed for the evening and I knew this was where I would find them. I had let myself in, using my own key. I placed it now on the table - I didn't intend to take it with me again.

I stood back, wary of their proximity when they both came to embrace me. "Please, do not come too near. I will explain in a moment."

I was acutely aware of the changes that the vampiric blood had wrought in me - my marble white complexion, my glass-like tapered fingernails, my teeth. Those damned teeth. I couldn't risk them noticing.

"Lyrica," my mother cried, more upset than angry.

"Where on earth have you been? Why did you not come home last night?"

"We only sense that the wedding ceremony went awry." My father added stood hesitantly a few feet away. I could tell that he was dying to cross the space between us and draw me into a big hug, but just like my mother he resisted the urge. "Your brother has been impossible to get a word out of since he came home in the wee hours of the morning."

"Clyde came home last night?"

I almost shouted it. I realized that I would have to be careful not to frighten my parents with any display of supernatural power. This included my voice, which I'm able to lower to a nearly soundless whisper or raise to fill a stadium.

Immediately, the infant hidden under my cape started crying. My parents both visibly tensed.

"Whose is this?" my mother demanded as I lifted him, still wrapped in a piece of Octavia's wedding dress. She was trying to search my face, but I wouldn't meet her eyes, fearful of the recognition I might see in hers as she realized I was no longer human.

"This is your grandson, the child of Clyde and Octavia." I placed the infant in my mother's arms, and he instantly seemed to grow calm. Undoubtedly, the warmth of a mortal body cradling him was infinitely more soothing to him than my marble-cold skin.

"Now where is Clyde? Where is my brother?"

"After locking himself in his room and sleeping all day, he rose as soon as dusk fell and took off," my father sighed. "He seemed in a daze, possibly still intoxicated from last night. I knew he had been drinking when he came home, and possibly worse. He pushed right past us both on the way in and on the way out."

"He didn't seem himself at all," my mother underscored. "We're very worried about him. When I looked at his face, it was very pale and completely closed off to me. Almost like yours is now, my dearest."

Blood tears welled in my eyes, threatening to spill down my cheeks. I fought them, knowing how hair-raising they would look to my already unsettled parents.

"The infant arrived prematurely and Octavia cannot care for him. She trusts you with his care and upbringing." I was rushing to get the words out. "He is a Thornhill by blood and will want for nothing. And neither will you, for the rest of your lives. The two of you and the child here are all that remains of our family." My voice had dropped to little more than a whisper, weighed down by sorrow. "I'm afraid this is the last time you will ever see me. I love you both, but I have to go."

My parents immediately began to protest and started racing for me, but I turned away swiftly, unable to bear their pain. "I am lost to you. Clyde is too. Please, don't search for us. Grieve for us and then let us go."

I vanished into the night with vampiric speed, the echoes of my parents' voices quickly fading behind me.

At the back of my mind, I was already devising a plan. There was no way for me to undo the curse that Venedict had brought down on us - but if his darkness could be contained, I could stop him from spreading it further.

CHAPTER
EIGHTEEN

I found Clyde later that night. He had taken refuge in one of the Thornhill family's warehouses on the banks of the Thames, near the old Execution Dock. Pirates were hung here until the 1830s.

Uncle Algernon had once told me about witnessing such an execution as a young child, an incident he recalled with a degree of fondness.

Clyde had hidden himself away in one of the large wooden crates used to transport coffee beans. As soon as I was in the area, my heightened vampiric senses told me precisely where I would find him.

I entered the warehouse through a small window under the beams. If I had still been mortal, I would not have been able to scale the wall, let alone climb down from the tiny window once inside. But the new blood in my veins gave me strength and agility I'd never possessed before.

I have to admit that a not insignificant part of me was relishing my newfound strength and the sense of freedom it gave me.

The warehouse was full of rows upon rows of wooden

crates of different sizes, most of them still filled with cargo, but some empty and waiting to be taken back across the seas.

Like a sonic radar, my senses guided me to the crate in which Clyde was huddled in almost a fetal position. His features were now drained of color and replaced by a haunting pallor.

"Lyrica," he whispered, his voice filled with despair, his eyes widening as I approached. "What have we become?"

I knelt down beside the crate, close enough to touch him but giving him space.

"Clyde, I'm here," I tried to reassure him, "you're not alone. If we help each other, we can find a way forward, surely, a way to exist as we are now. Don't you think? But we need each other."

I wasn't sure that I believed these words myself, not deep down, but the dark expression on my brother's face was breaking my heart.

"No, Lyrica." Clyde shook his head sadly, "I want nothing to do with any of this. I don't want to be a part of Venedict's world, or Octavia's, or even yours. I should have stayed in the chapel as it burned. We should all have gone up in flame along with Dorothea and Nathanael. I may yet decide to destroy this unnatural body."

I spent most of that night in the warehouse, slowly steering my brother's thoughts away from ending it all. I reminded him of the scientific curiosity that had always driven him, and I reminded him of the deep empathy that had inspired him to want to become a surgeon. Slowly but surely, I made him see a glimmer of possibility.

I also made him see that I needed his help to contain Venedict's evil, and in the last hour before dawn, we found ourselves trawling through the warehouse and the harbor, gathering chains.

We took swift action the following night. As soon as Venedict had retreated to his casket for the day, we wrapped layer upon layer of the chains we had gathered around it, securing them tightly with multiple padlocks. Then we carried his casket from the mausoleum in the cemetery and down into the mansion's hidden basement.

The plan proved effective in the following nights when he woke up. Even his muffled screams barely reached our ears.

Octavia, who may have protested our treatment of her brother, who she adored as much as I did mine, had slipped into a catatonic state from which there seemed to be no way to retrieve her. She withdrew from Clyde and me, spending most of her time in and around the cemetery, still wearing her red wedding dress and veil. Despite our pleas, she refused to speak to us, and on many nights she would not even rise from her casket in the Thornhill family tomb.

Clyde, after his initial crisis, slowly seemed to embrace his new reality. He returned to the Royal College of Surgeons, where he completed his training, attending only the night classes. He never approached our parents again, but at times he would come to their windows at night to catch glimpses of his son, whom they had named Augustine.

Yet, Clyde eventually decided that he couldn't bear to be so close to all the losses and pain he had endured, and so he packed his bags and moved far away, to the New World, where he would continue his studies of biology, science and medicine. He was determined to find a cure for vampirism, and as far as I know, he is still searching for it.

In a way, I had lost everyone. My parents were lost to

the divide that now separated my world from theirs. My brother, my cousins, Nathanael, whom I had considered a friend - they were lost in various ways, consumed by flames, driven to madness, departed to America or restrained by my own efforts in Venedict's case.

Truth be told, I couldn't live with the guilt of what I had done to him.

And so, not even a year into my vampiric existence, I made the decision to retreat from the world. I locked up the mansion, made my way to the family tomb, closed the lid on my casket and made a vow never to emerge again.

I kept my promise for more than a century.

As it turned out, the circle of protection that Venedict had spoken of, actually worked. It seemed to hold sway over other supernatural beings, but it had a limitation. It was completely ineffectual against the intrusion of humans.

In August of 1969, four human youths ventured into the cemetery and broke into my tomb. Their presence tempted me to break my slumber, and my fast.

I LET OUT a breath I had not even realized I had been holding. "So you were the so-called Highgate Vampire all along?"

1969 was when sightings of the entity known as the Highgate Vampire had first been reported, and in early 1970 the alleged vampire had been all over British newspapers. It sounded like Lyrica accounted for at least some of those sightings and attacks.

She shrugged. "Perhaps. But I am not the only vampire around these parts. There is Octavia, who still, as far as I know, rises to hunt on occasion before returning to her stupefied slumber. There is Gabriel, Venedict's maker. I know for a fact that he still resides nearby, in a beautiful villa in Queen's Wood. Unlike this place and the Thornhill family fortune, Gabriel's residence and business have continued to thrive. I have gone near his territory on a number of occasions but have never intruded. I have never confronted him with my questions about why he rallied a group of vampires against us. But then again, the answer seems obvious - he wanted to punish Venedict, his fledgling, for immediately adding several new vampires to his bloodline without involving his maker in the decision-making. At least that's what I think."

The sudden sound of footsteps echoing through the hallway reminded me that Sebastian had been gone for ages.

I'd been too engrossed in Lyrica's words to wonder what was taking him so long. Now my skin prickled and the hairs on the back of my neck stood on end.

The footsteps approaching through the house seemed to move with an unnatural speed, faster and lighter than Sebastian would be capable of. I rose from the sofa. Something wasn't right.

Lyrica sensed it too. Her body language was alert, like a vigilant animal watching for an attacker.

In a burst of energy, the library doors flew open, revealing a figure standing in the doorway. And as I had already sensed, it wasn't Sebastian.

The newcomer could only be Venedict. Lyricas's vivid descriptions of him, his energy, and his appearance left no room for guesswork.

Venedict Thornhill was surprisingly lithe, with aristocratic, refined, even androgynous features. His complexion, like Lyrica's, was as flawless as that of a marble statue, and his hair was cut straight across his shoulders, barely touching them. The dark aubergine color Lyrica had described had faded over the course of decades, giving way to a light shade of caramel.

Despite his slight build, Venedict radiated power as he moved fluidly into the room.

"Pardon my intrusion," he greeted us both in a pleasant, velvety voice, only slightly rusty from disuse, "but I have been staying out of the family's affairs for far too long. Now I am back and I fully intend to stay."

He fixed me with a pair of large honey-golden eyes. It struck me that his were the eyes I'd seen in the nightmare I had had at Eli's house.

As Venedict turned his attention to Lyrica, the details of the dream came flooding back to me. Venedict was the creature that had appeared to me and demanded that I come home. It also seemed obvious to me now that the burning chapel in my dreams had been the chapel at Highgate Cemetery. And the crying infant, the infant that turned to ashes just as I'd carried him to safety? Probably Augustine, Octavia's son, the last mortal member of the Thornhill bloodline.

Or, he had been at the time. Now the last mortal members of the Thornhill bloodline were myself and Sebastian.

"Sebastian!" I demanded. "Where is he?"

Venedict turned toward me, making a grand sweeping gesture with his hands. I noticed his slim, tapered fingers and the yellowed lace spilling over them from the sleeves of his coat. He had to be wearing the same clothes that he had worn the last time he climbed into his casket to sleep for the day - sometime in 1861.

"If you're referring to the young gentleman who kindly let me out of my confinement, then he is downstairs." He spoke casually, brushing some cobwebs and dust from his shoulders.

"Have you done anything to him?"

My eyes were fixed on Venedict, ready to act if he should make any sudden moves. I might be able to trust Lyrica, but her maker here? Probably not.

Venedict frowned, as if I'd offended him. "I have not harmed him in the slightest. I only put him in a mild trance and compelled him to let me out. I did take a little drink, of course, but he is hardly harmed by that."

That last sentence came as an afterthought.

Lyrica shot up from her seat, her voice flaring with an anger I hadn't seen in her before. "You dare to touch him! Sebastian and Harlan are the last of our mortal family. I swear, if either of them comes to the slightest harm by your hand, I will not stop at simply locking you away."

"What kind of greeting is this, dear cousin?" Venedict looked genuinely wounded. "I should be the one furious, making threats."

Worried about Sebastian, I left the two vampires to their reunion and swiftly made my way down through the house while their voices faded behind me.

I'd barely reached the ground floor when I heard Sebastian's voice calling out to me.

Then I saw him - he was staggering up the stairs from the basement, pale and shaky. I helped him up onto the marble floor of the entrance hall. He sank down at my feet.

"Harlan, I'm sorry, I'm really sorry I fucked up!" Sebastian was so full of remorse that it was radiating from every pore. "I just couldn't resist - his voice was in my head! Such a cliche, right?"

"I warned you not to go near the casket!"

I crouched down and used my sleeve to staunch the trickle of blood from two tiny puncture wounds on Sebastian's neck.

"Please believe me, I couldn't help it," he pleaded, wincing at the touch of the fabric. "I felt compelled to do it. He directed me to find a bolt cutter left behind by the squatters. I didn't think I could do it, but cutting through all those chains was easy."

"Yes, fortunately my powers haven't completely vanished,"Venedict's voice sounded from the dark staircase behind us. "But my ability to influence our young Sebastian seems much stronger, much more effective than with anyone else. Ah, all those times I've tried to summon someone from the cemetery to assist me in regaining my freedom! I got close on occasion, but I never could swing it. I must say it's convenient when someone shows up in your house and their blood already belongs to you. For this, Lyrica, I suppose I should thank you."

Venedict and Lyrica both stood at the foot of the staircase, a few feet behind us. Lyrica's arms were folded across her chest and she was shaking her head, her features obscured by her gleaming obsidian hair.

"Truly," Venedict continued, "I'm thrilled that the two of you have come to the ancestral home. You are the descendants of Augustine, correct?"

Reaching into his moth-eaten coat, he produced a lace handkerchief. He used this to dab at the corners of his mouth, where presumably a few droplets of Sebastan's blood still lingered. He then tossed the handkerchief to Sebastian, who just looked at it as it fell on the floor next to him, his eyes wide and disbelieving.

"Who's Augustine?" Sebastian whispered, probably

worried that yet another vampire was about to make his entrance.

Venedict's strange amber eyes glided from Sebastian to me.

"Apparently," I replied, speaking for us both. "Lyrica has told us the whole story, more or less. We've taken a DNA test to confirm it, and the results came back positive."

"Ah, yes. I've heard of DNA on the radio waves," Venedict nodded sagely. "I grasp the concept. Not that I need DNA to know you are of my blood. I can smell it, and I tasted it as soon as I sank my teeth into this one." He made a nod in Sebastian's general direction. "I was quite worried that our blood would have become utterly diluted as it trickled down through the centuries, but those fears have been allayed, for now."

"I resent that you just said that," Sebastian was hoisting himself up by holding onto one sturdy newel post, "But I also feel compelled to let you know, Venedict, that I'm your familiar, whatever that means. I'm not sure where the inclination to insist on this comes from either, but there you have it."

Venedict raised a quizzical eyebrow.

"This insistence on being your familiar," Lyrica said, addressing her cousin, "it seems to be something that happens to the first person you bite without killing after a long fast. The same thing happened to me when I awakened in 1969."

Venedict raised his eyebrows and his eyes glistened - he was clearly thrilled to learn about this.

"1969! And still so much we don't know about how this glorious vampirism works."

Sebastian and I exchanged a glance. Venedict might have heard of DNA, all right, but if he thought that this was

1969 he wasn't quite as clued in on current events as he seemed to think.

"I want to hear more about all of this familiar business, but first things first, I wish to find Octavia. I must say, right now I don't sense her presence anywhere in the vicinity, and this has me, for want of a better word, concerned. In all my long years of slumber, I've never once lost track of her energetic presence." "

"I'll help you find her," I offered, "But first I'd like to bring Sebastian to safety."

"He is perfectly safe here; I didn't touch a hair on his head!" Venedict actually rolled his eyes at me. "No harm has befallen him whatsoever - he's not even lost consciousness. Back in my day, we weren't quite so fragile."

Here Venedict paused, perhaps realizing that he was digging himself into a hole. "But I take your point," he added. "You have my word - both of you - that I will never again help myself to your vital elixir. Now, shall we go find my sister? I won't be at ease until we have located her."

"I haven't seen Octavia for quite some time," Lyrica's voice was gentle as she placed a slender hand on her cousin's shoulder. "I believe she eventually did what I did."

"I know what you did," Venedict said, closing his eyes and pressing his hands to his temples, as if he sensed a migraine coming on. "I know that it was you who locked me up down there. Then you went into the ground for over a hundred years, hoping that this act of contrition would somehow absolve you of your guilt. But it didn't work, did it? The hum of your guilty conscience has been like an ever-present oppressive energy that not even the walls of a reinforced casket can shut out."

Lyrica bowed her head, stung by his words.

"I intended to sleep and to return to the world when past sins and pain had washed away from me, yes."

"But Octavia had no reason to do the same," Venedict pointed out. "She would never have betrayed me and doomed me to confinement."

"What else would you have me do?" Lyrica responded, at once imploring and exasperated. "I had to stop you. You had caused so much damage. You tore our family tree up by the roots, just like aunt Helen predicted! I should have killed you, but I didn't have the heart to do it."

"It's not my fault that things went awry," Venedict rebuffed her. "I did the very best anyone could have done for you and your brother, for all of us. But wait-"

Venedict held out his hand, motioning for silence. Then he gasped.

"What is it?" Lyrica's brow furrowed with concern.

"The circle of protection around the family tomb - it has been broken, I'm sure of it." Venedict's eyes were open wide. "All these years, locked in my casket, I have been prowling the grounds of my territory. All of these years, I've been keeping my mind's eye on my property, on my family - but tonight, tonight I've been distracted. Without my presence, in spirit if not in body, I fear the family tomb is no longer a safe resting place."

"Let me come with you," Lyrica suggested. "We'll go to the cemetery right away. I feel at least partly responsible. I should perhaps have renewed the circle of protection and not let it weaken."

"Of course you should have." Venedict gave her a scathing look, already halfway to the doors to the outside. "You can thank your lucky stars that I'm here not to take revenge, but to clean up the mess. It's no wonder," he looked around, shaking his head, "that everything about the family has declined into this state of disrepair without me at the helm."

"Listen," I cut in, "Two of my, ah, colleagues are working in the cemetery tonight. I can call them right now and ask if they've seen anything unusual. If anything is amiss in the cemetery, they'll know about it."

"No," Venedict froze, shaking his head, his eyes narrowing. "Absolutely not. I know what they are. Octavia could be in as much danger from them as from anyone else. I refuse to put my trust in any vampire hunters - except you, once you have proven yourself." He stopped and squeezed his eyes shut. "Ah, I can't sense her presence at all. Let us not waste another moment. I need undisturbed access so I can retrieve Octavia - that's if she is even there. I fear she may not be, that something has already befallen her. Harlan, please come with me now. Distract the hunters for me."

My mind raced through the options. I couldn't allow Octavia, my distant foremother, to come to any harm. But trusting Venedict was another issue altogether, and helping a vampire was a moral gray area I'd rather not get into.

Still, how could I say no?

When I met his gaze, my decision was already made.

"I'll do it. I'll come along and keep them occupied. But remember, no harm should come to them. We're talking about friends."

Venedict's lips curled into a smile, but I couldn't tell if it was ironic. "Your friends will remain unscathed. I only ask that you trust me, and that you buy me the time I need. What bad could come of it?"

He flung the doors open on the moonlit night.

CHAPTER

NINETEEN

I f anyone had seen us making our way to the cemetery, they would have witnessed an odd specta- cle. Venedict, dressed in his velvety rags, led the way, followed closely by Lyrica, with me and Sebastian, still weak from blood loss, trailing behind.

I'd urged Sebastian to stay and wait for us at the mansion, but he was determined to partake in this bizarre family outing.

We maneuvered through the tall grass, weaving between the moss-covered statues until we reached the edge of the garden. Here we scaled the fence to the ceme- tery, Venedict and Lyrica effortlessly levitating over it while I made a nimble jump onto the fence before dropping to the ground on the other side. Sebastian struggled a bit as the strap of his camera got caught on one of the tall spikes. With a quick tug, he freed it and finally landed in the thick layer of dead leaves next to me.

I turned to him and said in a hushed voice, "It's impor- tant that you don't make any noise. And it would be even better if you stayed here near the fence to wait for us."

He shook his head. "I'll be quiet, I promise, but I've got to be there when you find Octavia."

It was a stalemate, and we didn't have time to keep going back and forth over it.

"Don't worry," Lyrica placed her hand protectively on Sebastian's shoulder. "I won't let anything happen to him."

I was only halfway reassured, but we proceeded cautiously through the silent pathways, heading for the Circle of Lebanon.

When we were close, I turned and whispered to the others. "I'll go up there first. Hang back here for a minute or two, then go get Octavia as quickly and as quietly as you can."

An eerie hush hung over the cemetery tonight, but I knew Jed and Carmen were somewhere in the vicinity. Probably in or around the Julius Beer mausoleum.

Leaving Venedict, Lyrica and Sebastian hidden behind a cluster of trees, I started walking up Egyptian Avenue, the gravel crunching under my boots. I called out to my friends. I didn't want them to just hear unannounced footsteps and draw the wrong conclusions. Or the right ones, considering that two vampires lurked in the shadows not far behind me.

As I drew closer, I noticed a thin, coiling mist, green and ethereal, flowing over my boots. It was seeping downhill from the Circle of Lebanon, slowly spreading its tendrils throughout the rest of the cemetery.

My pulse quickened.

Then a scream filled the air, followed by the sounds of running feet on gravel.

I sprinted towards the sound. If Carmen and Jed had encountered, awakened or angered something, or some-one, they needed my help. In that moment, they were infinitely more important to me than any distant vampiric relative.

I called out to them again but received no response.

Then, a figure stumbled toward me, moving downhill and away from the Circle. The dense mist had enveloped us fully, obscuring almost everything from view. It was only inches away that I recognized Jed. He had his hand pressed firmly against his face, blood gushing between his fingers. If he had any other wounds, I couldn't see them.

I reached out and grabbed him as he fell against me. Jed looked at me with a bewildered expression, blinking as if struggling to recognize me.

"Harlan," he stuttered.

"What is happening?"

"We've been attacked." His words were running together. "We didn't expect anything to happen, but suddenly all the equipment started going crazy and then, out of nowhere, this mist." He gestured around us with his free hand, the one not clutching his eye socket. "It rose up and engulfed us within seconds. We've called the head-quarters for support, but so far no-one has answered. Whatever we're dealing with here, we're on our own."

"Are you badly hurt?"

Jed didn't answer, but then he slowly moved his hand away from his face, revealing an empty, bloodied eye socket.

I quickly scanned the ground around us, but I couldn't see the missing eyeball. Hell, I could hardly even see the ground. We were probably going to have to consider Jed's right eye a casualty.

"Where's Carmen?"

"In the Beer mausoleum - she went in there to get weapons."

"Ah, a wounded soldier."

Venedict was suddenly standing beside me. Jed looked around, his bewildered gaze struggling to make out the figures in the now nearly impenetrable mist. He visibly stiffened when he noticed Venedict and Lyrica on either side of me. Sebastian was hovering a few feet away.

Helping Jed move around the corner, I carefully lowered him to the ground.

"Wait here," I instructed him. "I need to check on Carmen, make sure she's alright. Sebastian will stay with you and call an ambulance."

This time, Sebastian listened to me and he hurried over to where Jed was now slumped against an ivy-covered tombstone.

"Harlan, be careful," Jed warned me as I turned on my heel, ready to head back into the mist. "The guy who took my eye - he wasn't human. Vampire, I think. It happened so fast."

So Lyrica and Venedict, and Octavia, weren't the only Highgate vampires in the cemetery tonight. Great, just great.

"Is it just the one vampire?"

"Yes, just the one. Mind you, he's bad enough."

"It's Gabriel," Venedict seethed. "It has to be. He must be trying to gain access to the mausoleum. Why else would he be here tonight? He's after Octavia, and who knows what dark reasons drive him."

In the next moment, Venedict and Lyrica vanished, dashing up Egyptian Avenue.

Sebastian crouched next to Jed. "Go, Harlan, I'll look after your friend."

I followed the two vampires, who had already been swallowed by the wall of mist.

Where was Carmen? Had she confronted Gabriel as he tried to break into the Thornhill family tomb? Were they fighting?

I reached the center of the Circle of Lebanon where Venedict and Lyrica already stood in front of the tomb. The doors had been torn open and practically torn off their hinges, revealing a dark void within.

None of the caskets on their shelves appeared to have been disturbed, but I knew that surface appearances could be deceiving.

As the mist above us began to thin, I looked up, and a chill ran all the way into my soul.

Directly above me, on top of the tomb, stood the menacing figure of Gabriel Graves. He was wearing dark clothes, like a cat burglar, and his long, pale hair shimmered in the moonlight. In his arms, he held the seemingly lifeless body of Octavia Thornhill.

She was just as breathtaking as I knew she would be, with skin like illuminated marble and red hair gleaming like lacquered wood as it fell around her in perfect corkscrew curls. All her features were delicate and small, as if carved by an expert sculptor. She wore what I assumed was her red lace wedding dress. The serene expression on her face made it impossible to tell if she was dead or just unconscious.

Venedict's fingers tightened on my arm, confirming that he shared my shock and horror. Not sure if Gabriel had seen us, the three of us crouched down to let the mist hide us.

Gabriel, overcome by some private amusement that this moment seemed to hold for him, released a peal of laughter. His vibrant green eyes flashed in the moonlight before he, with a swift movement, disappeared behind the old cedar tree atop the tomb. In an instant, he was gone. Both the mist and the laughter began to clear.

Venedict lifted me by the arm. In the blink of an eye, we stood next to the old cedar tree, Lyrica landing softly beside us.

Gabriel was nowhere to be seen, not on either side of the tree or in any direction. But Lyrica was gesturing to draw mine and Venedict's attention to something I could have easily overlooked.

A large old flagstone, left slightly askew.

"I know where he went," she whispered. "I've noticed this tunnel before, though I've never had a reason to explore it. I believe it leads to Villa Graves in Queen's Wood. Let us follow him, but we must maintain a distance so he doesn't see us."

We waited for several tense minutes before descending the worn, windy stone steps into an underground tunnel. Brackets for torches lined the sides, but none were lit. Gabriel clearly navigated these passages without the need for light.

There was no mist down here. Instead, total darkness enveloped us. I couldn't even see my own hand when I held it out in front of me.

"Allow me," Venedict wrapped his arm around my shoulders and propelled me forward at an astonishing speed. Lyrica followed closely behind.

In front of us the tunnel stretched out seemingly endlessly. It had clearly been constructed long ago, perhaps around the same time as the cemetery, if not earlier. From Lyrica's account of Algernon's funeral, I knew about the tunnel connecting the two sides of the cemetery, but I hadn't known there were others.

The direction we were heading seemed to be ascending as we headed towards Queen's Wood.

WHEN WE EMERGED from the tunnel, we found ourselves under the branches of a giant weeping willow, its age and size mirroring the cedar in the cemetery. It was a perfect hiding spot, its cascade of branches concealing us from any potential onlookers in the grounds outside.

Venedict wore a furious expression on his face. "He has my sister," he declared. "We have to retrieve her from the villa, but it won't be easy. Gabriel is as cunning as a serpent."

"As vicious as one too." Lyrica added, painting a fuller picture of our adversary.

Lifting the veil of branches, Venedict revealed a beautifully manicured and landscaped garden. In the middle stood a white, imposing villa lit by floodlights.

Villa Graves was a Grecian dream of a house, rising four stories tall. At the front, ornate columns supported a majestic portico. White marble griffins, nearly as big as the lions in Trafalgar Square, flanked the doors. There were several outbuildings, all much newer than the original villa, villa being a misleading term for a property of this size.

All around us, pale moonflowers bloomed, releasing a delicate fragrance. The cascading waters from multiple garden fountains added a deceptively soothing melody. But somewhere behind all this tranquility, Gabriel Graves was carrying out his secret plans.

"This is how we'll proceed," Venedict turned to me with a serious but also hopeful expression. "I don't believe Gabriel saw you, and we must use this to our advantage. Your status as a mortal and as someone unknown will provide us with a way in. If I'm not mistaken," he continued, turning to Lyrica, "Gabriel still operates as an undertaker to this day?"

She nodded.

"I believe he has multiple locations scattered throughout London, but that he also maintains a workshop in his home, specifically for crafting his most exquisite and, of course, expensive caskets." Her eyes lit up as realization crept over her, and she added, "If you, Harlan, pretend to be a customer and give him a plausible reason for appearing at his door in the middle of the night, he just might let you in."

"Eureka, Lyrica!" Venedict exclaimed. "Our minds are finally aligned! Harlan, here's what you do: Ring the workshop's doorbell, and make up the tragic death of someone dear to you."

"Stroke his ego," Lyrica suggested, "A combination of grief and flattery will work. Gabriel is a singularly vain creature - and he loves consoling the bereaved."

"*Singularly* vain", Venedict emphasized. "And while you have his attention, we'll find a way into the villa to retrieve my darling sister. You'll be putting yourself in danger, of course - but it is the only way. Hold Gabriel's attention for as long as you reasonably can, then make your excuses and leave. We'll meet you back here, under the weeping willow."

I hesitated, my mind feeling around the perimeter of the plan, searching for a snag. There were loads.

"Harlan, please." Venedict's eyes and tone were imploring, "No matter what Gabriel's intentions for my sister are, I know they cannot be noble. Moreover, we're running low on hours before sunrise, and we cannot afford to waste them."

Minutes later, I found myself standing outside the home-based showroom of Gabriel Graves' undertaker business, Deep Graves, located in the largest of the modern outbuildings. I suppose finding family when you've never had one can really fuck with your sense of boundaries.

Most vampires are suspicious of technology, but Gabriel Gaves apparently was not one of them. A gleaming modern intercom sat on the wall next to the door. A sign next to it announced the name and nature of the business in ornate lettering.

I pressed the intercom button, my heart pounding.

Internally, I was cursing myself for not having brought more weapons when we went to the cemetery. Retrieving Octavia from the family tomb had seemed like such a simple task. I'd made an error of judgment, but there was no time to dwell on it.

A crackling sound filled the air, and then a voice - a smooth, cultured voice, a voice that seemed to have nothing in common with the wild and raucous laughter I'd heard in the cemetery - echoed through the speaker.

"Welcome to Deep Graves. Gabriel Graves speaking. How may I be of assistance on this moonlit night?"

I took a deep breath to steady myself before I replied, "Mr. Graves, I'm glad you're still up. I know it's the dead of night, but my dad has just passed away up at the Royal Free Hospital. I can't just sit around - I need to do something constructive, something to honor him. I heard Deep Graves provides the finest caskets and funeral services. Is this true? And may I come in?"

There was a brief pause, as if the vampire on the other end was considering my request. Then, the voice responded, "My condolences for your unspeakable loss. Please come in."

TWENTY

I made my way through the imposing doors, entering the dimly lit showroom behind them. Rows of gleaming caskets lined the walls, many of them ornate, each of them clearly handcrafted, with unique handles and detailing. Classical music at low volume drifted down from hidden speakers. A subtle fragrance wafted into my nostrils—a blend of polished wood with a hint of lavender.

"Welcome to Deep Graves." The vampire's voice was as soothing and reassuring as could be.

The tall and slender figure of Gabriel Graves seemed to glide forward from the shadows. His elegant, angular features were accentuated by whitish-golden long hair falling to his elbows. And at about six feet tall, he must have been considered remarkably tall during his lifetime - whenever that had been. I had no way of knowing his true age, but as Venedict's maker, I knew he had to be at least a few hundred years old. In other words, this was no sapling I was dealing with.

Remarkably, he seemed to have found the time between

his exploits in the cemetery and now for a change of clothes. Earlier, he'd been dressed head to toe in black, but now he wore an emerald green smoking jacket that almost swept the floor. Beneath it, the immaculately pressed collar of a crisp white shirt peeked out. Trousers in charcoal gray and a pair of polished black leather shoes completed the impression of a bona fide gentleman. The entire ensemble was a display of great taste and even greater wealth.

He extended a gloved hand towards me.

"Henry Hall," I shook Gabriel's hand, making the name up on the spot. I could feel the coldness of his vampiric skin even through the gloves, and it sent a shiver down my spine.

"What kind of monster would I be to turn you away in your grief, even if it is the middle of the night?" Gabriel's tone was pleasant and resonant, fully in line with the impression he clearly wanted to project. "Truth be told, you're not disturbing me at all. I'm somewhat of a night owl; I had no plans of retiring for several hours yet. As the owner and proprietor of Deep Graves, I am deeply committed to honoring the departed, and yes, this includes bringing solace to those they leave behind, no matter the hour."

"I appreciate your commitment, Mr. Graves." I gave him a smile that I hoped was full of the admiration he wanted to see. But I let go of his hand and let my eye slide away from his. "When others recommended your services, I had to reach you immediately. My father always wants, would have wanted, the best."

"Your father must have died before his time?" Gabriel's eyebrows arched. "Alas, none of us truly knows how much time is allocated to us. Please, allow me."

My skin prickled when I noticed it; the timbre of the

vampire's voice had shifted almost imperceptibly. It was now not just pleasant and soothing, but had taken on the quality of a silk ribbon slowly wrapping itself around my mind.

"I would like, if I may, to share with you a few important details about the history of Deep Graves and the craftsmanship that breathes life into each of our caskets."

I nodded, "By all means."

Gabriel guided me over to the corner of the showroom where, in a large illuminated glass display case, a simple wooden casket was on show. It looked downright antique.

"This is the type of casket that my family was known for building, back in the 1600s." Gabriel's eyes sparkled with nostalgia as he looked at the casket on the other side of the glass. "Ah, but those were tumultuous times. Still, I have to say, they provided the fertile ground in which my family's business took root and prospered. The first iteration of Deep Graves was nestled upon the Old London Bridge, and there was never any shortage of customers in those days. Why, there has never been a shortage of customers since. I hope I am not being insensitive when I say that death never goes out of style."

The vampire ushered me along to show me a much more detailed, expertly crafted example of his craftmanship. This casket was made of dark polished wood and had pure white satin upholstery. Its lid and sides were a tapestry of carved intertwining vines and roses. I recognized the style from the caskets I'd seen in the basement of Thornhill Mansion.

"When the old bridge was dismantled and the city evolved, our business found its new dwellings right here in Highgate." Gabriel, clearly, did not need any prompting from me to keep talking about his business venture. "By then, the Graves family had already dedicated generations to the art of laying the departed to rest and to honing a reputation defined by superior craftsmanship. As you can see."

"This casket is beautiful," I said, sensing that now was the time to start with the praise. And it was no lie; the level of detail was insane, not at all what you'd find in a run-of-the-mill undertaker's showroom.

Gabriel smiled proudly, but in a carefully cultivated way so that his fangs remained hidden. He leaned a little closer, his pale, green eyes luminous. "Craftsmanship and service, my young friend, remain the cornerstones of Deep Graves to this day. From the selection of the finest woods to the carving of the details that give each casket its unique personality. As a matter of fact, I do a lot of the work myself. I believe that every casket should be as unique as its occupant."

As I made my way along the row of gleaming caskets, my attention touching on each one, Gabriel followed my movements with an inscrutable expression, much like a cat watching a mouse. I was keenly aware of the deliberate indifference of his gaze, and I kept most of my attention on him while moving around the room. I was alert and ready to crouch down and reach for the knives discreetly tucked into my boots, concealed and always ready for action.

"These are all spectacular," I said, turning to face Gabriel fully. I'd made sure not to turn my back completely at any point. I'd only been in here for ten minutes at most, but my sense of unease was already intense.

Had Venedict and Lyrica managed to break in by now? They must have. Could they have already found Octavia and made their way back out with her to safety? Probably not yet. The villa was large and sprawling - even with vampiric speed, it'd take a little while to search through it all.

Gabriel accepted my compliment with an inclination of his head. "These are all fine, perfectly adequate caskets. But since you have gone to the trouble of coming here in person, I'll let you in on a little secret; my finest work isn't on display here." The tiny hairs on the back of my neck stood on end. "I have something in progress in my workshop, which is part of my private quarters. I'm willing to show it to you, if you'd like. You said it yourself," he added, eyes glinting with veiled amusement, "your dearly departed father would have wanted the best."

"I'm sure I can find a casket here among the ones I've already seen." I was hoping to politely turn down the vampire's invitation. I really didn't want to follow him deeper into his territory. I had my knives, but he had every other advantage.

There was a brief pause before his voice again rolled over me like a tide. "The casket I wish to show you still requires some finishing touches, that's true, but I can have it ready by the time you need it. I'm capable of working quite swiftly when time is of the essence. I don't want to rush you, of course, but I was in the midst of working on this particular masterpiece in my workshop when you rang me on the intercom. I'd like to get back to it soon, and you are more than welcome to join me. You are, of course," Gabriel splayed his hands in a disarming gesture, "more than welcome to take your leave and come back tomorrow instead. I can book you in for a consultation with one of my assistants at the Deep Graves premises in Highgate Village."

He watched me, a shadow of a smile playing about his lips. His proposition was clear: Follow me deeper into my domain or leave.

He knew he had me.

"Well," I responded, drawing out the seconds as I turned from the oak wood casket adorned with inlaid marble that I had been admiring. I'd gone this far - I couldn't chicken out now. "You're right. Lead the way."

I didn't have to ask twice.

Gabriel led the way to the far end of the showroom, through an arched doorway and into a glass corridor overlooking an atrium garden. Lush greenery climbed its walls and the sound of trickling water drew my attention to a fountain surrounded by purple plumes of lavender.

The glass corridor took us to the villa itself, and soon we were standing in a lavish living room.

After the brightness of the showroom, it took a moment for my eyes to adjust to the unlit space. When they did, I could see that Gabriel's decorating style was a tasteful if ostentatious blend of antiques, chinoiserie and modern glass and steel. In the middle of the room stood a large, low-slung sofa arrangement gathered around a glass coffee table. It was laden with a curated collection of antique nick nacks and old photographs - Gabriel's face smiling back at us from different eras.

I froze when I sensed movement in the corner of the room.

A blond-haired child vampire sat in an armchair in the dark, kicking his short legs, completely engrossed in reading a book. He glanced up from his reading, flashing green eyes at me and Gabriel as we stood in the doorway.

"This is Dwight, my nephew," Gabriel introduced him. Leaning for a moment against the doorframe, he addressed the younger - or at least smaller - vampire. "Dwight, as you can see, I have a visitor. I'll be showing him what I am working on. You keep an eye on everything up here. Oh, and turn on some light, would you? How many times have I told you?"

"Ah, yes, of course," said the child, Dwight, sounded amused. With a fluid movement, he reached out and pulled the braided cord of a lamp. "I mustn't strain my eyes in the dark. Tsk-tsk. I always forget."

Gabriel turned to me again, "Let us get a move on." He gestured with his hand toward the dark corridor that would take us deeper into the villa. Then he started walking ahead of me, his pace quickening with every step deeper into the shadows of Villa Graves.

"You have a beautiful home," I noted.

"Thank you. The Graves family has worked diligently for centuries to amass the fortune that I - and Dwight - now get to enjoy." I could hear the note of pride in his voice.

"I can only imagine."

I was starting to understand Gabriel's penchant for revealing fragments of truth veiled in secrets and white lies. According to what Venedict and Lyrica had shared with me on our way here, Gabriel had been posing as his own descendants, tirelessly accumulating wealth over countless years. Dropping hints about this seemed to be his way of keeping himself amused.

We made our way through the long corridors of the villa until, suddenly, Gabriel stopped in front of what appeared to be a solid, impenetrable wall.

He reached behind a portrait painting - of himself in the 70's, wearing a green velvet suit with flared trousers and green tinted glasses, his gloved hand resting on a whimsical dog-headed cane. Behind the painting, Gabriel pressed something in the panel. Immediately, a section of the dark wood whispered open, revealing a glass elevator.

"Step inside," he invited. "We're nearly there now."

My blood was singing with apprehension at the sight of the gleaming glass box, but I still stepped into it.

If Gabriel was going to attack me, he was going to do it whether we were here in the corridor or somewhere else in the building. Right?

The doors closed soundlessly behind me, sealing us within the confined space. A panicked voice at the back of my mind was screaming that this was a mistake. But it was too late to turn around now. The feeling of my stomach leaping into my throat told me that we were already descending.

CHAPTER

TWENTY-ONE

The air subtly changed as we descended further, the enclosing dark wood panels transitioning to rugged rock and eventually to a vast subterranean cavern.

Towering stalactites and stalagmites sprouted from an underground lake, evoking the grandeur of an ancient cathedral. Frosted glass platforms and walkways, lit from beneath by submerged lights, seemed to hover over the water. A hushed silence enveloped the space, punctuated only by the soft hum of the descending elevator and the gentle lap of the lake's waters.

Clearly, Gabriel had invested time crafting this neat little refuge. It was the perfect sanctuary for a vampire; no matter what time of day or night it was outside, it'd always be night down here. I wouldn't be surprised if he kept his own casket down here somewhere.

The elevator came to a gentle halt, its glass doors whispering open. Gabriel stepped out onto a sleek, frosted glass surface and motioned for me to follow. Vampire or not, he had the demeanor of the perfect host.

I stepped out after him. "You're not some kind of secret superhero, are you?"

He chuckled, delighted by the idea. "Far from it. I simply inherited this old villa and found it full of secrets. Tunnels, trapdoors, stairwells, even this. It was really just a subterranean lake, but I've had it built out with all these platforms, stairs and lights that you see. And I set up my workshop down here so I can work undisturbed."

I bet you did.

Gabriel indicated an illuminated but narrow gangway that ran along the wall. I strained my eyes, trying to see as I walked behind him, our footsteps reverberating softly against the rocky walls.

A cold sense of foreboding had settled like an invisible weight in my chest and on my shoulders. Not a soul in the world knew where I was. I was deep underground with a powerful, adversarial vampire. Gabriel would have nearly all the advantages if he decided to attack me now. This was his home turf, a place he probably knew as well as the back of his hand.

The further we went, the less likely it became that he was actually taking me to a private workshop - and the more more likely it became that he was simply luring me away from the world outside.

I was suddenly very conscious of the sound of my own blood rushing in my ears. Probably, Gabriel was too.

What he didn't count on, of course, was what I was. Thinking that I was just another mortal foolish enough to fall into his web could prove his fatal mistake.

His back was confidently turned to me as we walked, as though he had nothing to fear.

Reacting to my silent thoughts, Gabriel halfway turned and broke the silence. "I would ask you to tell me a little more about your late father, your family, yourself, but why don't we wait until I have shown you my work in progress? I'm convinced that it will provide a much more interesting starting point for our conversation."

He hadn't revealed a single glimmer of supernatural power, but I could feel it like a faint electric hum in the air.

"Sure," I said, noticing what appeared to be an island of natural, ragged rock rising out of the dark water.

We stepped from the gangway onto it.

"Here we are," Gabriel announced, "My workshop, my sanctum."

With a flick of his hand, he must have pressed a remote or flicked a switch, because the space surrounding us became bathed in light.

Industrial-style chandeliers were suspended from the soaring vaulted ceiling far above us. There were many of them, all hanging from solid chains at different heights. Some of them were dangling above the water, creating the illusion that there were even more .

Other than that, the space was bare, except for two clear glass coffins sitting side by side on a raised, altar-like podium ten feet or so away from where we stood. Sickeningly, I noticed the glass tubes connecting them, forming a macabre lifeline between them.

But what sent my heart racing like a trapped bird in my chest was this: In one of the coffins lay the still figure of Octavia, her slender fingers folded upon her chest.

"Not what you expected?" Gabriel's voice coiled through the air. "But as I told you, this is where I keep my most important project."

Gabriel approached the bizarre twin coffins, his facial expression full of tenderness. His eyes fixated on Octavia's impassive face. Standing beside the podium that the coffins rested on, the vampire brushed a wayward, ruby red curl away from her forehead, an almost reverent gesture. The air was thick with anticipation - mine or his, I wasn't sure.

As I stood there, my eyes trained on the twin glass coffins and the tall figure leaning over it, Gabriel's true intentions seemed to crystallize.

Our eyes met over the coffin and a wicked smile spread on his lips.

"Yes, this, this is my masterpiece." Gabriel's voice was every bit as cultured as before, but with an underlying intensity creeping into it like a vibrant thread. "It may not be as beautifully intricate as some of my other works, but it will serve the most beautiful purpose. And you, Harlan Thornhill, have an important role to play in effectuating the miracle I have in mind."

I took a step back as the realization settled over me, squeezing the air from my lungs. He knew my name.

I met the vampire's penetrating gaze as he started walking around the podium and approaching me slowly. "The time for pretenses is at an end. Isn't that a relief?"

He had put the raised podium behind him and was standing in the space between it and me. There were only three or four feet between us, a distance I knew he could close in the blink of an eye.

"Yes, I know who you are. And not only that." He gave me a smile that showed his fangs, a detail he no longer cared to hide. "I know of your reputation, your profession, your family... such as it is. I can even make a rather solid guess as to your true purpose for showing up on my doorstep. No doubt you have come looking for her. I cannot say I know why, but your sense of timing is impeccable."

His words had thrown me but my years of training had

me crouching down and drawing the hidden blades in one fluid movement.

Gabriel raised one eyebrow, as if implying that he had been expecting more.

"If you know who I am, why did you let me in? Why turn your back to me?"

A soft chuckle. "You may consider yourself to be a masterful vampire hunter, so forgive me if I seem coy. The so-called Van Helsing Society only deals with lesser vampires and minor psychic disturbances while leaving the truly powerful ones, such as myself, well enough alone. And wisely so, I might add. Even a skilled mortal hunter is no match for me and I rather doubt you have ever been up against, let alone defeated, one as ancient and powerful as I." When I didn't stop him, he went on, "To fear you would be beneath me. Yet, I have not been taking any chances. You may not have noticed, due to your flawed and dull mortal senses, but even with my back turned, my senses were fully alert. I always kept far enough in front of you that even the slightest disturbance of the air would have alerted me to your attack in plenty of time."

"What do you know about my family and about me?" I genuinely wanted to know, but mostly I was hoping to stall him.

My two blades were long enough to pierce his body through from one side to the other. If I was lucky enough to get my aim right, I might use his own forceful strength against him when he came for me, as I knew he would.

Alternatively, though this seemed much less likely, keeping him talking might give Venedict and Lyrica time to find us here. If it was three of us against him, I was fairly confident of the odds.

Right now, though, I only had myself to rely on.

"I know you are a Thornhill, and that you grew up without knowing. No doubt Lyrica has wanted to shield you from the truth, just as she has previous generations. And yet, here you are, in this neck of the woods, and I you clearly know that you belong to that accursed family. You know who I am, too. And somehow - and this, I must say, this baffles me - you know that I was at the cemetery tonight on an errand. Why else would you have come here?"

Taking a few, deliberate steps closer, he added, "Yes, I have been keeping an eye on the Thornhill descendants through the years. I should, of course, have been preoccupied with keeping an eye on my own, but unfortunately, cruel fate has not allowed me such comfort. Dwight, my nephew whom I introduced you to upstairs, is the only family I have left. There are no mortal descendants." He let out a small sigh, suggesting that this was a truly regrettable state of affairs and he expected me to feel sorry for him.

Newsflash, I did not. "Oh, so jealousy has made you stalk me instead of your own descendants?"

I knew I was provoking him, but if I could stir his emotions, I figured I could keep him off-balance. He shook his head, as if offended by my word choice. "I prefer to think of it as keeping an eye on all the pieces on the chessboard - even the peasants - so I can anticipate my opponent's next move."

"And how's that working out for you? I mean, here I am, a surprise to you."

A split second passed during which Gabriel appeared to be on the edge of losing his composure. But then he grinned at me, flashing his fangs in the glow of the chandeliers.

"Rather an unexpected gift than a surprise. Tonight is the night that I revive the body of Octavia Thornhill, and for that, I need blood. An abundance of blood. When the vital elixir flows between the two sides of this coffin behind me, you see, her immortal but dormant body will be infused with the life-giving essence it requires. And whose blood could be more suitable, more symbolically apt, than the blood of her own descendant?"

And just like that Gabriel's twisted plan was coming into full view. Apparently, he intended to drain my blood, using the tubes as conduits to feed my lifeforce to Octavia. Oh, fuck.

"That's right, my young friend. You will serve as the catalyst for her resurrection," Gabriel's voice had become infused with a chilling excitement. "It will be your blood flowing through these delicate glass veins."

The reality of what was at stake was pressing down on my chest like an unbearable weight. And perhaps Gabriel was right - perhaps my experience as a hunter counted for nothing against him. As if he could smell my wavering, Gabriel let out a burst of laughter that ricocheted off the walls.

"Ah, Harlan. You cannot escape what has now become your destiny. But you *can* take comfort in the knowledge that your ancestress will rise once more, reborn from your sacrifice. Though, I should probably mention," He paused, taking yet another step towards me, almost playfully, "that the vampire that will awaken tonight will not really be Octavia. It will merely be her body. The spirit inhabiting it will be that of my darling Elizabeth."

I took a step back, both wary of his proximity and of the madness of his ideas.

"Who the hell," I demanded, "is Elizabeth?"

Hadn't there been enough surprises for one night?

"Elizabeth, why she's my beloved sister." Gabriel's eyes

glinted with sudden tenderness. "Unfortunately, she has been without a body of her own for quite some time. I won't go into the details except to say that she requires a new one. I consider it my obligation, as her brother and protector, to provide her with a suitable replacement. And this one is beautiful, wouldn't you agree? Born to immortality on the precipice of womanhood and perfected by my own immortal blood. I feel a sense of ownership over it, to be perfectly honest."

In my time as a hunter, I'd run into plenty of objectively frightening situations, but what Gabriel intended to do, aiding the spirit of his sister in taking possession of a body that wasn't hers, sounded particularly twisted.

I took another couple of steps back, conscious that the gangway, my only potential means of exit, was behind me.

"But why not just create another vampiric body for your sister to... occupy? Wouldn't that be easy for someone as powerful as you say you are? I mean, you could easily find another young and beautiful female body. Why steal Octavia's?"

I wasn't suggesting that Gabriel go out there and steal a human victim to replace Octavia, but I had to bide my time.

Soon one of two things were bound to happen. Either Gabriel was going to attack, in which case I'd do my damnedest to make him regret it. With one blade, if I could only get it angled correctly, I figured I'd be able to pierce his heart while slicing through his throat with the other. Or Lyrica and Venedict were actually going to show up.

Gabriel shook his head, as if dispelling the possibility that they might. He glided yet another step towards me, as though we were engaged in an agonizingly slow, coordinated dance.

"You don't seem to grasp," he scolded mildly, "that this

body holds sentimental value for me. This body belongs to the sister of the one who betrayed me. Haven't you ever heard of ancient warriors consuming the brains or hearts of their enemies? The symmetry, when I call my own sister's spirit into Octavia's body, couldn't be more spiritually prudent. And since you're so curious, Octavia's spirit is barely attached to this immortal flesh anymore. It's a tenuous connection at best, which will make it so much easier for Elizabeth to not only enter, but to take root."

I could taste bile at the back of my throat. His words sickened me.

"Now that you know my intentions," Gabriel's tone was soothing now and completely reasonable. I imagine he used the same tone of voice when discussing funeral packages with clients at Deep Graves, "you *could* choose to cooperate, to accept your demise as a necessary sacrifice to bring my sister back to vibrant and eternal life. But, alas, I know that you won't, that you will attempt to resist me and cling to life."

Taking one more step back, I found myself backing onto the gangway. My eyes were locked on Gabriel.

"It is a shame, really, that I will have to snuff out your life while you are still so young and vibrant. But my dear Elizabeth has already been waiting for so long. Now is her time to live again."

"You're insane." My voice came out low through gritted teeth. "You really think this is going to work? What if your sister's spirit is gone - what if she's traveled on long ago?"

The moment hung in the air between us, heavy with tension. Anger animated Gabriel's features.

"You're wrong, this will not fail! Elizabeth's spirit is already with me, waiting for me to work the miracle."

Then he lunged forward in a blur of movement.

TWENTY-TWO

T he smoking jacket billowed behind Gabriel as he lunged forward. Ready for him, I struck out with both knives - but he was out of my reach again before either of the blades could touch his skin.

Or so I'd thought.

As he danced backward, regaining his bearings and readying himself for a second attack, I saw him wiping his throat with the back of one emerald sleeve.

"You might be a little better than I thought," he conceded, with a note of surprise and a graceful inclination of his head. "Perhaps that werewolf mentor of yours has taught you a thing or two, after all."

"He's trained me well, all right. Come near me again and I'll sever your head. The alternative is that you let me leave now with Octavia." I nodded toward the glass coffin.

"Is this supposed to intimidate me?" Gabriel threw his head back and laughed uproariously. The monster from the cemetery was starting to show through his carefully polished facade. "You know I will not let you go - and I will not relinquish the body. What you've accomplished here is barely a scratch. So no, you're dreaming. You're dreaming if you think you'll ever leave this place, except in spirit."

I only had one threat up my sleeve that might make him rethink his position. The problem was that if I used it, I'd reveal my only sleight of hand. If Gabriel knew that Venedict and Lyrica were somewhere in the darkened villa above us, he might let me walk with Octavia, but more likely, he would press on, forewarned and expecting their arrival. So no, I couldn't afford to play this vital piece of information into his hands.

I bit down hard on my lip and did my best to steady my breathing and my frantic heartbeat before Gabriel lunged at me again.

This time his movements were almost too fast for my eyes to follow, but again I parried him, slicing through one of his sleeves. Our dance began in earnest. Centuries as a vampire had lent Gabriel the superior strength and agility I would have expected. My training and my sheer desperation were just enough to keep up with him, for now.

Gabriel's attacks were becoming more ferocious, fuelled by his burgeoning frustration as he realized I wasn't easy prey. And there was the time constraint. Morning couldn't be more than two hours ahead of us. Even this far underground, a deathly sleep would steal over Gabriel at sunrise.

Again he came flying at me, and again I parried him. My flashing knives would have frightened off a lesser vampire. It was just a shame Gabriel wasn't one.

For a while there were only the sounds of my blades and of my breathing. A few times, Gabriel let out a gasp when I managed to nick his skin and draw blood. He hadn't touched me yet, but we both knew that it was only a matter of time. We were only a few minutes into our standoff and I already knew I wouldn't be able to keep this going for long.

Unlike Gabriel, I'd tire sooner or later. Besides, one powerful strike from him would be enough to throw me back against the rock wall fifteen feet behind us. I hoped to high heavens he hadn't noticed the slight tremor in my arms from holding and wielding the knives.

But of course he sensed my wavering. The second I lowered one of my blades just a fraction, he was coming at me again.

His movements were so fast this time that he became a blur. He ducked under my right arm as I struck out at him, and then he came up behind me. With brutal force, he kicked my legs out from under me, sending me crashing to the stony ground.

As I lay stunned, momentarily disoriented, Gabriel towered over me. His pale green eyes radiated malicious glee as I struggled to regain my breath.

Where were my knives? They were no longer in my hands. I felt for them on the uneven ground around me, but wherever they were, they weren't within reach.

"We're done playing games." Gabriel informed me, still looming over me with a wide and unbearably triumphant grin. "We must get on with my sister's resurrection."

Over his shoulder I could make out the glass coffins, one still holding Octavia, and the other empty, waiting for me.

"I thought you were smarter than this. I know why it's bound to fail. It's because... because..." I deliberately fumbled for the words, hoping to give Gabriel that I was still disoriented.

"Because what?" Irritated, Gabriel leaned in a little closer, bringing his ear closer to my mouth. Yes, thank you.

With a swift motion that demanded every ounce of my strength, I threw my upper body forward.

Gabriel realized too late what I was up to, and then I clamped my teeth down on his neck. His entire energy field tensed with shock. Apparently it was news to him that two could play this game.

I'd already nicked his throat, and that made it possible for me now to bite through his skin. I tore at his throat like a rabid dog until I felt blood gush into my mouth and down the front of my shirt. His blood was black as liquid night - vampire blood.

With his powerful fingers, Gabriel pried my jaws open, forcing me to release him. I only let go when I was fairly certain that he was getting close to crushing my jawbone in his hands.

He stumbled backward, instinctively reaching for the wound. It looked like a wet, jagged mouth against his pale flesh. He seemed stunned at the sight of his own blood staining his hands and he stumbled against the podium holding the twin coffins. The impact caused them to shudder, but they remained unharmed. Octavia didn't stir at all, still blessedly oblivious to the turmoil unfolding around her.

This could be the only chance I was going to get.

As Gabriel clutched at his throat, I forced myself to get to my knees and then to my feet. My knives, where were my fucking knives? I wouldn't make it far without them.

They were on the rocky ground, of course, one of them about five feet to my right and the other halfway between me and Gabriel. I lunged for it. Then, propelled by Gabriel's blood and with the gleaming knife high above my head, I rushed forward.

He saw me and the flashing blade, but it was just a little too late. I bore down on him, the knife steady in my hand, when something cool and slimy wrapped itself around my wrist.

The sudden force of the powerful grip forced me to let go of the knife's handle. I watched incredulously as my weapon fell jangling at my feet.

I looked at my wrist and saw the serpentine tentacle encircling it. My eyes must have bulged with shock, because what I was looking at was as thick as a very large man's wrist, but its iron grip was much more powerful. My muscles strained against the sudden restraint, my mind racing to regain a sense of control over the situation.

What the hell was this?

Following the length of the tentacle with my gaze I registered first that it had erupted from the depths of the underground lake and second that it belonged to a sea-creature whose slick and muscular body was now emerging from the water.

Great, just great.

Above the waist, the new arrival's head, torso and arms looked mostly human. The skin, though, had a pale, translucent quality to it, as though he - and this was definitely a he - spent more time deep underwater than he did on land. A mane of dark blond hair flowed around his shoulders in a wild tangle, interwoven with strands of seaweed. The Grecian nose and high cheekbones were like a slightly rougher sketch of Gabriel's features.

From the creature's waist a sleek, muscular mantle extended into eight powerful tentacles that swayed and rippled.

I'd seen some strange things in my life - but I'd never seen something, someone I suppose, like this.

"You dare to threaten my brother?" the sea creature seethed, now gliding fully onto the rocky platform. His voice was deep and strange, but the words and the threat they contained were perfectly clear. One of his sucker-lined tentacles was still firmly wrapped around my arm, immobilizing the downward thrust of my knife.

The tables had turned, the tide of the battle shifted in an instant. Gabriel, every bit as conscious of this as I was, was quickly regaining his bearings.

"Thomas!" he exhaled, clearly relieved as he brushed dust from his sleeves and smoothed back a few loose strands of hair. "You've joined us just in time to meet Harlan Thornhill before, well, before he must be on his way."

Thomas? That seemed like a jarringly ordinary name for whatever kind of creature he was. Apparently sensing my disdain, the creature tightened his tentacled grip on my wrist. I gasped at the strength of it.

"But what in the world is he doing here?" Thomas demanded. As if my being here was the only thing strange about this situation.

"He rang the doorbell and asked to be let in, if you can believe it! I suppose he thought he was going to slay me." Now that his brother was here and had me in a death grip, Gabriel appeared to have rediscovered his sense of humour.

"Quite a coincidence," Thomas's voice was deep and roiling.

The sea-man turned his attention to me, and shook me as if he expected an answer to fall out. All he managed to do was make my teeth bite hard together with every shake.

Gabriel was the one to answer, according to his own theory, "Well, yes. He was pretending to be someone else - a customer. But I decided that we could use his blood as well as anyone else's. In fact, the blood of a Thornhill is symbolically ideal, don't you think? And now we can save those kindergarteners for another time."

Thomas's eyes, shockingly green in his otherworldly face, narrowed. "Do you think Lyrica is up to something - that she might have sent him?"

Gabriel shook his head no, not even deigning to entertain the possibility. "Lyrica hasn't been up to anything for well over a hundred years! I doubt she's up to anything tonight. She lacks daring. Besides, why would she send a mere mortal to torment us? Even one as admittedly skilled in battle as this one here?"

"But he found us somehow," Thomas pressed on, the wheels of suspicion churning in his mind. "He knows who you are and where we live. Who would have told him if not Lyrica?"

My mind was racing for an escape plan. With Thomas's arrival, my already dismal chances of making a successful escape with Octavia, let alone surviving the next hour, had dwindled dramatically. My best bet was to distract and delay as much as I could until either my unlikely cavalry arrived or the sun rose and cut the number of my opponents by at least one.

It seemed possible that the merman, or whatever he was, was going to die with the sun like Gabriel. But I probably shouldn't be pinning my hopes on it.

"You two are brothers?" I fired at my captors, hoping to delay and keep them talking.

"We are," Gabriel confirmed, but unfortunately for me, he seemed to have tired of our conversation and was moving over towards the glass coffins on the podium. He motioned for Thomas to follow. "Bring him over, Thomas. Get him in the coffin. There have been enough delays."

More powerful tentacles wrapped around my arms. I

strained against their cool grip but to no effect. Thomas lifted me effortlessly from the ground as if I was weightless. The room spun briefly as I soared through the air, and then I landed painfully on my back in the glass coffin next to Octavia's. Its sides were high, clearly to allow the space to fill with blood. My blood. I could already feel my veins shrinking in protest.

Despite both my training and my better judgment I started panicking. Thomas's tentacles held me down as I thrashed and struggled. Gabriel deftly tied me with leather straps attached to the coffin's sides. With the straps in place around my ankles, chest and wrists, I could barely even wiggle.

I didn't want to die in this place, but unless I found or thought of an escape hatch, soon, I was going to. I forced myself to stop thrashing and straining, knowing I would need to conserve my energy and strength in case an opportunity came into view.

Gabriel bent over the coffin. "I see the fight has gone out of you." He said it as though it disappointed him slightly. "I must say, you surprised me. For a moment there, you even spooked me a little. But in the end, we have still arrived at this moment, at the threshold of Elizabeth's resurrection."

"Soon, your blood will nourish our sister back to life," Thomas emphasized.

Gabriel positioned himself at the head of the twin glass coffins, his eyes ablaze with anticipation as his gaze gliding between me and Octavia's lifeless form. Thomas moved to stand at the foot of the podium.

"We must be thorough," Gabriel instructed his brother, "and we must be careful. As you've seen, Harlan here is no commonplace mortal, easy to overcome and subdue. As his blood drains, his strength will soon slip away from him, but until then you mustn't take your eyes off him - even when Elizabeth begins to stir! This is very important. You saw how I underestimated him."

"I'll be watching him like a hawk."

Gabriel redirected his attention to me again, his whitish blond hair falling around his face and framing his piercing eyes. "How I would love to taste your blood, but I will let Elizabeth have it all. Every last drop of it."

Sensing that I was running out of time, I reached for anything that would delay us.

There was something unsettling, almost pitiful, in the way Gabriel had confessed to surveilling the Thornhill bloodline, lacking any mortal family of his own. He had been keeping tabs on his enemy's bloodline, not out of affection but with feelings of hatred and disdain.

"Why did you turn Venedict?" I asked, hoping to provoke Gabriel and distract him. "Why did you give him your immortal blood? You were in love with him, weren't you? I mean, why else turn someone into a vampire if not to keep them with you. Did you imagine some kind of romantic shared eternity?"

Gabriel's movements froze, his stance rigid, but only for a fleeting second. "I've had enough conversation for tonight," he said curtly.

"You can plead, accuse and theorize all you want, but none of it will grant you another minute of life," Thomas barged in, adding his two cents.

My words had struck a nerve, clearly offending Gabriel and denting his pride. I sensed that I had touched upon something significant. If I was right, it likely explained Gabriel's insatiable thirst for revenge. It might even shed light on why Gabriel was so determined to possess Octavia as a vessel to house the spirit of his own sister. Venedict had been lost to him in flames of hatred, but Octavia was innocent, a familiar token of connection. But what good was any of this to me now?

I looked up and saw Gabriel, with air of reverent concentration, withdrawing a small, black Chinese lacquered box from an unseen inner pocket in his smoking jacket. He turned it over in his hands and I saw that it had a mother of pearl heron on the hinged lid.

"I bought this for Elizabeth, once upon a time," he explained as he opened it. "And this, too."

He withdrew something that looked like a hairpin, also made of lacquered wood and mother of pearl. But then he removed a cap from its tip and revealed a thin, needle-like knife.

Bending over the coffin - but not close enough for me to attempt the same dirty trick as earlier, not in these restraints - Gabriel grabbed my wrists one at a time. He easily punctuated my skin by placing the hair-thin needle knife against it and applying pressure. The cuts themselves barely registered, the adrenaline coursing through me making them feel like mere paper cuts. After each cut he replaced the knife with a clear tube hooked up to the glass veins connecting the two coffins.

"You said you knew things about me." The words came rapidly, nearly running together, "Do you know who my parents were? Do you know who killed them? Was it you?"

If I was going to die in this place, I preferred to at least take some answers with me. But Gabriel shook his head, his pale hair shimmering like a curtain.

"No, I did not. Trust me, I wouldn't mind taking the credit. Now, this could be an interesting conversation, if only we had more time. Alas, we do not. The night is wearing on and you have served your purpose. You might even have shed a ray or so of redemptive light on your accursed family - in my eyes, at least."

Through the transparent sides of the coffin, I saw Thomas reach down a tentacle and gently caress Octavia's face. "Elizabeth, Elizabeth, not much longer now," he reassured the sleeping vampire. Turning my head to the side, I saw blood already flowing through the tubes between me and Octavia, my life draining into her.

"And now the final touch." Gabriel reached into the black lacquered box again and took out a small glass vial. Whatever the substance was, he poured it into Octavia's mouth. Then, he flung out his arms and in a commanding voice he called out, "Elizabeth, heed my call! Come and claim this vessel. Embrace the new immortal life it offers you."

"Hear us Elizabeth, Elizabeth, come to us!" Thomas joined in, imploring the spirit of long-lost Elizabeth Graves.

My heart skipped a beat as I noticed a field of ethereal, softly glowing energy forming above Octavia, swirling and pulsating, before concentrating in the area above her heart.

Next came the subtle movement of her chest gently rising and falling. Whatever dark magic was at play here, it seemed to be working. Gabriel and Thomas had both noticed, too, and they were transfixed.

Riveting as this was, I still had my own life or death situation to worry about. I was starting to feel weak and lightheaded, and if I stayed here much longer, my fate would be sealed.

If you've ever had to face your own death, you know that in those desperate moments, you find yourself bargaining with something beyond, some higher power, even if you're not religious. I'd never been religious, but as I lay there, strapped into the glass coffin and gazing up at the distant rock ceiling with its swaying chandeliers, I found myself making promises, pleading for any other way out than death. I silently vowed that if I survived, I'd do better. I would become more generous, more forgiving, more patient, kinder to everyone.

I could only hope that someone or something out there was listening and would be amenable to giving me another chance.

No answers or pointers arrived from the cosmos, but in the depths of my own mind, an idea sparked.

I wriggled my bleeding wrists in their restraints, pulling against the tubes and feeling the tug on my arteries, hoping that my slick blood would make this easier. I would free my hands if I had to break all my fingers to do it.

By pressing my fingers together and forcing my hand into the narrowest possible shape, I managed to pull it through one of the restraints. My heart was in my throat. If either of the Graves brothers noticed what I was up to, it'd be game over. But for now, they were both captivated by the awakening that was happening in front of their eyes.

Gabriel's face radiated a mix of awe and relief as he reached out to touch Octavia's face. Blood tears glistened on his cheeks. "Elizabeth," he whispered, his voice raw with emotion. Beside him, Thomas was equally rapt.

Now I had one hand free. I was still trapped and I had no weapon, but if I threw my weight against the side of the coffin, I might be able to tip and shatter it. I would then have splintered glass at my disposal, but would a shard be enough to fight myself out of the corner I was in? The odds seemed low, but they were all I had.

I had to try.

CHAPTER

TWENTY-THREE

G abriel and Thomas stood on either side of the
glass coffins, their eyes and attention fixed on
Octavia. Presumably my blood, infused with the
spark that would restore her immortal body to glorious
vitality, was already coursing through her veins.

"Thomas, I believe our miracle has been granted!"

Gabriel's features were twisted into an expectant
grimace as he turned to his brother. He seemed both tense
and elated, while Thomas released a held breath as a subtle
tremor rippled through Octavia's limbs. Her eyelids fluttered, and then she opened her eyes. They were green, just
like the eyes of her two brothers.

I didn't know what color Octavia's eyes were supposed
to be, but green wouldn't be my guess. Suddenly they rolled
back in her skull, and when they rolled back down the color
had changed to hazel with flecks of glowing amber. Then
they rolled back again, and once again they returned green.

"Elizabeth, dearest sister, you have returned to us."
Gabriel reached out a tentative arm towards Octavia or
Elizabeth, who looked up at him, bewildered and a little

afraid. She didn't seem to know where she was - and who could blame her? If she'd been without a physical body for as long as Gabriel had implied, this moment must seem to her the beginning of a whole new life.

"Your return is a miracle, Elizabeth." Thomas bent over the coffin and gently touched her cheek with one of his two human hands. For now, his tentacles were hidden away under the podium and out of view. It was probably a wise move.

Elizabeth, in Octavia's body, gradually sat up, her movements sluggish and clumsy. Thomas supported her with one muscular arm encircling her back. Surprisingly gently, he helped her to sit.

Her green eyes darted between her two brothers, recognition slowly blossoming behind them. Then she extended both of Octavia's delicate hands towards them. "Gabriel, Thomas, you are both really here! And so am I! But where are we, what is this place?"

Blood tears welled up in Gabriel's eyes and he quickly wiped them away. "Oh, Elizabeth. The world has changed a thousand times since the three of us were gathered. Thomas and I will help you adjust to this new age. Believe me, it holds so many wonders - you're going to love it!"

Thomas echoed his brother's sentiment, his voice overcome with emotion.

It was clear that the two Graves brothers had forgotten all about me. For the past several minutes I had been lying quietly in my coffin, seemingly still and already unconscious. Really, I had been digging deep and summoning all my willpower and strength. I sensed that this was my last chance. I would get one shot at this, and that was all.

In an adrenaline-fuelled surge of desperation, I twisted my body and threw its full weight and force against the side of the coffin facing away from Octavia. The glass tubes that bound the two coffins broke immediately, and blood started splashing out.

The twin coffins had been separated, and for a split second, mine teetered precariously on the edge of the podium while the two Graves brothers looked on, their faces frozen in shock.

We all held our collective breath, and then gravity took hold.

With a resounding crash, the coffin, with me still in it, fell and shattered on the ground. Fragments of the once pristine coffin flew and scattered absolutely everywhere.

I was dizzy and weak from blood loss, but I still had some fight left in me. I wasn't sure how much, though, so I didn't waste a second.

I scanned the ground in front of me, searching for the biggest, sharpest shards that the shattered coffin had produced. And there they were - to large gleaming pieces, one as long and slim as a sword, the other shorter and curved like a jagged sable.

While all of this was happening, I hadn't looked up once to see what Gabriel and Thomas were doing, whether they were already moving in to stop me. If I didn't have a means of defending myself, it didn't matter. I only lifted my eyes once I had my two improvised weapons in my hands.

Apparently, Gabriel and Thomas had shaken off their initial disbelief and their collective focus and fury were now directed at me. Two pairs of green eyes blazed with hatred and disbelief.

All three of us seemed to understand the gravity of the situation. My life hung by a thread, but perhaps Elizabeth's awakening did, too, now that my blood was no longer flowing into her veins.

"No!" Gabriel's voice filled the silence like a thunder-clap, his face contorted with rage. "She still hasn't fully crossed the threshold, she still hasn't lodged. Thomas, our plans are in jeopardy!"

Thomas hissed in frustration, an unearthly sound that no human throat could have produced.

Elizabeth, or Octavia, looked terrified, but I couldn't tell whether the source of her fear was me, or the two actual monsters in the room.

I rose to my feet, my eyes locking with Gabriel's. It might be a trick of the light, but I thought I saw green flames dancing and writhing in their depths.

"This was a foolish move, Harlan." His voice came out controlled, but the fury roiling beneath the surface was only thinly disguised. "We will not be stopped so easily, and while I took no pleasure in having to kill you, now I will relish making you suffer."

"You're the one who will suffer." My voice was calmer than it had any right to be, given the circumstances. I was like a mouse in a corner with no way out, turning around to attack the cat.

"Look at you!" Gabriel let out a contemptuous laugh. "You're in no condition to threaten me or anyone here. You're as good as dead! But you are wasting your precious blood on the ground, and for that I cannot forgive you."

He had already started walking around the podium, and now Thomas was closing in on me from the other side. I knew I could only keep my focus on one of them at a time. And that's if I managed to keep my lights on at all. I was trying to fight it, but my consciousness was flickering, my vision growing dim. I shook my head, trying to stay alert.

Glass crunched under my feet as I took a staggering step towards Gabriel, my shards of glass lifted and pointing at his jugular. If he was careless I might be able to slit his throat or even cut his head clean from his body. Silently I was daring him to come on.

I didn't get to test my theory. A sudden howl broke the cord of concentration that had formed between me and Gabriel.

Both of our heads whipped around to the other side of the platform, where Thomas was bowled over in pain. He was clutching, in one of his human hands, a severed and still writhing tentacle, his mouth and eyes open wide in pain and disbelief.

Behind him, rising out of the water, was Venedict. In his right hand, he held, of all things, an antique bayonet. He hadn't brought one to the cemetery, so I could only assume that he'd found it somewhere in the villa.

Lyrica appeared at his side, also dripping water and holding a similar, long-bladed bayonet. The tip of hers rested pointedly against the tender throat of the child vampire, Dwight, whose small body she was holding in front of her own like a shield. The small vampire's head was painfully tilted back, and he was trembling under the threat of having his immortal life severed.

Thomas let go of his amputated tentacle.

"Dwight!" He cried out. "You demented witch, let him go! My son has no involvement in this, he's innocent."

"Innocent?" Lyrica scoffed. "He's a vampire who has stalked the world for nearly half a millennium. He's as far from innocent as any of us. Now, back away from Harlan, both of you. Now!"

Her tone of voice was firm and commanding. During the past few nights, I thought I'd gotten a rounded impression of her character - but this side of her was new to me. Right now, I welcomed it with open arms.

"Father, uncle, I'm sorry!" Dwight whimpered. "I wasn't able to stop them. They must have come up through the garden, because they were suddenly there, coming through the window. They took the bayonets from the display and forced me to lead them here."

Gabriel shook his head vigorously, his jaw taut and working like an unconscious tic. The situation had finally shifted in my favor, but none of us seemed certain of what that meant. The Graves brothers, both of them wounded, had stopped in their tracks. They, too, were calculating their next moves.

A real sense of hope flickered within me, but the awareness that I'd lost a lot of blood held a bushel over it. My blood glowed in the cheeks of the reanimated Octavia and glistened dimly on the shards littering the ground.

Tension coiled through the air as Lyrica stepped onto the rocky platform, still holding Dwight in her grasp. Gabriel's eyes had gone narrow with fury while Thomas released another guttural growl.

"Let my son go!" He halfway pleaded, halfway demanded, but Lyrica was shaking her raven-haired head.

Gabriel's voice, taut with controlled anger, repeated their request, "Release the boy, Lyrica. If you don't, the consequences will be more dire than you could possibly imagine."

Lyrica's gaze, steely and resolute, met Gabriel's. "I'll release him, but we will leave this place unharmed, Gabriel. Myself, Venedict, Harlan *and* Octavia. Is this understood?"

She pressed the tip of her blade more forcefully against the skin under Dwight's chin.

The Graves brothers both wavered. Triumph had been within their grasp only minutes ago, but now they found themselves backed into a corner. They both seemed to struggle to grasp and come to terms with it.

"You know we don't have long," Lyrica said, flicking her long, wet hair behind her shoulder. "We have an hour at the very most. We need an answer. You can let us go in peace, or you can resist us and Dwight will die. Choose now."

She tightened her grasp on the child vampire and pressed the sword tip into his skin until he cried out.

"And get this," Venedict added, "We are going to leave either way. You might as well let us."

"You'll pay dearly for this, Venedict, Lyrica!" Gabriel was outraged, "You clearly cannot conceive of the consequences of your actions, which I assure you are coming."

Sadness flickered across Lyrica's features. "Enough of your threats, Gabriel. Step aside now, you and Thomas both, and let Harlan retrieve Octavia."

"Thomas, get them!" Gabriel cried out, holding his protective stance in front of Octavia in the coffin.

"No!" Thomas's voice rose in a desperate roar as Lyrica, with one swift and decisive motion, drove the blade upwards through Dwight's chin. She did it with such force that it pierced through the top of the smaller vampire's skull only a fraction of a second later. She pushed the blade to the hilt before withdrawing it effortlessly. Blood gushed in a black ribbon from Dwight's crown and from under his chin. With an inscrutable expression, Lyrica stepped aside and let the child vampire fall to the ground like a marionette whose strings have been severed.

Thomas' wordless cry echoed off the walls of the chamber. Overcome by a primal fury, he struck out with his tentacles toward Lyrica while releasing a stream of jet black ink, not too dissimilar to vampire blood, that spattered us all. But Lyrica, swift and agile, evaded the worst of it.

Thomas lunged at Lyrica again with a ferocity that finally matched his monstrous form. His tentacles thrashed and writhed as they tried to ensnare her. Lyrica dodged the tentacles and countered with swift strikes of her already bloodied bayonet. She managed to cut deep into another tentacle, but Thomas retracted it before it, too, could be severed.

Gabriel faced off against Venedict, who was trying to get to Octavia. Venedict had his bayonet while Gabriel was unarmed, his elegant attire already tattered and stained with blood and ink. But he stood his ground, refusing to let Venedict get access to the coffin.

"You don't understand," he insisted. "The immortal beauty you see here is no longer your sister, but mine."

"How dare you spew this mad nonsense at me!" Venedict snarled as he and Gabriel danced around each other. "Harlan, get Octavia from the coffin and be quick about it! We're leaving."

With Venedict facing Gabriel and Lyrica facing Thomas, the obvious move for me was to go and lift Octavia from the coffin. If only I wasn't so dizzy, and if only everything didn't seem so dim and far away.

I willed myself to move, commanded my legs to take one step at a time. Octavia was sitting upright, with a look of bemused shock painted on her face. I couldn't tell what she was thinking, but when I neared the coffin, she reached her arms out towards me.

"Don't bite me, okay?"

As I stepped up to the podium, I caught a fleeting glimpse of Lyrica out of the corner of my eye. With a swift, brutal strike, I saw her plunge her blade into Thomas's shoulder as he crouched over Dwight's small form. This potentially deadly attack on his brother finally shook

Gabriel's resolve to guard the coffin. Up until now he'd been trying to keep near it even while dancing around Venedict's blade. Now he turned his attention to Lyrica and to Thomas.

Just as Octavia had wrapped her arms around my neck and I'd lifted her from the coffin, the ground leapt up and swallowed me.

~

WHEN I CAME TO, I was being carried through the garden outside, the air blessedly cool on my face. Venedict and Lyrica each had an arm wrapped around me and were carrying me between them.

Octavia appeared to be fully awake now and was following along on her own two feet, Venedict leading her along by the hand. Her feet were bare as they ran through the grass and I wondered idly if her shoes had rotted away in the grave or if she'd simply left them behind.

My vampire companions were moving swiftly, their steps purposeful as they closed in on the weeping willow and the hidden tunnel underneath it. Without as much as a backward glance, we descended into the darkness, the damp earth smell filling my lungs.

"What happened?"

Lyrica turned her face to look at me, surprised that I had regained consciousness so soon, or perhaps at all. She smiled. "We escaped. Once Thomas was wounded, Gabriel had to admit defeat. He was out of options."

"Our plan worked!" Venedict declared, triumphant. "But of course not without cost." He didn't turn to look at me like Lyrica had, but instead kept his eyes firmly on the narrow passage in front of us.

"You've lost a lot of blood, and I really mean a lot of it." Lyrica's brow furrowed with concern. I wanted to ask her how bad she thought it was, but I slumped into their supporting embrace and went out like a light again before I could find the words.

I kept floating in and out of consciousness the rest of the way back to Thornhill Mansion.

I was distantly aware of us emerging from the tunnel beneath the ancient cedar tree in Highgate Cemetery, and of the moonlight shining on the weathered tombstones that lined the path. Then came the wrought-iron fence looming in front of us with its intricate patterns of acanthus leaves. Venedict and Lyrica lifted me over it gently, leaving the world of the dead behind. The mansion's sprawling garden welcomed us with the scent of night-blooming flowers carried on a cool, pre-dawn breeze.

I couldn't keep my eyes open and they fluttered closed. But I heard the creak of the heavy wooden doors as they swung open, and the sound of footsteps on the marble floor.

"Where've you been? You found Octavia! But oh my god, wow, what's happened to Harlan? Is he-?" I was floating on a sea of darkness, but I could hear Sebastian's voice quite clearly. It carried.

"No, no, he isn't, and no, we won't let it happen." This was Venedict's voice, reassuring, but with a hint of panic only thinly disguised. I wasn't sure Sebastian could hear it, but I could.

TWENTY-FOUR

T could hear the distant sound of footsteps as they carried me, not upstairs to what I'd come to vaguely consider my bedroom, but down into the crypt-like basement.

I was placed on a blessedly cool stone floor. Through my half-closed eyelids I sensed the outlines of Venedict and Lyrica hovering over me. Octavia had remained upstairs with Sebastian.

"How bad is it really?" I managed through clenched teeth.

"Quite horrifically bad." Venedict's eyes were floating above me like two orbs of amber. They were burning with concern. It was just like in that dream I'd had, I couldn't remember when. The dream about the burning chapel.

"An ambulance would never get here in time. You've lost too much blood." This was Lyrica. "You deserve the truth, and the truth is you are on the threshold."

"You know what we must do." Venedict was addressing her, not me.

"But he doesn't wish to become like us. Becoming what

he has spent his life hunting would surely kill his spirit, don't you think? Perhaps we should simply let-"

"I am making an executive decision," Venedict cut her off. "Get hold of Sebastian, let him know what is happening here. Once the usual slumber has crept over you and I and Octavia, he will have to ensure Harlan remains in one of the caskets, or at least that he remains down here, while - you know. We do not have time before sunrise to make sure of this ourselves."

Lyrica hesitated, filled with doubt and half-formed protest, but then there was a rustling of skirts as she apparently got to her feet and left the room.

"Harlan, you understand what I am about to do." It wasn't really a question. I was still on the floor, too weak to move, my head resting on Venedict's lap and he leaned over me.

"You won't live unless you accept the dark transformation that I am about to foist upon you."

"No."

My teeth had started clattering but I still managed to get my objection out. I couldn't open my eyes anymore, couldn't see Venedict's expression or anything at all. I wanted to tell him to at least attempt to call an ambulance, but the words had already floated away from me, dissolved like mist.

"Harlan, listen. I understand that you have a few psychological hangups pertaining to our kind, but surely they can be worked out in time. I do not even have to drain you, merely to fill you up. Now, drink this."

I felt the firm pressure of his wrist against my lips. I'd never felt this parched in my life, and I longed to drink of the dark essence that he was offering me, but no. I couldn't.

This was not what I'd signed up for, not the fate I had envisioned for myself.

Summoning all my willpower, I managed to give one shake of my head, my lips pressed tightly together.

Venedict sighed with impatience. "You must, Harlan. And it would be better for our relationship if you drank willingly. You and I are going to be around each other for a long, long time. Let's not start off on the wrong foot."

The room was suffused with an otherworldly energy, crackling with Venedict's dark power as he, gently at first, placed his slim, strong fingers under my chin, and started prying my jaws open. He held my mouth open while he let the first few shimmering drops fall onto my tongue.

Each drop landed like an explosion.

"Embrace it," Venedict's voice laced with a persuasive intensity that sent shivers down my spine. "What could be so bad about embracing this unexpected twist in your destiny? My blood will transform your body, but not your soul. You can still be who you wish to be, in fact more than ever. There's nothing to fear."

I resisted. His words were meaningless, as far as I was concerned. Lyrica had been absolutely right in her assumption that becoming what I'd spent my life dedicated to hunting would destroy me. It would be the end of me. I would rather die than be taken over by the surging darkness.

My heart pounded in my chest, weaker now, a rhythmic reminder of my dwindling time.

I thrashed mindlessly, wanting to crawl away, but Venedict held me down easily with one arm while feeding me his blood with the other. I sputtered and tried to spit, the metallic taste filling my mouth and spilling down over my chin. But most of it was still disappearing down my throat as Venedict intended.

He was laughing softly to himself, apparently finding my struggle amusing.

He wasn't much less of a villain than Gabriel, was he?

Lyrica must have come back into the room, because her voice, soothing and comforting, spoke suddenly very close to my ear, her words threaded through with regret, "Harlan, please try to understand, this is the only way to save you. There is no human life for you to return to - tonight that bridge has been burnt."

I wanted to argue with her, to remind her that she herself had called the vampiric blood a curse up until a minute ago. But I couldn't speak, couldn't see her, could barely even hear her anymore.

The loss of control, the insatiable thirst that would soon consume me, these things frightened me much more than anything else I'd ever faced. As my senses threatened to fail me completely, I reached deep within myself, searching for the reserves of willpower I knew I had honed over the years. But even calling on all my strength was not enough.

It was too late. I was gone.

I realized to my horror that I must have been drawing on Venedict's blood without meaning to, because suddenly he was prying my jaw open again and exclaiming, "I said let go, Harlan! My *god*, you're greedy. A true Thornhill in every way."

The dark, vampiric blood was coursing through my veins, extinguishing the light of my humanity as it went. I could feel it.

My body trembled as a new and unfamiliar power shot through my bloodstream like adrenaline. My eyes burst open and the entire room around me seemed to be glowing.

"My god!" I exclaimed, my hands flying out in front of me. I realized that I was sitting up, and that Venedict and Lyrica were kneeling on either side of me. They were both vivid and beautiful, and everything in the room was humming with electric energy.

Of course Sebastian chose this exact moment to cautiously push the crypt door open, his oval face appearing around its edge. His eyes widened when he saw me.

"Can I come in?" he asked in a slightly tremulous voice. His gaze was fixed on me with utter fascination.

"Sure, join us." Venedict waved him over. "I trust Lyrica has explained everything to you, given you sufficient instruction?"

Sebastian nodded. "Yeah, I think so. I'm to help Harlan into your casket and make sure he stays put until tomorrow night whether he wants to or not."

"Exactly!" Venedict beamed at him.

"All right, so I know we've got other things to deal with right now," Sebastian said with a slight shiver. "But I should probably tell you that there's a bit of a situation upstairs. Basically, Octavia has killed a cop."

Venedict and Lyrica exchanged a weighty glance.

"It happened so quickly - I couldn't stop her. She wanted to see the garden, and there was this policeman outside on Swain's Lane. She made him come over to the fence and within seconds, he was dead. He just fell over like a ragdoll."

Venedict wiped his brow with a yellowed lace handkerchief produced from an inner pocket of his waistcoat. How many of these did he own?

"Well," he said, "I'm afraid you'll have to deal with it, Sebastian. It's time for Lyrica, Octavia and myself to go into hiding for the day. We've all had quite a night, and sunrise is mere minutes away. Just make sure the detective has no modern electronic signaling devices on him that could attract others of his kind, and then bury him in the garden. At the back, between mine and Octavia's windows is best."

Sebastian looked understandably dumbstruck. "But-but it's a crime and I've never dealt with a dead body!"

"As my familiar, I don't think you have a choice? There's a shovel somewhere in one of the cupboards." Venedict rose to his feet and dusted himself off, just as Octavia emerged behind Sebastian and stepped into the room.

"I'm sorry," she said, looking anxiously to her brother, "but I was hungry, positively starving."

"Haven't I told you, no cops? They're risky prey. But for now, it doesn't matter. We are all just relieved you are home again, and that our family is united."

"I'm the only human remaining. It isn't fair!"

We all looked at Sebastian with varying degrees of bewilderment.

"You wish to give up your humanity just like that?" Lyrica asked, incredulous.

"Yes, of course!" Sebastian almost yelled it. "I know I didn't nearly die tonight, but I'd also like to embrace darkness, thank you very much. I've already been drawn into all of this, the mansion, all of you, so why should I be the only one to remain, as you would probably call it, a mere mortal?"

"Sebastian," Venedict said, his voice straining to conceal his amusement, "now is not the time. I have just expended all my energy and power to ensure Harlan's successful passage into our world. I need you to keep watch over him while we sleep and his body dies. We'll discuss the matter, but not tonight."

Sebastian's disappointment was palpable. "I get it," he murmured, heaving a sigh. "Harlan's transformation comes first right now. But I won't let you all forget."

Venedict and Lyrica exchanged a brief, understanding glance before returning their focus to me. Sebastian, too.

The three of them watched me with fascination as the deep cuts Gabriel had dealt me began to close. The pain, once searing and consuming, was already becoming weightless and lifting off me like dew in the morning sun.

The best way I can describe what was happening to my senses would be to say that a veil that had covered me my entire life seemed to have been ripped away, allowing me to perceive the world with absolute clarity and richness for the first time.

I could see every detail, every intricate pattern in the chamber and in the faces of Venedict, Lyrica, Octavia and Sebastian. To my newborn vampire eyes, each of them seemed incredibly beautiful and miraculous in their own way, each radiating a vital energy, its quality and imprint distinct from the others.

And it wasn't only my physical senses that were different. Every corner of my consciousness was illuminated and accessible to me. As I moved over towards the nearest casket, the one with the Clyde Hartenbrook name plate affixed to it, my steps were effortless and graceful.

Actually, my entire body felt weightless, as if if I'd be able to soar right up into the air - maybe tomorrow night, I'd try.

But wait. Wasn't I supposed to hate this? Why did this transformation feel so good, so comfortable, so right?

I froze in my steps, a wave of guilt washing over me. My face fell. I felt myself frozen to the ground.

Lifting my hands out in front of me, I saw that the

wounds Gabriel had inflicted were completely gone, as if they had never been there.

My hands and forearms were smooth and white like marble, and my fingernails were gleaming like glass.

"No, no, no!"

Horrified at the sight of my own hands, no longer human, I stumbled back against the wall. I let myself slide down, my monstrous hands covering my face.

Sebastian came over and knelt down in front of me. He was shaken by the situation, yes, but completely, touchingly unafraid of me as he put his hands on my shoulders. "You'll be okay, Harlan. You're just having a panic attack. I used to get them all the time."

"A panic attack?" I snapped, and released a bitter peal of laughter. "I think this is a bit more than a freaking panic attack, don't you?"

"Try to enjoy the wonders that come with your turning, Harlan," Lyrica said in a quiet voice. "Savor this moment, if you can."

Somewhere behind my panic, my newly transformed senses were alerting me to a subtle shift in the atmosphere, a warning that the first rays of the sun were piercing through the horizon outside.

As if in response, a deep pain pierced my insides, making me curl up in pain. I let out a yelp before I could grit my teeth to stop it.

"It is just your body, Harlan." Lyrica's voice was infinitely gentle. "It has to shed all its human tissue before it is fully immortal. Remember how I described it? It is awful and messy, yes, but it will not last long. And then you'll have forever. *We* will have forever, as a family."

"Well, I'm retreating for the day." Venedict declared, clapping his hands together. "Harlan can have my casket or any of the others. We'll burn the insides clean tomorrow night. We'll burn the whole casket if necessary! I'll be sleeping... elsewhere. Given my many years of confinement, I am sure you can all understand that it will take me a while to trust Lyrica again."

In a flash, he was gone.

Lyrica came over and knelt next to Sabastian. "Harlan, come, let us guide you over here to lie down, where you will be more comfortable."

She held out her hands to me and I allowed her and Sebastian to pull me to my feet.

The pain in my gut was intensifying, quickly becoming excruciating. This actually felt worse than anything the Graves brothers had put me through.

They guided me over to Clyde's beautifully crafted casket, which Octavia had already propped open before climbing into her own beside it and closing the lid. The interior was lined with silk as black as the night itself.

Lyrica and Sebastian all but lifted me into the casket, its soft cushioning enveloping me like a cloud.

Lyrica's melodic voice sounded in my ears and her cool fingers stroked my forehead. "Close your eyes and surrender to sleep. The daylight will pass, and tomorrow night when you awaken, all pain and fear will have left you. I promise. But I must go and sleep now, myself."

"Isn't there a way to undo this?"

I realized that Lyrica had gone, and it was Sebastian's face outlined in the darkness above me.

"Shhh. They can't take it back even if they wanted to. And maybe you could try to look at the silver lining. I'm pretty envious, to be honest. If the dark blood was given to me, Irene would take me back in a heartbeat. No, actually, I think she would chase me."

"Could you close the lid?"

"Oh, sure. I just thought it'd be more comforting for you if-"

I'd fought against the wave of unconsciousness for long enough. Now it crashed over me with full force, carrying me away from Sebastian's voice - farther away than I had ever gone. I wasn't too convinced that I would even come back. Perhaps Venedict's efforts had been too late, after all.

CHAPTER

TWENTY-FIVE

"You've been avoiding me," Eli grumbled, his voice on the phone seeming to reach me from a far distance as I stood amidst the tangled vines and tall grass in the overgrown garden of Thornhill Mansion.

My newly heightened vampire senses enhanced the beauty of the twilit landscape that surrounded me. Even the air felt different, somehow charged with an otherworldly energy.

"Bullshit, Eli, I've not been avoiding you. It's just that I've been caught up in some pretty complicated experiences here that I've needed some time to process. I still do. But you don't have to worry about me, that's one thing I *can* share with you now."

Eli hesitated. "Complicated experiences? No doubt, but why don't you tell me a little about them? Lyrica Hartenbrook and Thornhill Mansion must have yielded some of their secrets by now, I imagine."

With Eli's voice in my ear I crouched down in the tall grass to admire one of the many old statues that stood half-hidden in it. This one was a gargoyle, looking up at me with

a curious expression. Even inanimate objects like this creature made of stone seemed alive and full of energy from my
new vantage point.

When I didn't immediately respond, Eli pressed on.
"You've been there for three days, Harlan. You must have
spoken to her by now, and you must know more about
what you're dealing with. I'm relieved to have actually
reached you, but you're being, well, evasive. If I didn't know
better, I'd say you were hiding something from me. Maybe
even something important."

How could I even begin to explain to Eli what had
happened to me over the past few nights? It would be hard
for me to tell him at all, but there was no way I'd be able to
get the right words out over the phone.

"I'm not hiding anything. It's just that Thornhill
Mansion has a complicated history and it'll take me some
time to tease everything out. I'd like to just be left to it. I
promise I'll keep in touch, and when the time is right I'll tell
you the whole story. Warts and all."

Eli sighed. "So you definitely don't need my help and
you don't want me to come? I was almost ready to jump on
a plane to London when you finally decided to answer one
of my calls. Damn it, Harlan, you're grown, but I still feel
responsible for you. Guess I always will. If you're in over
your head in some mysterious way, you should just come
right out and tell me. You know you can rely on me and that
there's no need for beating around the bush."

"I know. But this is my job and I want to handle it on
my own, in my own way. You need to let me stand on my
own two feet. What you should be more worried about is
the Van Helsing Society and what Ramsay Fairweather is
up to."

"Don't try to make this about the Van Helsing Society or

about your rival, or whatever is going on there. This is about you - otherwise you wouldn't be this defensive. Can I share my honest thoughts? I sense that you've been drawn in by something sinister, something that you can't see your way out of. If I'm wrong, why don't you tell me what you've been up to, and what or who you've encountered in that crumbly old mansion. Put me at ease."

Eli was refusing to be deterred. He was like a dog with a pig's ear. Good luck to anyone trying to pry it away from him.

"Jed and Carmen are here," I offered. "Well, not *here* here. They've been working in the cemetery, apparently reinvestigating the Highgate Vampire case."

"But that case is done and dusted!" He frowned, finally taking my bait. "I was there! There was a dark entity stalking the cemetery, and there were local vampires, all right, but this is nothing unusual in a big, ancient city. Let me just make one thing perfectly clear; the entity itself was no vampire, just a mass of dark energy attracted by some rather amateurish black magicians. Putting it to rest was child's play. If Ramsay chooses to waste the Society' resources and the time of two excellent hunters going over that cold old trail again, he's dumber than I thought." Eli had gotten all fired up now and was bristling.

"Or he's actually up to something. Jed and Carmen think so, too. They say he's trying to keep them distracted and away from the Society's headquarters while he... well, this is what we don't know."

Eli sighed. "I've already packed my bags. Perhaps I should visit the headquarters and try to find out what might be going on."

"Please. And Eli, keep me in the loop about anything you find out. I have to go now. Lyrica's expecting me."

"All right, Harlan, look after yourself. Don't turn a blind eye to any potential danger, though, and stop ignoring my calls. Don't go around thinking you're immortal." He chuckled, "You sometimes seem to forget that you're not."

After wrapping up our conversation I just stood there for a moment, looking up at the mansion towering over me. Somewhere to the side, there was a freshly dug grave. With my heightened senses, it was easy to pick out where it was. Sebastian, wanting to do a thorough job of it, had even gone out of his way to purchase a rose bush and plant it on top of the disturbed soil. He must have carried all of this out in the early hours of the morning.

Octavia had marveled at the rosebush and the garden in general, but disappointingly, she didn't seem to remember anything about the family, the mansion, or even herself. Venedict insisted that she was just suffering from temporary amnesia, but I wasn't so sure that the creature we had brought home from Villa Graves was Octavia Thornhill and not the unknown entity of Elizabeth Graves. Her eyes seemed to change between green and hazel with the light, so they were no help either. I supposed time would tell who she really was.

Time would tell about a lot of things.

Speaking with Eli on the phone had seemed so normal, so everyday. But it was an illusion, and I had no real way of knowing how the future of our connection would play out. He might very well reject me now that I was no longer human.

Sure, he wasn't fully human himself, but being a werewolf is different. A werewolf is only a part-time monster, and the moral implications just aren't the same.

I let my thoughts drift and caught myself imagining the

possibilities of moving into the mansion, becoming a true part of the family.

I needed to rethink most aspects of my existence in light of what had happened last night. There was no rule saying that I couldn't keep living in my own flat in Edinburgh, but what would I do there? I was no longer a hunter, was I? My license was already suspended - now I'd never get it back.

As the identity crisis crept up on me with frightening force, a familiar presence broke through my reverie. It was Carmen, standing outside the tall wrought iron fence, her figure backlit by the streetlights dotting Swain's Lane.

Seeing her here both comforted and unnerved me. Her being here seemed to confirm that my mortal life, with all its connections and patterns still existed - it was just that I'd been plucked right out of it and now stood beside it, observing it with a sense of detached bewilderment.

I walked over toward the fence and Carmen, trusting that the friendship that connected us was still there, still solid. I felt like a child climbing out onto the limb of a tree to test whether it would snap or carry me.

As I stepped close to the gate and allowed myself to become illuminated by the streetlights, Carmen's eyes widened. She was a hunter; she knew instantly what I was.

"Harlan!" Her voice carried the barest hint of alarm.

I approached her slowly, hoping to show her that I had only good intentions, that I was still me.

Our eyes met, and for a fleeting moment, we both froze. Then, a faint smile tugged at the corners of her mouth and I felt a surge of relief.

"You've changed," she said. "New haircut?"

"New everything."

"Not *everything* I bet. But no wonder you were being cagey when we spoke. What the hell have you been up to in there? And what are you gonna do about the Van Helsing Society?" She arched one of her narrow eyebrows. "I hope I'm not shattering any illusions here, but I think you'll have an even harder time getting your license back now."

"No doubt. Is Jed all right?"

She gave a shrug. "Sort of. He was whisked away to the Royal Free Hospital after your cousin called the ambulance. I rode along with him - there was no point in me remaining at the cemetery, not with our attacker gone. He lost an eye, but he'll live. He actually seems pretty thrilled at the prospect of having to have a glass eye."

"I'll pay him a visit," I said. "But I should probably give him a heads up first."

Silence enveloped us for a moment before Carmen broke it. "Say, you still owe me a tour of the mansion." She tilted her head back and gazed up at the building behind us. "And since I'm here, why don't we make it now? Then you can also tell me how this happened to you. I'm honestly dead curious. Pardon the expression."

"I don't see why not," I said, opening the gate to let her in. As it creaked open, a quote from the Dracula novel popped into my thoughts and it fit the moment too perfectly to not say it out loud. "Welcome to my house. Come freely. Go safely; and leave something of the happiness you bring. Only I actually mean it."

Carmen stepped through and I let the rusty gate jangle closed behind her.

"Don't get offended, Harlan, but I think the change might actually, weirdly, suit you. At least you have a sense of humor about it."

"Gallows humor you mean. And it's too soon to say. Right now, I'm not exactly sure who or what I am anymore."

But I was determined to find out. My path through the universe had been irrevocably changed since last night. The very fabric of my being had been twisted, and now nothing was in its familiar place.

It was all disorienting and terrifying, but I had to admit that there was a powerful sense of excitement in it, too. The door to my old life had been sealed behind me forever, but a new door had appeared. And who knew, it might turn out to be broader and wider than the previous one.

Maybe this was not the end but the beginning.

Also by Lucius Valiant

Dark Roots

Deep Graves

Foul Moon

Grim Games (Publication date TBA)

ABOUT THE AUTHOR

Lucius Valiant is a Danish-British author.

The first real book he recalls reading is Bram Stoker's "Dracula." And that, as the saying goes, was that. There would be no turning back.

Lucius's literary inspirations include classics of Gothic fiction, such as Mary Shelley's "Frankenstein" and Oscar Wilde's "The Picture of Dorian Gray," as well as horror, supernatural, and speculative fiction by writers such as Anne Rice, Poppy Z. Brite, and Stephen King. He also draws much influence from Britain's rich history, folklore, and legends.

All of these influences shine through like glittering, dark fairy dust in his writing, which readers have described as vivid, visceral, and cinematic, with a sprinkling of wry humor.

Visit his linktree to learn more, join the mailing list, and be kept in the loop about upcoming releases and secret subscriber treats: https://linktr.ee/luciusvaliant

AUTHOR'S NOTE

Thank you, dear reader, for taking a chance on a new and unknown author! I'm honored that you picked up my book among the millions that are out there.

If you enjoyed "Dark Roots," here's the best way to show it: Reviews are to indie authors what lifeblood is to vampires. I'd be super grateful for your honest review wherever you buy and rave about books.

If you want more of my writing, my world and my characters, let's stay in touch. I have a newsletter you can sign up to via https://linktr.ee/luciusvaliant and I'm almost certainly haunting your favorite social media platforms.

Lucius Valiant, October 2023